FIRE AND VALOR BOOK

THE KING'S DRAGON

W.M. FAWKES
SAM BURNS

FlickerFox
Books

Content Warning: this book is intended for adult audiences only, and contains graphic violence, swearing, and graphic sex scenes.

Trigger Warnings: alcohol abuse, child neglect and abuse, violence, torture

Cover art © 2019 by Natasha Snow Designs; www.natashasnowdesigns.com
Editing by Clause & Effect

TRISTRAM

Some days would be forever pressed to the forefront of Tristram's mind. The day he met his cousin, Prince Reynold. The day his mother told him he was a half-dragon bastard.

The day of King Edmund's funeral.

All kings were beloved in theory, but Reynold's father, Edmund, had been a truly great one. He'd been a bland man, dull and uninteresting in conversation, without half his son's charisma, but he'd been exceptionally good at the daily tasks of ruling a kingdom. The people loved the image of handsome, impeccable Reynold hosting tourneys and throwing lavish feasts in the palace. They had loved what Edmund had done for them.

That wasn't to say Tristram thought his friend an incapable leader. He simply wasn't the workhorse his father had been.

Tristram's black velvet doublet and matching hose were some of the finest he owned, as much as he couldn't stand the sight of them. They were strangely comfortable for clothes he hardly ever wore, but they made his pale hair look white by contrast, and that made him stand out more than he cared to. He finished pulling on his boots and stared down at them.

His dagger lay on the bed, shiny and eye-catching, like a beacon. It was rarely far from his mind, but the fact that he'd chosen such a flashy thing made it hard to forget.

Was it appropriate to wear on his person to the king's funeral?

It was not.

He turned and headed for the door, but before he'd even made it half-way, he'd turned and headed back for the bed. With hardly a conscious thought, he had the dagger in his hand, and he was tucking it into his boot.

"A good idea," said a voice from the doorway, startling him.

He looked up to find Reynold standing there, looking tense and unhappy. He'd been like that since the beginning of his father's illness, but it was still strange to see. Reynold had always been good at accepting surprises as they came, but since last winter—since his father's illness had taken a turn for the worst—he'd been closing himself off. Maybe he was preparing himself for the trials to come. Ruling all of Llangard was a burden Tris couldn't begin to imagine.

"Good idea?" he asked.

Reynold motioned to Tristram's hand, still on the dagger hilt. "Coming prepared. You never know who is about, or what their intentions are." His hand clenched and unclenched, eyes on the dagger, as though he wanted to snatch it for himself. That was a feeling Tris knew all too well, but he'd never seen it on his cousin before. Reynold never left the palace grounds without at least two guards by his side, and this day would be no different. While he had trained with a sword, he had never had much use for one. The Spires, the main seat of the Cavendish line, was impregnable, drawn straight out of the earth in huge towers by the magic of Athelstan Cavendish himself.

"Shall we walk out together?" He suspected the answer would be no, since Reynold was always concerned about pageantry. Even on this, the day of his father's funeral, his first concern was likely to be the appearance of things, and it was custom for the new ruler to walk alone up the hill outside the city to the Cavendish tomb. Reynold's attention to detail was a good reason for him to be king, and never Tris.

Surprising him, Reynold nodded. "Yes. I would speak to you about the training of the guard. You practice with them. I want your opinions on their skill."

"You've cultivated the finest personal guard known to Llangard, Your Highness." The answer required no thought. Reynold's methods for training and culling the guard were extreme, but none could doubt that the result was the most skilled fighters in the land.

Reynold waved dismissively. "Things are different now. I need my most faithful men at my back, and you know them better than anyone. We should speak on each of them."

There was nothing Tristram could say to that, so he inclined his head and shoulders in acquiescence.

He did know the guard well. Since he'd arrived at the palace more than a decade before, he had trained with them almost every day. He didn't know how things were different now, but it was clear Reynold wasn't interested in discussing it, and one never tried to press for answers with Reynold. At best, it would result in the prince being unhappy. Worst didn't bear contemplation.

Reynold was destined for greatness. He was intense and charismatic and drew people to him like moths to a flame. But no one who knew him would have called him a kind man.

The walk from the Spires to the Cavendish tomb was not long, though most of the realm's peers would have taken carriages. The court would be there already, seated, awaiting their new king to bid farewell to the last.

It was a quiet day in the kingdom. Overcast, as Tris always thought sad days ought to be, but more than that, the usual bustle of the capital was hushed and still. Reynold's guards trailed after him once they left the palace grounds. The market was closed, the smithies cold, and when they arrived, the funeral was filled with silent people wearing their very best clothes.

Reynold had declared it a day of rest for everyone in the kingdom, and the people were out in force, showing their love for the man who had led them in prosperity for nearly five decades.

They walked among the people side by side to the magnificent family mausoleum. It had been built by Reynold's ancestors when Llangard was young and magic was plentiful. The Cavendish line had always been particularly impressive with stone magic, and the sloping arches of the building were a testament to their artistry, seeming to slide up out of the ground as though they had naturally formed that way.

They walked together to the head of the crowd, where the most important lords were waiting, including Tristram's own mother, sitting with Reynold's son, Roland.

Reynold paused there, straightening his spine and lifting his head, then reaching out to squeeze Tristram's shoulder. He nodded, Tristram gave a small bow, and they parted ways, leaving Tris to go sit with his mother and Roland, and Reynold to do his duty.

Tristram took the empty chair next to Roland and tried to give the boy a hopeful smile. The princeling was always a clever, thoughtful, well-behaved child, but on this day, he was especially quiet. He had seen more death than any nine-year-old should, between his mother and his grandfather. Generally, Reynold would have had the boy at his own side, but things would be different now.

Reynold was king.

The prince reached out and took one of Tristram's hands in his, then Tristram's mother's, but he didn't say anything. She met his gaze over the prince's head, and he saw his own concern mirrored there. The boy needed more support than ever before, and his father was no longer in a position to offer it.

Reynold had begun to speak of remarrying. He'd been widowed for three years, and now that he was king, the fact that he had a single son was of some concern to the people of Llangard. Remarrying was the sensible thing to do, but Tristram couldn't help thinking that would leave Roland more often on his own.

No second wife would be interested in spending her time coddling the child who wasn't hers, but who would one day become king.

"He was sad," the prince whispered, barely audible even in the silence. "He didn't want to go."

"We never want to leave the ones we love," Tristram's mother told Roland.

Tristram wasn't sure that was true. His father—or rather, his mother's husband—had been a miserable ass who'd seemed all too happy to shuffle off the mortal coil and leave everyone behind. Little wonder Tristram had been the product of an affair, really. The only actual wonder was how his mother had forced herself to care for such a man at all. Even dealing with the shock that he was the product of an affair, Tristram had never held her infidelity against her.

He'd have sought comfort in the arms of another man too, in her position.

The prince—no, the king, he must remember that—King Reynold's sister, Princess Gillian, drifted up to sit on Tristram's other side. She looked as though she hadn't slept in days, and given how she'd spent her father's final days at his side, Tris didn't doubt it.

"I don't know where to be," she said, her voice lost and a little frightened. "I always sit next to Reynold."

Tristram glanced across the aisle to where King Edmund's brother, Prince Laurence, sat with his wife and son. There was space with their family, but if the princess stood before him, they weren't company she wanted.

With his free hand, Tris reached to take one of Gillian's. "Then you should stay with us, Your Highness."

She offered a weak smile, but her hand squeezed his with strength he hadn't realized she possessed.

Reynold stepped up in front of the crowd, head high and shoulders straight, the very image of a powerful king. The way he scanned the crowd, pausing now and then, made every person there think he was looking at them, thinking of them. He bestowed a soft look on Roland, and the boy leaned against Tris.

Finally, Reynold gave a sad smile and bowed his head to look at his father's casket. When he spoke, his voice was commanding, but quiet enough to show the people that he was hurting with the loss of his father, just as they were. "I thank you all for coming to see my father off on his final journey. He would have been deeply honored by your presence."

He spoke to the crowd about principles and duty, and how his father had been the very essence of both—how he only hoped he could fulfill the promise that lifetime of service had made. He'd always been excellent with words, and the speech would have made King Edmund proud.

Admittedly, Reynold had thought his father old and unwise, but at least he did him honor in this.

As the honor guard, led by Prince Laurence, carried the litter with King Edmund's casket into the royal mausoleum, to be entombed there next to his queens and across from his own long-dead parents, Tristram wondered if he'd be doing this again in forty years.

Likely not, despite the fact that he would be that long-lived. Once everyone realized he was a half dragon, he'd likely be run out of the country, forced to live with dragons he'd never met.

Well, if they would have him.

He only hoped his mother didn't live long enough to have to deal with it. He didn't want her punished for seeking out a tiny bit of comfort in her lonely youth.

The procession moved into the mausoleum, and he dropped his head to say a quick prayer to the gods for another year of peace. It was what their people needed, what Reynold needed, in the first year of the reign of a new king.

2

GILLIAN

For the first time, Gillian was free to decide what to do with the rest of her life on her own terms. Her brother might want her to make an advantageous marriage, but not too advantageous; she would still be in the public eye, but no longer a contender for the throne. His Majesty would be too busy to pay her much mind. She could spend her days reading, on charitable acts, hosting parties, or practicing magic parlor tricks, and no one would pay her half as much mind as they'd paid her yesterday.

She felt awful about it. It wasn't that she wanted the attention, but her father was dead, her brother was king, and Prince Roland would be officially installed as heir apparent. Barring unthinkable tragedy, Gillian no longer stood to inherit anything. She was no longer of such import to the realm.

Hells, what a relief that was. But as she stood from her plush seat to follow the procession into the Cavendish tomb, worrying her bottom lip with her teeth, blinking tears from her stinging eyes, she could hardly be glad of it.

Tristram's thumb stroked her knuckles when she stood. Her hand was still locked around his, and he wouldn't let go of her until she pulled away. He was too decent to set her adrift.

Tristram Radcliffe was a good man—one of the best in the realm—

always there to be the steady wall to lean against when things were diffi-cult. She took a breath that jumped in her chest and let go of him with a weak smile. "Thank you," she whispered.

For years now, Lord Radcliffe had been her brother's stalwart companion—the kind of noble, honorable knight a king would want by their side in battle.

Reynold, of course, did not only cultivate friendships with the honor-able, but Tristram and his mother had been allowed to sit through the ceremony with what remained of Gillian's small family. Less savory companions were relegated to the shadows under a nearby tree and barred entry to the tomb entirely.

"Come now, little dove," Gillian said, bending a little to be closer to Roland's height. He was far from a man, but he'd already been twice to this sad place. Heartbreak was written all over his soft face from the tears in his light blue eyes to the way he pressed his lips into a thin line to hide the tremble. "We must follow the king."

She held out her hand to her nephew. Her fingers were free of rings that might scratch his soft skin. Reynold was of the opinion they were gaudy on a woman as young as her; she was of the opinion that arguing with Reynold was as useful as arguing with a rock.

With Roland's small hand in hers, they joined the procession, falling in line just behind Reynold, who cast the perfect mold of a grieving son, his head bowed under the weight of his new crown. His coronation wouldn't be for months, until their mourning was over, but he'd borne the weight of it from the moment of their father's last breath.

The Cavendish family tomb rose naturally from a hillside. Legend had it that Brandon Cavendish, son of Athelstan, the first magician to come to Llangard, fell to his knees over his father's body. In anguish, he called up the earth and veins of quartz that ran within it to entomb his beloved father. It curved broadly across the landscape, long and low with gilt doors hidden in the shadow of a crest of glittering stone.

For centuries after, the Cavendish line had carved their tombs from the stone with their magic. Inside the mausoleum, the oldest tombs were farthest back—enormous, natural, craggy growths that proved there was no perfection in magic, only raw beauty and power. They were more than three hundred years old, and it was hard to imagine anyone wielding that sort of power.

Now, Reynold had to commission a stonecutter for their father's tomb. Her brother didn't have any magic of his own, and Gillian hardly more than that. But the ceremony still required a show of power from their bloodline. In decades past, their skill had become unnecessary, their strength diluted, but if they were to lose it entirely, there was no telling how the people would react. Magic was the only weapon they had against the beasts of legend that would enslave and murder them. Gillian had no doubt that Reynold would have traded Roland's legs to see him show any magical talent at all.

The large cavern was lit by torches. The hushed murmurs of the guests devoted enough to follow echoed softly off the walls as Gillian drew in a slow breath and rolled back her shoulders. She could only breathe so deep before her corset stopped her, but it was enough.

At Reynold's nod, she stepped forward. Roland shuffled to his father's side and pressed his cheek to the king's thigh. Reynold set a hand fondly on his head. Here, in front of the peers of the realm and their enemies, there'd be no hint of his dissatisfaction at Roland's frailty.

The men who carried the casket lowered it into the tomb beside her mother's, then shifted the heavy stone slab on top. Prince Laurence stood over the tomb, frowning. Four decades ago, her uncle had been in much the same position as she was. When King Gerald had died, it had secured her father's succession to the Llangardian throne, and Laurence had been freed of that responsibility. Now, he ran his broad hand over the stone that hid her father, then rejoined his family.

Gillian's throat tightened, and she looked away. Far toward the back of the cavern, the firelight flickered off crystal formations her ancestors had carved with power and grief. Toward the front, where her father—and where someday Reynold and Roland and even she herself would find their rest—the tombs were more subdued. Plainer. Aweless.

As Gillian approached the smooth slab of her father's final resting place, she flexed her fingers. Every time she called on magic, she doubted it would come. Worry slithered in her gut. It hadn't left her yet, but she had a fear that the monotony of life would leech any wonder that remained out of her. There was no rhyme or reason to magic. She didn't know why she had it and Reynold didn't, or how to make what little she had grow.

She closed her eyes and ran her fingers lightly over the marble. The top was even and smooth, but she reached beyond it, feeling for her father, calling the memory of his craggy, broad features to the front of her mind.

For all her life, he'd had wrinkles around his eyes. When she'd been small enough that he could sweep her up onto his shoulders, she'd only seen them when he smiled. He'd had hair like hers, jet black and straight as the arrow flew, but his eyes were Reynold's—a blue so light it mirrored the snowy peaks of the Mawrcraig mountains on icy winter nights. He'd been broad and sturdy—the kind of man who required an especially strong horse for longer journeys. He hadn't been handsome, exactly. Not like Reynold with his teasing smirk and rust-red hair that caught the sun. But King Edmund had been beautiful, even when his black hair turned dull gray and his lines were deep from exhaustion and rarely from smiling. At least Gillian thought so.

As she drew his shape out of stone, she did not breathe. The magic trapped in the space between her fingertips and the cool stone was all she could feel, all that mattered. Straining like she was trying to lift the man himself—a whole head taller than her and thrice as broad—her brows puckered. When she dragged the shape of him from the stone, she gasped, sucking a deep breath into her clenched lungs. She sagged against the tomb, bracing her hands on the curve of her stone father's arm. Laurence's arm wound around her shoulder, and she turned into him. Warmth rushed through her when he pressed his lips to her forehead.

She blinked her eyes open to see that Lady Radcliffe had given Roland a flower. He stepped forward and settled it over King Edmund's chest. A tear slipped down Gillian's cheek. Unthinking, she wiped it away.

The casting had drained her, but once the mourners had filtered past the tomb, setting trinkets and offerings on her father's form, she allowed her uncle to guide her out of the mausoleum and into the light.

Outside, her breaths came easier. She steadied on her own feet and smiled serenely at the mourners gathered. It was an expression she had practiced—one that came easily, even when she was ready to crawl into bed and sleep for a day or two. She might be able to make her own choices like she had never before, but Reynold needed her now, and there would be far fewer choices to make if either of their stars fell.

"Are you well, Gillian?" her uncle asked softly, leaning toward her ear so others would not hear. She nodded, and he stood firm as she stepped away to address the crowd.

"Today was a day to mourn the passing of a great man, a great king, and a wonderful father," she said, raising her voice for all to hear. "Tomorrow, we celebrate the rise of a new one." She turned toward Reynold, who tilted his chin up a fraction.

"We invite you to join King Reynold Cavendish for a tournament." A smirk tilted the left corner of her lips. "I hear there will be prizes."

The energy of those gathered shifted. The idea of a tournament piqued the interest of lords with sons who wished to win the king's favor. It seemed an untoward moment for a celebration, but with so many foreign guests in attendance, her brother had assured her it was necessary to present a strong front and prove the resilience of Llangard. Reynold dismissed the crowd, but people continued to approach to offer their condolences.

At least, that was the intention of most of their guests.

When Reynold's man, Bet, approached—clad as ever in his black leather jerkin and matching trousers, his dark hair curled and unkempt, shadowing his obsidian eyes—Gillian frowned. This was the sort of unsavory company her brother kept in secret. He was not an appropriate guest for their father's funeral.

"Your Majesty," Bet said lowly.

That was all it took for Reynold to begin to extricate himself. "You'll have to excuse me—" he said to Lord and Lady Lovell, who both dipped in a bow.

Her strength returning, Gillian reached out and grabbed Reynold's wrist. "It is hardly appropriate for you to abandon—"

He cut her off with a glare, but he did not pull away, only stared long enough for her to lose her nerve and release him on her own.

"It is hardly appropriate," he drawled, "for you to order your king, Gillian. Excuse me."

Gillian watched him step away with the miscreant, scowling. Even she had heard rumor of what Bet Kyston was to her brother—a dagger in the night, a murderer. Her brother would call him a necessary evil. Princes and kings could not always move openly against their enemies, and they could not afford to suffer too many of those. To her, it seemed dishonorable, but Reynold was as much a knight as his son was a magician.

"Your Highness," Lady Radcliffe said softly, approaching from her left. She paused a moment, just long enough to give Gillian time to shake off her frustration. "Should I take Prince Roland back to the palace to rest?"

Gillian started. The boy looked beyond tired.

"Please," Gillian agreed, squeezing her arm softly. Tristram stood at his mother's side, somber and appropriate—not skirting off to talk to assassins at a gods damned funeral. "Thank you for your help today."

They bowed to her before taking their leave, and Tristram swung Roland onto his shoulders the very way King Edmund had once lifted her. The Cavendish's resting place was outside the city walls, but within the half hour, they'd have Roland tucked in bed and safe. She wished she could follow them home.

❦ 3 ❦

BET

Under normal circumstances, Bet Kyston would never have interrupted King Reynold at his father's funeral. He would not have attended at all, if not for the large number of Torndals—strangers whose intentions had yet to come out—in attendance. King Reynold's wariness had grown as his father's health deteriorated. He'd asked Bet to keep watch for anything suspicious, but Bet had tried to stay out of sight. He was not fool enough to think King Edmund would be pleased by his presence.

Now, Princess Gillian glared at him as he took her brother away, her lips pale and set into a firm, disapproving line. She looked as severe as he'd ever seen her in her black dress, the bodice covered in simple thread-of-gold brocade in the shape of fern leaves.

But Bet had the king's trust, and His Majesty knew that he wouldn't interrupt them without cause. There were those at court who thought Bet reached too far above himself, but he knew his place better than anyone and kept to the shadows when he wasn't needed.

No sooner had they left Princess Gillian than Lord Tristram and his lady mother approached her to scoop up the little prince. Bet sucked in his cheeks, watching their retreat from the corner of his eyes. Lord Tristram, who moved so smoothly through these crowds, carrying secrets Bet could not guess.

Since he'd been a boy darting down hallways he had no business sneaking through to avoid the kitchens, Lord Tristram had held his attention. The lord had come to Atheldinas with his mother, stepping out of the carriage with a glare like there was no place he loathed more than the capital city of Llangard—perhaps nothing at all he loathed more, save his father, whom he shouldered past.

If his fair hair and molten eyes hadn't caught Bet's attention while he crouched in the carefully manicured shrubbery that day, Lord Tristram's fury on the training field would have.

He had been smaller than the knights—not yet a man, but more of one than Bet had been—and he had not won his sparring matches. Had not come close. But when he fell, he rolled to his feet and sprang again. At the time, Bet had already learned not to get hit. But Tristram, only a few years older than Bet, had been hit again and again. Every time, he had stood up.

By some special magic, Lord Tristram did not bruise. Bet didn't notice at first, but having borne a number of blows himself, he could see Tristram had always recovered faster than normal. A sound strike to his head, and Bet was dizzy for days. Either the knights Tristram fought went too easy on him, or the young man was hardier than he should have been.

Bet had always dealt in secrets, even as a kitchen boy darting between the legs of lords and ladies, scampering under tables. His hearing was impeccable, his penchant for trouble unmatched. And still, after a dozen years, Bet couldn't parse out all that Lord Tristram kept hidden.

He certainly couldn't be as perfect as he seemed—a hardy fighter, a clever companion to a prince—now to a king. Handsome. Gods, far too handsome, from his perfect bowed lips—that smirk saved for the sparring field—to his blasted calves. Bet had rarely had opportunity to see those calves, but they were muscled, graceful.

Tristram's hair reminded Bet of his mother, fair and beautiful. Bet looked nothing like her, dark and craven as he was. Seven hells, when Tristram had been a youth, Bet could've mistaken the fine line of Tristram's nose, his sharp cheekbones, for elven. It was little wonder that others at court made that mistake. But elves bruised.

"Bennet," Reynold said coolly, drawing Bet's attention from the trio of Lord Radcliffe, his mother, and Prince Roland. Bet licked his lips.

"When you led the procession into the tomb, the Torndals stayed behind. I heard Jarl Jorun speaking to Jarl Katrien with something less than admiration for your late father and for you. She is a sorceress and known to be versed in the brewing of unguents . . . and poisons." They shared a look. Bet did not even have to cock his brow for King Reynold to understand him.

"You believe they poisoned my father?"

The contingent of northerners from Tornheim had been with them for a fortnight—long enough to see King Edmund through the end of his illness. Now that he was dead, they showed every sign of staying. Bet would wager every coin in his purse that it had less to do with the upcoming tournament and more to do with the chance to cause unrest as Reynold took the throne.

Bet frowned. Before he could reply, Reynold continued.

"My father was old. Sickly. It was his time." A muscle in his jaw had begun to twitch.

That was, after all, precisely what Reynold wanted to believe—it was finally his turn. His divine right had come to fruition. Bet had never developed a habit of arguing with him. People who did, did not tend to last long at court.

Bet's eyes flicked up to the golden crown resting on his king's russet curls. It fit him perfectly. Even in the gray of the overcast day—perhaps because of its somber tone—Reynold gleamed like the sun. Who was Bet to imply that his ascension to the throne was anything other than right and proper?

After a moment, his gaze fell back to Reynold's demanding one. "I did not mean to suggest that your father's death, though tragic, was anything other than natural. I am only saying I do not trust the northerners."

At that, Reynold frowned. His eyes darted their way, and he rubbed his palm over his lips.

"Nor should you," Reynold agreed when he dropped his hand. "What, exactly, did Jorun say?"

Bet's nose flared as he drew in a breath. He'd learned not to stoke

Reynold's anger unnecessarily. In this instance, it seemed unavoidable, however unlikely that that anger would fall upon his own head.

"He likened your father to a farmer. More shepherd than king—lord over wayward beasts. He said that King Edmund had outlived his usefulness, but that Your Majesty was not likely to."

The lands of Tornheim, to the north past the high ridge of the Mawrcraig Mountains, past even Lord Radcliffe's seat at Merrick, were harsh and unforgiving. There, the mighty ruled. There had been whispers of a jarl who could call the wind. That the Cavendish line had not produced an heir with significant magic in generations would signal to their enemies that the kingdom was weak. It was only a matter of time before they tried to take advantage of that weakness.

Reynold considered him a moment. The king's tempers were much more dangerous when they swept cool as a wind out of the frozen north. He nodded shortly.

"And Jarl Katrien?" His Majesty asked.

"Said very little."

Behind his closed lips, Bet could see the king run his tongue over his teeth. Never let it be said that Reynold did not weigh his options before acting.

"Jarl Jorun flaps his tongue too much," Reynold said casually. "Bring it to me. If it's still in his skull, all the better."

With a dismissive wave of his hand, Reynold turned back to the lingering mourners. Bet bowed deeply, even as he stepped away. "Yes, Your Majesty."

❧ 4 ❧

RHIANNON

A ccording to legend, the people of Llangard had once had magic enough to bring a mountain down on Rhiannon's ancestors. Now, Gillian Cavendish hardly had enough power to draw her father's image from the stone. Rhiannon could scarcely imagine the cause of any dragon's trepidation with these people, though she herself had spent decades fearing and revering them in equal measure.

Of course, human magicians weren't only skilled in manipulating earth and stone. Most dangerous by far were the ones who sang to the wind. They made it impossible to fly and guided bolts and lances true. Earth and water magics could be troublesome to her kind. Fire magic was largely a joke. No human magician could conjure a flame that burned brighter than the one in Rhiannon's own throat. It was hard to imagine Rhoswyn, her dearest sister and a formidable dragon, cowed before the Llangardian princess.

"They just . . ." At her side, Hafgan frowned. A line puckered between his light blond brows. "They leave him there?"

Around them, mourners began to filter out, moving back into the daylight, but Hafgan stood, trapped by the sight of the solitary stone tomb, set apart from the late queens', and the carving of the late king in repose.

Rhiannon was not often moved by sympathy, but the exception in all things was Hafgan. Children were rare among dragons, and though Hafgan wasn't hers and couldn't be called a child anymore, his hatching had been a miracle. It was the only one she'd ever seen.

Rhiannon had been among the dragons Queen Halwyn sent to Wynford when that village had gone quiet and they'd seen smoke curling high past the mountains to the west.

When the Summer Clan had landed amongst the rubble, they'd found devastation. The vulnerable bodies of dragons' smaller forms—so like those of humans—discarded like scraps of trash. Dragons in their true forms with necks pierced through by lances, their chests torn open.

The dragons of Windy Pass had traded often with humans. It was there, when she had only seen fourteen summers, that she found her hoard. It was late for a dragon to begin their collection, but nothing had ever called to her like a sterling silver locket half buried in dirt and ash. She'd pocketed it and kept the thrill of finding it to herself as their group searched somberly for survivors who weren't there.

In that ruin, they'd found Hafgan's egg. Its light gold and green scales weren't cracked, and though an egg without its mother rarely survived, the Summer Clan had cared for him with nest and fire and the heat of their bodies until a tremor ran through it, and Hafgan was born.

She reached out and settled her arm around his shoulder, though already he was taller than her—older than she'd been when they'd found him. Gently, she twisted her fingers through the soft golden hair, shorn short at the nape of his neck.

"Their ways are not ours," she said, too low for anyone close to hear. On her toes, she leaned in to kiss his temple. "Sweet song, you worry too much. They believe his spirit goes to their gods. He will be reunited with his people one day."

Hafgan only stared at the smooth marble, lines of worry creasing his brow. "He is alone and trapped."

"And it is not our concern," she whispered. Nevertheless, she wrapped her arms around his waist and squeezed him close until she felt his arm slip around her shoulder, the huff of one last sigh, and knew that he'd recovered.

Dragons did not bury their dead but burned them and sent their ashes scattering on the wind where they could lift up the wings of their people. Hafgan's first clan had been a part of the wind since before his hatching.

Stepping outside, into the free air, was a relief. The hillside was grassy and lush. On a far slope, wildflowers still bloomed, though the season was beginning to turn colder.

The funeral was over, and Rhiannon was not there to parley with a dead king, but the living one. She scanned the crowd for russet hair and a crown that held light even on this dark day. It was finer than any piece of gold in the queen's hoard.

Relations between the dragons of the Mawrcraig Mountains and Llangard were contentious at best. The kingdom relied on the dragons to turn back any invaders from the north, and the dragons expected to be left alone for their trouble. A new monarch provided an opportunity to improve things. They didn't have to stay trapped in their villages. Dragons were meant to fly. And the path to their freedom was in the hands of a man she knew nothing about. It was time to change that.

Craning her neck, she finally caught sight of him standing apart from the rest of his people, speaking to a man who looked as if the black clothing he wore was a second skin, not the trappings of mourning the courtiers wore.

King Reynold stepped away from him. As he moved, he twitched his hand to beckon a knight to his side. She came at once, armor as gray as the skies above.

Perhaps he feared trouble. A ruler was never more vulnerable than in their first days. Halwyn had fought and killed no less than three usurpers before the first full moons of her reign. The knight—a woman with hair like strawberries in high summer and a gaze as sharp and exacting as brass tacks—looked well equipped to keep him safe.

Rhiannon grabbed Hafgan's wrist. "Come on," she hissed as she pulled them both into the king's path. When His Majesty startled, she did too.

"Excuse me, Your Majesty." At once, she dropped into a curtsey.

He waved a hand, and Rhiannon could feel his gaze bore into the top of her head. "You needn't bother with such formality today. Rise, my lady."

"My condolences for your loss," she said to the ground before she stood. When she rose and met his eyes, she smirked. "Heavy though it may be, I can see that the crown rests well on your head. And handsomely."

Pale as King Reynold was, a faint flush colored his cheeks. "Do I know you?"

"I doubt it. We hail from the north. I am Rhiannon gan Derys, and this is my ward, Hafgan."

"Your ward?" the king echoed. "I would have guessed brother." Reynold looked Hafgan over. He stiffened beside her. In his whole life, there were only a handful of times that anyone had looked at Hafgan with anything short of complete affection. "Or that you were his ward instead."

Rhiannon fought the urge to roll her eyes. She knew that things were different among humans than among her own kind. It wouldn't do to offend him. "I have no need of a keeper."

"Enviable," Reynold said, glancing toward the knight beside him with a wry smile. "Are you from Tornheim?" he asked when he turned back to Rhiannon.

"Do I look like the kind of lady who'd keep company with those brigands?" Rhiannon asked, cocking her head.

Though he didn't flinch before her as she'd have liked, Reynold laughed, and the sound was deep and pleasant. "I don't know," he admitted. "You don't look like any sort of lady I've ever seen before."

It was a complete falsehood intended to sway her, and still, she preened. "Well, you can hardly count on a man, even a king"—she dragged her finger down the front of his doublet, across buttons made of silk—"to understand a woman." Suddenly, she turned to the knight at his side. "What do you think?"

"Me?" she asked.

Rhiannon lifted her brows and nodded once. The knight licked her lips and swallowed. She said nothing.

"Well, Sidonie?" the king demanded.

Sidonie—gorgeous name, Sidonie—glanced between the pair of them. After a moment, her armor shifted as she regained composure. "I think you look like trouble," Sidonie said, her chin lifted, her freckles a warm, gorgeous brown.

Rhiannon could not help but grin. She bit her lip to hide it and, no doubt, failed miserably. "Too right!" she announced. She rocked onto the balls of her feet, turning back toward King Reynold. "Does that concern Your Majesty?"

Their eyes locked as, slowly, Reynold shook his head. "I was made to withstand trouble such as yours."

Rhiannon laughed. "No doubt, Your Majesty. No doubt. Now, if you'll excuse us—" She linked arms with Hafgan, quite aware that she had yet to be dismissed.

"Where are you going?" the king demanded.

"I'm famished, sire. I'm afraid I must retire."

As she turned away from him with Hafgan, King Reynold reached out and caught her arm.

"Then I will escort you." Authoritative. Not a quality she particularly liked in men, but with the crown atop his pretty curls, perhaps he was drunk with his new power.

"Your Majesty," she said on a breath, slipping her arm from his vise grip, "I would love nothing more. But you have a mourning sister to look after and subjects ready to follow at your whim."

He scowled, but as he glanced around, he remembered himself and nodded.

"I would see you again."

Rhiannon hummed a moment, staring at the hollow of his throat before raising her eyes to look up at him through her thick lashes.

"You are hosting a tournament," she said. The king nodded curtly. "We intend to stay for it. Perhaps, if you put forward a champion strong enough to win the day, I will honor you with my company."

Reynold's jaw clenched. From the hard look in his eyes, it was clear he thought she should be honored by his instead.

"Or we can return north tomorrow . . ." she suggested, listing to the side like a wilting flower.

"No," the king said sharply. "Stay. Watch the tournament. You'll find there's much in Atheldinas to recommend it."

"And its king," she assented. With a small curtsey, she backed away and pulled Hafgan on toward the city walls. There were carriages for the courtiers, but they would walk. The gently sloping hills were nothing to the crags of their mountain home.

"I thought you wanted to talk to him," Hafgan whispered in her ear. "Is that not why we're here?"

"It is, but the king does not seem the sort to give favors when he's already won his prize. It is a game, Hafgan, and one I intend to win." Her assurances did nothing to wipe the worried look from his face. She squeezed his forearm. "Don't fret! We'll watch the tournament. It'll be fun. And when the time is right, I'll turn the king's ear."

The coldest man alive—and she hoped Reynold was far from that—would not forge treaties standing so near his father's tomb, after all.

5

SIDONIE

Perhaps Sidonie was old fashioned.

Or perhaps she had loved the previous king too much, hard worker and supporter of the people that he had been. But a tournament to celebrate the new king starting the day after King Edmund's funeral left a bad taste in her mouth.

Reynold was her king now. She owed all allegiance to him.

That did not mean she had to like him.

If she privately thought him a vainglorious brat not fit to clean his father's boots, no one ever needed to know. All she had to do was smile and nod and protect him with her life. The relative value of his life versus his father's was meaningless; Edmund was lost, and Reynold was king. His life was certainly more important than hers.

"Sir Beaufort," her squire chided. "I need your foot." He was a good lad, and not going to point out that she'd been woolgathering.

"Sorry, Tobias." She propped her foot up for him to finish his lacing, and tried to pay attention to the matter at hand.

A tourney.

She'd fought them before, many times. It was how she'd gone from being a member of the city guard to a member of the prince's guard. Now, she led the king's.

Any farmhand could talk to the right people and get a job in the city guard if they were so inclined. Working at the palace was another matter entirely, and people who were born on farms rarely managed to work their way up those ranks.

Her family was constantly in a state somewhere between bemoaning the loss of her hands during harvest season, and proudly telling everyone who would listen that their eldest child was a member of the king's guard.

"You mustn't be nervous, Sir Beaufort," Tobias said a little timidly, as though he expected her to be angry with him for speaking his mind. "The only other knight of the realm with a chance against you is Lord Radcliffe, and you've beaten him before."

She chuckled at that. "And he has beaten me before."

He shrugged, dismissing it. Tobias was new, and her squires always started out thinking she was determined to prove herself against the powerful lords of Llangard's court. She couldn't care less if she won or if Tristram Radcliffe did, so long as one of them defeated the lot from Tornheim.

Preferably both of them.

The important part wasn't her pride, it was protecting her country from greedy, grasping northerners, who would cherish any opportunity to make a fool of her king, and therefore, of her kingdom. "I trust Lord Radcliffe and I will both make King Ed—Reynold proud."

The sadness that washed over Tobias's face at her slip was a mirror of how she had been feeling during the days since the king had passed. Edmund's death was such a loss to the common people of Llangard, she feared for their future.

He nodded before motioning to the tent flap. "You're ready, sir. Luck be with you."

She inclined her head to him and left the tent. She tried hard not to think of the flighty creature who had so turned the king's head the day before. Rhiannon, she had named herself, and from the north.

Sidonie was from the southern reaches of Llangard, where they did not have women like that. There, women were hard workers with strong backs, field-roughened hands, and leathery skin. Rhiannon had seemed like a bauble worn by a noble lady, glittering and beautiful.

And not for the likes of Sidonie.

Still, she found herself scanning the crowd for signs of golden, almost white-blonde hair. Lord Tristram was from the north, wasn't he? Perhaps that was simply the look of northerners. Most of the women in court were regularly aflutter over his pale hair and golden eyes, including Her Highness, Princess Gillian.

She supposed among men, Tristram was a decent choice. He had fine features and full lips that most men did not. Sidonie had never seen the appeal of blunt, angular, masculine features. Give her a soft curve and a round cheek any day.

Golden-blonde curls twirled on the breeze in front of her, followed by their owner, the beautiful sylph from the day before. Her eyes were bluer than the sky, like the wildflowers that grew along the roads, and of course, she had a few of those tucked behind her ear to show them off. The smirk on her face was downright dangerous. His Majesty was wrong if he thought this woman was trouble he could handle. She was too much trouble for any man.

"M'lady Rhiannon," Sidonie greeted, trying to remain formal. His Majesty had attempted to pretend indifference, but clearly, he had found Rhiannon charming. There was no point whatsoever in Sidonie pinning her affections on one she could never have.

Rhiannon gave her the same coy smile as the day before, cocking her head to one side at an angle that looked almost painful. "Off to compete in the king's tournament?"

"His Majesty wishes me to win it," she agreed. She wouldn't flatter the woman by saying it had anything to do with her. Sidonie wasn't planning to win it for her, after all. She was planning to win it for the pride of her country, on the orders of her king.

Without so much as a word, Rhiannon pulled the flowers from behind her ear and leaned forward to tuck them into Sidonie's braid. "For luck then," she said, that smirk telling Sidonie she knew exactly what she was doing. "I'm sure you'll emerge the hero of the day."

"As ever, my sword is for Llangard." She should take the flowers out of her hair and give them back. It wasn't appropriate for her to accept any lady's token, since she was fighting on behalf of the crown, much less this lady's.

Rhiannon nodded, face serious but eyes still sparkling with mischief that Sidonie thought might prove the end of her. "Of course. For king and country."

She didn't know why, but she reiterated her statement. "For Llangard." It was the sort of assertion that, taken wrongly, could have her sent packing back to the farm—or worse, beheaded, if Reynold were looking for betrayal behind every corner. He hadn't given indication of such previously, but one never knew what a lord would do with power until they had it.

She sighed, inclined her head, and took her leave of the still smiling Rhiannon.

It did not matter. The flowers did not matter. She had a tourney to win, for her people.

Lord Radcliffe gave her a salute from where he sat across the field, astride his horse and ready for his first opponent.

She glanced to the other end of the field to see what he faced.

Jarl Jorun.

Sidonie shook her head in disgust. The jarl was a horrible creature, oversized from both hard work and too much wine, and his breath was constantly sour. He never let her pass him by without making a reference to her "womanly assets," usually followed by comments about how a woman was wasted on the field, when women were much better suited to politics and matters of money. Sidonie had no talent with either, and she almost hoped Tristram failed to beat him, so she would have her own chance.

Almost. She didn't want any member of her court to fare ill, and in the end, Radcliffe beating the man was as good as anything. And he would, because arrogant though it might seem of her to think it, Tristram Radcliffe was the only competitor on the field who had a chance against her through skill alone. Perhaps if he had a run of bad luck, she would have to joust someone else at the end of the day, but it was not likely. Radcliffe didn't seem to suffer bad luck as often as most people.

It would be interesting to see which of them came out the winner this time. He always gave her a good competition.

The joust was a quick thing in practice, and surprisingly simple, given the immense pomp of the average tourney. It was merely two people, two horses, two shields, and two lances. Whichever rider had the better grace, the stronger, steadier arm, and the most skill in their aim won the day, unless they were faced with faulty equipment or distractions.

Not that the jarl was above cheating to win. Some miscreant had once poisoned her horse on the morning of a tourney, and she was not convinced it hadn't been him.

Radcliffe and Jorun readied their horses, and the crowd went silent.

Sidonie looked to King Reynold in the stands and saw that his eyes weren't on the match about to commence, but scanning the crowds. When his gaze locked, she followed it and found, of course, Lady Rhiannon. She couldn't fault his taste as far as the woman's beauty; she was impeccable. But he had ordered the tournament, and Radcliffe was one of his closest friends, so ignoring the joust seemed a little—

There was a crash and a gasp from the crowd. Sidonie looked back to find Jorun on the ground, his horse dancing nervously around him. The crowd, however, was more interested in Radcliffe, still on his mount despite the fact that the jarl's lance was lodged in his visor. It was deep enough to have taken an eye out, or gods forbid, kill him.

When he hit the end of the tilt, he hopped off his mount with more dexterity than most men could ever manage, let alone in armor, and whipped off his helm. His lovely face was completely intact, and while Sidonie was close enough to see fury in his eyes—an unusual emotion for the placid lord—there was a performer's smile on his face.

The crowd cheered and Radcliffe gave a sweeping bow, which only prodded them into cheering louder. The man knew how to perform for the people, of that there could be no doubt.

Jorun pulled himself up, muttering and dusting off bits of splintered lance, which appeared to have hit him square in the middle of the shield, if the scratch in the paint was any indicator. She cursed herself for getting distracted by a pretty face and missing what had happened.

Likely, Jorun had been aiming for Sir Tristram's face instead of his shield, as was the rule of the joust. The jarl knew full well that the people of Llangard didn't follow the northern style of jousting, which seemed designed to take off the head of one's opponent. He would smile and claim to have made a mistake, and the king would have to let the matter drop, despite what had been a clear attempt on the life of his cousin and vassal.

Jorun might have to get away with it physically, but he didn't have to get away with it entirely.

"Do you need help, dear jarl?" she called from her place next to the crowd of her people. "It seems you've fallen from your horse. How embarrassing."

The crowd burst into raucous laughter, and she smiled sweetly at him as though making a genuine offer. He glared at her and stalked off the field, leaving his horse behind.

Perhaps he had the right of it, and politics were the place of a woman.

❧ 6 ❧

TRISTRAM

Tristram knew Jorun had never liked him. It had never been in doubt; the man tried to impugn his masculinity and his honor at every turn. Tris wasn't sure why, exactly, but it was no secret. But trying to kill him in full view of the entire court was new.

It was clear that had been his intention. His lance had been squarely aimed at Tristram's head, no sign of quavering. That Tris had managed to avoid most of the blow and knock Jorun from his own horse had been nothing short of a miracle. Luck, as much as skill.

He took a deep breath as he left the field, where he was joined on the walk by Sir Sidonie Beaufort.

"I'm not mistaken that he just tried to kill you?" she asked.

He shook his head and had to pause for a moment. His hands were trembling, and he was unsure if it was anger or fear. He decided anger was less shameful. After a few deep breaths, he turned and faced her. "Is something happening that I don't know about? Attempting to murder me makes no sense. He can play it off as it is, but if he had killed me—"

"If he had killed you, it would have put the king in a bad position. Do nothing and look weak, or have Jorun executed and look like a petulant child angry at losing a tourney." She glanced around them to make sure no one was listening and lowered her voice. "Because that is what the northerners would have called it. Losing a man in a tourney is nothing there, and they consider themselves the better for having culled a weak fighter."

"They know that isn't how we are," Tristram complained, but she was entirely right, of course. And she knew he was aware, because she didn't repeat herself. "There's nothing to be done."

She smacked him on the shoulder, bright smile on her face. "You did what was to be done, m'lord. You bested him despite his attempt and made him look a fool."

"I think you did rather better at that," he said, his return smile weak. "And I thank you for it."

He had done his best to pretend he wasn't smarting, that the side of his face wasn't numb and he wasn't in shock that someone had tried to kill him, but upon his life, he couldn't have opened his mouth. He might have screamed at the man, and then where would they be?

He breathed in slow and stretched his shoulders as much as the armor allowed. "You had best get back to the field. I think you're up soon."

"No doubt I'll see you in the final round," she answered with a wink, and left him to head back to the field.

He wasn't so sure. He thought he might have used all the luck he had in him that day, simply by escaping his first joust with his life.

Tristram wasn't a man for politics. He rarely knew the right and clever thing to say. He didn't know how to speak to courtiers; sometimes they seemed to be speaking a foreign language. He was more like King Edmund had been, he feared, than like Reynold. He wondered if Reynold would bore of his ineptitude and send him away eventually.

He would end up back in the northern border fort in Merrick where he'd been raised, likely, in the same situation. His mother's husband had angered the king and been sent to the outer reaches of the kingdom for over a decade.

All things considered, it wouldn't be so bad. He might even meet a dragon, something that wasn't likely to happen in the heart of Llangard. Maybe he could meet his true father. He usually thought he was angry with the dragon who had impregnated his mother and disappeared, but his mother was no child, easily swayed. If she had wanted to go with the dragon, she likely would have. She bore the dragon nothing but fond memories, perhaps even still love, so it was not Tristram's place to question that.

"My lord?" his squire asked, voice cracking with concern. "Are you quite well?" Tris had almost forgotten the boy was there, and he felt like an ass for it.

"I am, thank you." He patted the boy on the shoulder. "You needn't worry about me. I've had worse."

It was true enough. Reynold—His Majesty, Tris must get used to calling him that, even in his head—His Majesty had always been hard on his personal guard. Tris sparred with them regularly, and sometimes the man who did the worst on the field went without supper. Worse yet, sometimes the king summarily dismissed him. It meant that every sparring session was a fight for one's future, and it certainly accomplished the goal of making sure everyone did their best.

While Tristram's own supper and livelihood had never before been in jeopardy, it had made for some tense moments on the practice field over the years.

He was concerned that he had used up his all for the day in those ten seconds of avoiding death, but he didn't want to embarrass the king by losing his second bout, so he needed to calm himself and prepare.

"Could you get me some wine, Alf?" His squire's eyes went wide, and with good reason. Tris never drank wine before or during tourneys. He stuck to watered ale that didn't dull his senses. At the moment, though, the important thing was calming his nerves.

The best of squires, Alf nodded and ran off instead of asking questions. It was obvious enough why Tris was asking for the stuff. He just had to toe the line of calming himself without getting intoxicated.

He caught motion from the corner of his eye, and his head snapped up to make sure he wasn't in danger. When he took in the motion's source, danger remained to be seen. His Majesty's shadow, Bennet Kyston—known to everyone as simply Bet.

There wasn't a person alive who invoked more turbulence in Tris. He was dangerous, obviously. Tris didn't know what he did for Rey—for the king—but no one spoke of it in polite company, which included himself. He seemed perpetually angry, and seemed to particularly dislike Tris.

On the other side, the man was beautiful beyond all, and no one seemed to notice it. Those shining dark curls and intense black eyes, the way his lips curled up in a combination of smile and sneer when he felt . . . emotions of whatever kind it was he felt.

But not right then. Bet's expression was blank as he marched right up to Tris, grabbed his chin and tipped it to the side so that he could inspect his face, specifically the side that Jorun had nearly removed. "The eye?" he asked tersely.

Tris blinked for a moment before he realized he was supposed to answer. "Fine. It's fine. Are you—" How could he ask if the man was concerned about him without seeming ridiculous? "Is something wrong?"

Bet wore an unfamiliar scowl, with no hint of that smile to tame the curl of his upper lip. Tris didn't think he'd been at fault, but Bet's sneer could make a man apologize for being born. It was all he could do to keep his mouth shut.

After a long, silent moment, Bet nodded sharply and turned to march off.

When Alf came back with the wine, Tris downed the goblet, sobriety be damned.

❧ 7 ❧

HAFGAN

Seated in the stands above the field, Rhiannon was drinking again. Humans drank a lot of things that made Hafgan dizzy and ill, and he didn't like it. When he asked for water, they looked at him like he had asked for a cup of mud. Come to think of it, the river that flowed below the Spires was dank and slow moving compared to the crystalline streams of Brynaf, where the Summer Clan lived.

It had, perhaps, not been his best decision to accompany Rhiannon on this trip.

The visit to the human kingdom was a good idea, in theory. They could improve relations between their people and work together against the grumblings from the north. Tornheim was an inhospitable place, and both humans and dragons from those lands were hard, weather- and life-beaten. They looked to the green meadows and plentiful crops of the south, and hungered.

But the humans and dragons of Llangard had been at odds since long, long before Hafgan's hatching. Stories of fearsome magicians were passed around fires when it was too cold to spend nights outside, but humans avoided the mountain wilderness as much as dragons avoided the plains of Llangard.

The crowning of a new king seemed a good time to try to turn things around. They could hope that the new king was more forward thinking than his predecessor, willing to make new allies and work together for the good of their people.

But Hafgan had no idea how Rhiannon intended to succeed when everything she did seemed to annoy the king as much as please him. The man kept turning his intense gaze upon them, a half frown twisting his lips every time Rhiannon's eyes weren't upon him in return.

Immediately after the tourney, when the king's lady knight won the day, the man stood from his throne and headed toward them. Hafgan wasn't sure he'd noticed any of the drama of his other man being nearly killed, or the pronouncement of his champion being the winner. He was too interested in Rhiannon.

"Maybe we should go," he whispered to her as she pretended to ignore the king stalking toward them, lifting a goblet to her lips. "We could be home by tomorrow."

She turned and laughed at him in that way Rhiannon had that didn't allow one to take offense. It was as though he'd said something funny, not as though she thought him a buffoon. "Sweet summer song, you worry too much. He might be human and king, but he's still just a man. He's nothing to fear."

Hafgan thought humans were plenty to fear, otherwise dragonkind wouldn't be hiding in the mountains, pretending they didn't tremble in fear of magic they couldn't use and didn't understand. Rhiannon had been underwhelmed by the princess shaping stone into the image of her dead father, but Hafgan saw the potential there.

She could reshape stone with nothing more than her will and the energy of the universe at her command. What was to stop her from reshaping the mountains themselves? Hafgan shivered, despite the warmth of the air and the people around him.

Rhiannon raised one eyebrow, and he gave her a tight smile in return. He was not going to share his fears. Rhiannon thought him childish enough without him telling her he was worried about the very mountains where they lived.

While there were stories about human mages and their might, most dragons thought the mountains impenetrable since the death of the first human king, Athelstan. Only he had been able to use the very earth against them. Or perhaps his son had been disinclined to destruction, and the rest had merely forgotten that power.

Most dragons hadn't been orphaned and adopted before they hatched. He was grateful to the Summer Clan for taking him in; they were his family. But he would never forget that humans had scattered his first family to the winds.

The soft creatures who surrounded him, drinking intoxicants and cheering feats of agility and daring were not threatening, but they were a threat. There were mages among them who could destroy everything Hafgan loved. Rhiannon might be willing to dismiss that, but he could not.

"Did you enjoy the tourney?" the king asked when he arrived in front of Rhiannon.

He ignored Hafgan entirely, as he mostly had the day before. Insulting as it was, Hafgan felt safer without the king's sharp eyes on him. He had never been in love, but he was fairly certain Rhiannon wasn't the kind of person he would fall in love with. She was too much for him—overwhelming in every way, and she often left his head spinning as much as a cup of human drink.

"Your Majesty," Rhiannon answered coyly, with a curtsey. "Your champion was positively masterful."

The king glanced back toward the field, as though he'd forgotten there had been a tourney at all. Considering the tourney had been to celebrate him and his ascension to the throne, that was off-putting. Perhaps Hafgan was naive. He often thought their queen, Halwyn, was cold and emotionally uninvolved too. She was a good leader, so he supposed King Reynold might be the same.

Still, he couldn't imagine being so cold about his people's successes. Or more importantly, the other champion who'd fought in his name, who had come so close to mortal danger. The man had handled himself magnificently, and he'd been so familiar when he pulled his helmet off to show the crowd that he was unwounded.

Rhiannon was still doing her strange dance with the king, so Hafgan took a quiet step away, and then another. She was distracted and didn't notice. Was it inappropriate for him to leave her alone with the king? There was a crowd surrounding them to keep the man from doing anything untoward. Or was Hafgan the one not supposed to be alone, since he was the ward? Hafgan didn't know much about human culture other than that it was confusing. Humans were so fast, so passionate, and so changeable, he often felt as though he'd been left behind before he even met them.

Still, it was hardly a challenge to slip off while Rhiannon was distracted by the king, and wander away in search of the knight from before. He had hair even paler than Hafgan's, which seemed unusual among humans. Dragons were prone to only the darkest and lightest colors of hair when in human form, often mimicking the color of their scales with golds and pitch blacks. Meanwhile humans had a sea of beautiful and varied red and gold and brown tones that reminded Hafgan of autumn in the mountains.

Hafgan slipped between two tents, turning to look in every direction as he went, and still almost ran into someone anyway. The crowd was thickening, growing raucous and loud as the humans got further into their cups.

For a moment, Hafgan paused and considered returning to their room at a local inn. Rhiannon would look for him there, surely, and he would be able to avoid all the noise. The city was too loud for him sometimes.

He caught sight of the knight from earlier, looking exhausted. Not defeated, exactly, though he had lost his final match against the female knight, but as though he wanted to go to his cave and hibernate like a bear. Some older dragons did that during the coldest winter months, but this man didn't qualify for that.

"I'll be in my rooms if you need anything, Alf," he said back into the tent he'd come out of. "Don't work too hard. There's a celebration. You should enjoy it. Things can be polished and relaced tomorrow."

He turned, listened for a moment, and shook his head in amusement. His eyes caught on Hafgan watching him, and he smiled. It was one of the friendliest gestures Hafgan had seen from a member of the human aristocracy.

"Can I help you with something?"

Maybe Hafgan should have stayed with Rhiannon. "Um." He paused and swallowed. "You—you fought well. Is that what you call it? Fought?"

The man shrugged and then winced, putting one hand to his shoulder. "As good a term as any. I presume you aren't from the capital?"

Hafgan shook his head. "We're, um, from the north."

The man brightened at that. "I grew up in Merrick. Where are you from?"

He definitely should have stayed with Rhiannon. "Um, a very small town. Near the mountains." He tried to remember how humans named their towns, but they all felt so random to him. He spit out the first thing that came to mind. "Halwyn's Den."

Halwyn would be disgusted with the notion of a human town named for her.

The knight looked disappointed, but he covered it quickly. "I haven't heard of it, I'm afraid. I hope you're not too close to the mountains. They can be dangerous."

That was true, particularly for humans, who were vulnerable to changing temperatures, so he nodded. "Oh no, um, sir."

The man laughed, and his smile was happy and genuine. His warm brown eyes caught the light and looked almost golden—like a dragon's. "It's Tristram."

"Hafgan," he introduced himself, offering a small bow. That seemed to be how the humans did things, and the gesture was returned in kind, so hopefully he'd done it right.

The look on the knight's face when he looked back up at Hafgan was odd. "Hafgan. That's so familiar. Not a common name, though. I wonder if I might have visited your town and don't remember it."

Hafgan had serious doubts about that. "It's a very northern name," he suggested. He was awful at lying, and the way the knight raised an eyebrow at him confirmed it.

Thankfully and horribly at once, that was when one of the king's many knights came ambling up. "Hafgan?" he asked. When Hafgan nodded, the knight motioned toward the castle. "His Majesty has invited the Lady Rhiannon and yourself to stay with the royal household a while, and she asked me to retrieve you, as well as her things."

When Hafgan looked back, Tristram was smiling at him. "That is excellent news. It's been years since a lady caught his attention." There was some concern in his tone, but his expression was open and hopeful. "Perhaps your Lady Rhiannon could be the next queen of Llangard."

Hafgan hoped not. Or perhaps he hoped that if it were the case, he didn't have to be around to witness the uncomfortable way Rhiannon danced back while the king pursued.

He offered a strained smile in return. "Perhaps I'll at least see you again before we go, Sir Tristram."

"I hope so!" the knight agreed, patting him on the back as he headed toward the palace.

The knight was friendly enough, and maybe Hafgan was simply too timid, but he was starting to think he'd be lucky to escape the capital with his wings intact.

8

BET

Rarely in Bet's long career did he have any personal vendetta to play out against his mark, but he would enjoy killing Jarl Jorun.

Bet had stood in the shadow of the stands to watch Tristram's joust, had seen the jarl lift his lance too high, viciously sturdy, and with sinking horror, had watched Tristram's head snap back. For one breath, he had thought Tristram might be dead, and he could have killed Jorun right there in front of every lord and lady of Llangard and the whole contingent from Tornheim—slit his throat and stained his coarse gold hair with blood before anyone could stop him.

But Tristram had kept his mount. Jorun had fallen. And Bet allowed the Torndal a few more hours of life.

Now, he watched from different shadows, steam swirling tendrils through the air around him. Bet stood naked in the bath, water moving gently past his waist. Under it, where no one could see, he twisted the wooden handles of his garrote between his fingers.

Columns rose directly from the bath itself, providing alcoves and a sense of privacy despite the pool of hot water half the size of the tiltyard. Beyond the one Bet hid behind, Jarl Jorun grunted. He flinched away from the woman sponging his shoulder.

In the hours since his joust, his skin had turned a deep, ruddy purple.

Bet felt a small twist of pride to see the bruise. Radcliffe's victory was a boon for Reynold; that was all. And Jorun's lack of honor was an insult. Llangard had lost nothing thanks to their knights' impressive fortitude.

"Get off," Jorun growled. "Get away."

The woman flinched, blinking at her lord with wide, startled eyes. "Go!" he shouted, drawing attention to them from other warriors and fighters soothing their aching bodies on the other side of the bath. People narrowed their eyes to peer through the steam, but the northerners had no friends in Llangard, and Jorun had no friends among his own people when he was in such a foul mood.

Tense, she backed away from Jorun, swam to the edge of the bath, and pulled herself onto the tiled floor. Water dripped off her glistening skin as she rushed away with her head bowed.

On the far side of the bath, men were laughing, boasting, making promises of the taverns and brothels they'd visit once night had fallen. As servants brought them wine, they grew louder, rowdier. And Jorun remained on his own to sulk over his loss. When he turned to the bath's wall, his hands braced on the edge, Bet saw his opportunity.

With slow, smooth motions, he approached Jorun.

"I told you to leave," Jorun growled. In one second, his arms tensed to push off the wall and rebuke the young woman, but before the second passed, Bet was upon him.

He pulled the handles of the garrote apart and slipped it over Jorun's throat. The man was thick all over, his throat sinewy and strong. Behind his neck, Bet crossed the wire ends and pulled. Jorun choked. He struggled and splashed, but all his sounds were drowned out by the men at the other end. The sight of him blocked by steam and, for good measure, Bet dragged him behind a column.

He braced his back on the stone as Jorun kicked his feet. His fingers, strong and thick, dug viciously into Bet's arms, his sides, anywhere Jorun could reach, leaving deep scratches.

Bet hardly noticed. All his interest was in the resilience of skin, muscle, and tendons in Jorun's neck. All Bet's strength went into pulling the wire tighter, until he felt the muscles give, the breath nothing more than a soft vibration in Jorun's throat, and the jarl's flesh gave way to the metal.

Blood blossomed from the line of wire choking him, seeping down his neck in a ruby curtain. It was slicker than the water splashed on both their bodies, and it blossomed in a cloud as Jorun's body sank lower in the bath. Slowly, slowly, the fight seeped out of him.

When he was still, his breathing stopped forever, Bet carefully peeled the wire from his neck. With efficiency, he cleaned it off in the water and wrapped it loosely around his wrist. Then, he turned his mark over.

Jorun, who'd long sought to embarrass Llangard, who'd insulted and threatened Reynold, who might have a hand in King Edmund's death—no matter how timely.

Bet touched his face. His beard was long and braided—a habit of the Torndals. Despite the dark blond of his hair, he looked nothing like Tristram, who had hair spun of purest gold and silver, with features carved by the hands of the greatest sculptor. Bet considered what this man might have done to Tristram's high cheek, his bright eye—a brown so light it might be molten gold—brighter, even, than King Reynold's crown.

In one move, Jorun might've denied Bet the sight of Tristram's perfection forever, and resent that perfection though he did, Bet could not allow a brigand to steal it.

He cupped Jorun's cheek, ran his thumb over his brow, and dug into his eye. With gritted teeth, he pressed, tense and hard until the eye, too, gave. Sunken and bloody, the pad of his finger stained red, Bet released him with a disgusted sound.

The body floated away, toward the far end of the pool where men still laughed and clapped each other on the backs and slipped through the water closer than Bet would ever be allowed. Steadily, Jorun's body turned the water red.

Bet looked down and in the ripple of water, saw blood splattered over his own face. He splashed his cheeks, and by the time he heard the first scream, he'd left the pool behind, shrugged into his dark robe, and disappeared.

TRISTRAM

People were staring at Tristram.

They often did that; he wasn't ignorant of the attention people at court paid him. With his pale hair and bright eyes, he was unique looking. When one combined that with his title and relationship to the royal family, it meant that he was often considered admiringly.

Two days after the end of the king's tourney, however, they were staring at him for an entirely different reason.

No one was going to miss Jarl Jorun, likely not even the man's wife or children if he had those back in Tornheim, but his death was the only thing courtly gossips were talking about. Even the fact that the king was courting a beautiful young woman hadn't earned as much attention, but Tris supposed that wasn't quite as dramatic.

So as Tris wound his way through the Penrose Festival, he had to ignore stares and quick, quiet whispers of suspicion that he'd murdered the man.

In truth, he'd avoided the baths after the tourney, knowing that Jorun would be there and in a foul mood—a foul mood aimed squarely at Tris.

Where Tristram had been at the time of the murder mattered little enough, since apparently the man had been disfigured in precisely the same way as he'd attempted to do to Tristram.

Because of that, people were looking to Tris for answers in Jorun's death, as though he could know anything about such a horror. Tristram might have wanted to break Jorun's jaw, but kill him? No.

Tristram's mother didn't enjoy the Penrose Festival—she always said it was for people younger than herself—but she had offered to go on this day, to keep him company. He had wanted to be alone, so he had turned her down and wandered into Atheldinas on his own.

He usually enjoyed the festival.

It marked the time of year when the winter moon began to eclipse the summer one. Penrose had never covered Nye completely in Tristram's memory, despite the fact that stories said it had happened in the past. It seemed unlikely that the tiny white moon could ever truly eclipse his huge blood-red brother, but Penrose did seem unusually large this year. Every winter, Penrose came to the forefront, a brilliant white spot on a red backdrop to say that the month was to be a cold one.

While he had never been much for making flower crowns, Tristram enjoyed the music, the harvest foods, and the apple wine brought down from the north for the occasion. Reynold thought the last mediocre and possibly boorish, but Tris had grown up on the stuff. It was one of the happy memories from his childhood, watching the people in the nearby town make it.

There wasn't much reason for the festival other than to mark the passing of summer. People made flower crowns with the year's last blossoms and gave them to favored loved ones. Some joked that if one made a flower crown for the object of their affections, there would be a baby by spring, since many young people used the festival as an excuse to pair off for the coming winter cold.

Not that Tristram could blame them for that. He rather wished he had someone handsome to pair off with.

"—killed the jarl," he heard from one side, and he felt his shoulders slump.

When he glanced over at the speaker, though, a young woman standing with a few of her friends, she wasn't looking at Tris. He followed her line of sight and there, on the hill where the townspeople had gathered flowers in great baskets—and sometimes just in heaps—was Bennet Kyston.

The king's shadow was being dragged along by Prince Roland, right into the thick of the flowers. After a moment, the young prince stopped in front of a likely basket, filled with fluffy pink blooms, and pointed to them.

Kyston looked thoroughly uncomfortable, but when the prince shook his head and grabbed some flowers, he held his hands out for them readily enough. With impressively nimble fingers for a boy his age, Roland followed the instructions of a vendor to weave the stems together into a ring.

Tristram watched, entranced, as the man stood there. He was in all black, as always, like he was on his way to a funeral, and he looked like perhaps he'd prefer to be literally anywhere else—maybe even his own funeral. He twitched at loud sounds or movement nearby, but at the same time, carefully didn't crush any of the flowers lying in his outstretched palms.

Against his will, Tris found he'd drifted closer and closer to the odd pair while watching them. At any moment, Kyston would notice him, the spell would break, and Tris . . . well, Tris wasn't sure how he felt about that. The young woman had likely been correct about Bet killing Jorun, and Tristram had to suffer the consequences of that action. Tris wasn't sure he wanted to face them yet.

When Roland finished tying off the last stem, Bet's hands were finally freed. He reached into his sleeve and pulled out a few coins for the old woman. She hesitated but accepted them, careful not to touch the man as she took the coins, whereas she'd put her hands over the young prince's to teach him.

It seemed strange to Tris, being unwilling to touch those hands. They looked callused and strong, no surprise given the man's ability with a blade, but they'd held the flowers for Roland so very gently.

A flash of heat went through Tris at the notion of what else they might be able to do gently. Or possibly not gently.

Roland and Kyston were standing there talking, and finally, the prince waved his hand in a very clear "come here" gesture. When Bet leaned over as demanded, the prince reached up and unceremoniously set the flowers in his hair, beaming at them when they fell right into place in the man's ebony curls.

Bet looked stunned, as though the crown on his head weren't the obvious result of the prince's work. Perhaps he'd thought it hadn't been for him, but it weren't as though Roland had anyone else handy. Also, the prince rather liked the man. He might be one of the only people in the kingdom who did, but Tris thought Roland might count for any other five people. Perhaps more.

Roland tucked his hand back into Bet's and dragged him off in another direction, pointing at something out of Tristram's eye line.

He wasn't going to follow them about, so he sighed and turned away. Perhaps he should give up and go home. As much as he usually enjoyed himself, if the best part of his day was watching the prince make a flower crown for the king's shadow, that said nothing good of his time at the festival.

GILLIAN

The Penrose Festival had always been one of the best days of the year, ushering in a season of revels in great halls warmed from giant hearths. When she was little, she'd been allowed to stay up late and her father had let her sneak tiny sips of sweet blackberry cordial from dainty glasses that looked like they belonged in a doll house, not her father's broad hand.

The past year, the Penrose Festival had lost some of its charm. Her father's illness took a turn, and he was unable to attend. It'd been the first year that he had not made a crown for her, bowed low, and set it on her head. She'd spent the whole festival last year listless. Eventually, she'd made her way to Tristram and Reynold and spent the evening listening to them arguing about the merits of the north.

This year, though her father was gone, Gillian was determined to make new traditions. She'd spent the last weeks at his bedside, and this felt like her first chance to move toward her own future. Though her heart continued to ache, she could finally see past all the time spent in that dark, cloistered room with tears stinging her eyes.

"Who will you give it to?" her lady-in-waiting, Marianne, asked, leaning over to inspect the handiwork on her lap.

"Lord Radcliffe, of course," Gillian replied.

As the ladies began to titter behind their hands, she glared. "He is a dear family friend."

"And your cousin," Susan added.

"The king's cousin, not my own." Reynold's mother and Tristram's had been sisters, though the former was long since passed. Gillian was, quite luckily, completely untied to Lord Radcliffe. For now.

"Well, you'll want to hurry," Susan said. Her eyes flicked somewhere beyond Gillian's shoulder. She twisted to see Tristram cutting his way through the crowd. He was heading back toward the Spires.

Gillian cursed under her breath and scrambled from her seat. "Excuse me," she said to her ladies, already turned to go after him. Marianne scrambled after her, it being improper for her to rush around in public without any kind of escort.

She caught him before he left the square and touched his arm. He froze and turned to her, scowling, but he bowed when he recognized her. "Are you leaving already, Your Grace?" she asked, her tight throat choking on the words.

"I'm afraid I'm not fit company at present, Your Highness," Tristram said lowly. His smile was soft, resigned—the smile of a man able to bear when things did not go precisely his way.

"Unacceptable," she said, one hand on her hip. From the other, she dangled a chain of flowers with jewel-toned blooms. "I've made this for you, and you must stay so that the people can enjoy my handiwork. Trying to find blooms that wouldn't look wan in your fair hair was agonizing. Don't tell me you don't appreciate my efforts, my lord."

Tristram chuckled and ducked his head. "I'm afraid your efforts were in vain, Your Highness. You ought to give it to another."

Gillian frowned. "If Reynold weren't busy with his new lady, would you be so set on leaving?" She didn't like to think Tristram's only interests were jousting and King Reynold. He was, if nothing else, her friend. Certainly.

He shook his head. "The king's new courtship has nothing to do with—"

Gillian sighed. "One drink, and a walk around the square. Then, you may leave with my blessing. Yes?" She offered him an arm. Tristram's lips twitched into something like a smile, and she seized victory.

"Fine."

"And you must wear the crown," she amended.

"You drive a hard bargain, Highness."

He lifted it delicately and settled it atop his head. She grinned. "Very pretty. Now, a drink?"

He seemed more comfortable as they walked around the square together. At the very least, he did not flinch, duck his head, or slump his shoulders like he had before she'd found him. That, if nothing else, was heartening.

She caught him staring at the king and Lady Rhiannon once they'd taken a pass at a vendor's cart and balanced goblets of apple wine in their free hands. "Do you know her? I heard she's from the north. Anywhere near Merrick?"

"I have never met her," Tristram said tightly.

"Do you not like her?" Gillian hadn't had the opportunity to spend any time with Lady Rhiannon to form an opinion of her own. She seemed charming and laughed readily. In bleak times like these, they could all use a little more of that brightness at court—especially Reynold.

"Honestly, I do not know her, Your Highness. She seems—"

"Bold?"

Tristram laughed and shook his head.

"I thought you would have liked that in a lady," Gillian hedged. To be frank, she didn't know what he favored in ladies at all. That she was aware, none had ever caught his eye. Determined as she was to change that, a place to start would have been useful.

"I think Lady Rhiannon is perfectly lovely, but I am curious where she came from. I've never heard of her house, and to travel so far with only that young man for company seems . . . dangerous."

"Perhaps she is simply formidable."

"Perhaps," he agreed.

They talked of small things—the changing season, the stores the council had put away and whether they would be sufficient to get the city through winter. Her father had had a keen mind for those sorts of considerations; Tristram was hardly the only lord curious about how the first winter of Reynold's reign would go. With their father's dwindling health, Reynold had been responsible for most of the preparations for this year's winter.

He obliged her for one drink and a turn around the square before he removed his arm from hers. "Thank you for the lovely evening, Your Highness," he said softly. Disappointment pulled at the corners of her mouth, but it did not bear any childish griping.

"Thank you for keeping me company, Tristram," she said.

He lifted the flower crown from his head and settled it atop her own before he took his leave.

As she watched him walk away, Marianne drifted to her side. She'd followed them at a distance on their walk but left enough space to pretend privacy. "Take heart, Your Highness. Lord Radcliffe is merely in a foul mood. You heard about the jarl? I'm sure he would stay if not for the whispers."

"He had nothing to do with that," Gillian snipped, tipping her chin up. "We all know who killed the jarl."

Gillian's glare found her brother's shadow, looking pale and out of place at the festival—a crown atop his pretty curls and a scowl on his face as Prince Roland led him by the hand.

The prince ought to have a proper guard, like Gaspar, who stood apart from her own ladies, frowning. His eyes tracked her every move.

Unreasonable as it was, Gillian knew that Kyston would never allow harm to come to the king or Prince Roland. Her nephew was every bit as safe with him as he would have been with Sir Gaspar or Sir Sidonie. Nevertheless, Kyston's presence here, especially in the aftermath of the tourney, was unsavory.

Marianne's lips pursed. For a moment, her green eyes followed Tristram's back as he walked away. Then she shrugged. "You think? I only mean, well, you heard—with his *eye* . . ." Marianne grimaced. "The jarl was a disgusting, awful man, but he didn't deserve that. Even Kyston doesn't usually relish in—"

"You think there's some limit to that villain's taste for violence?" Gillian demanded.

"Well, no, m'lady."

"Lord Tristram is far too—far too *noble* to have dealings with the likes of Bet Kyston, and I'll thank you not to disparage His Grace in the future, Marianne."

"Yes, Your Highness."

Gillian crossed her arms. With a huff, she tipped her head back to catch the chill breeze that passed overhead.

While they'd woven their crowns and sipped their apple wine, the sky had darkened from peach to purple. Soon, the moons would rise, and Penrose would start to cover Nye. She heard that, some years, the little moon would cover the larger one entirely—a fable that promised resilience to the small and weak, or the unavoidable return of trouble, depending on who you asked. That year, the bard who'd come to court had been telling different tales of the two moons night after night. He even had one that claimed they were dragons, brothers, Nye chasing after troublemaking Penrose through the skies overhead. That story hadn't gone over especially well with the king.

Maybe the moons weren't dragons or anything like them, but a lady chasing a lord who seemed determined never to look her way too long. This year, their coming together would bode well for her; she was certain.

BET

The tourney melted into the Penrose Festival, and the merriment in Atheldinas lasted another two days. The court had spent the last year mourning King Edmund throughout his slow decline. It seemed almost a relief that he was finally gone—at least from where Bet sat, on a bench in a quiet courtyard, sipping wine and listening to the banquet inside. Fewer still were mourning the loss of Jarl Jorun, though the Torndals were sulking.

King Reynold would hardly cancel the festivities to account for a few angry foreigners. But the company from Tornheim was at odds with the throne. Their entire group remained in their chambers rather than partaking in the festival. Jarl Katrien was demanding action, and while the king went through the motions of finding the villain who had attacked Jarl Jorun in the baths, he had yet to put Bet in chains.

In the meantime, Bet avoided them. His rooms were among the servants'; his preferred haunts were streets behind those the lords of Llangard frequented when they wanted a fright. There was no reason for anyone to come looking for him. Anyone with sense already knew of his guilt and upon whose orders he acted.

Best he wasn't seen with the king until the Torndals were gone. That meant avoiding the banquet in the courtyard on the far side of the palace.

He sat back on a carved stone bench, stretched his legs out in front of him, lifted the pitcher of wine, and tipped it toward his goblet. He'd pilfered both in the kitchens.

As he set the pitcher aside, he took a deep gulp of honeyed wine, sighed, and slumped in his seat. His back arched over the stone behind him, and he stared up at the stars and the nebulous swirls high in the sky. He understood that most people didn't hear quite as well as he did, but he couldn't imagine it. It felt as if, if he tried just a little harder, he could make out particular sounds, maybe even a conversation. He'd never managed it at this distance with such a din, but the attempt did bring a soft rustle to his attention.

Bet sat up. From a nearby shrub, he saw the whites of eyes. His lips twitched.

"You should be in bed," he said, taking another small sip and putting the goblet down beside him. Bet leaned forward onto his knees, clasped his hands before him, and stared into the bushes yards away. "Or at the celebration."

"Gillian said I'm too young to go," the prince said as he climbed through the green. When he approached, twigs in his hair and dust on his nightshirt, Bet plucked the mess from his auburn curls and brushed his arms off brusquely.

"Pity, that."

"Why aren't you there?" the prince asked, as if there weren't a reason in the world that Bet would be unwelcome.

"I don't like revels," Bet said.

"Everyone likes revels."

"How would you know? You're not allowed."

Bet had to bite his tongue to keep from smiling when the prince scowled at him and crossed his arms.

"Trust me," Bet said gently. "They're not amusing at all. No one says what they mean. It's like a play, but the actors aren't very good."

The prince's frown deepened. "I like plays. Anyway, no one ever says what they mean."

Bet considered that. People lied. In fact, he generally assumed them more likely to lie than to tell the truth. But he did not think that was what the prince meant. What would it be like to be small and important? When

Bet had been Roland's age, he had not heard enough lies. The prince likely heard too many.

"Too true, young prince."

"Do you say what you mean?" Roland asked with pursed lips.

Bet chuckled. "Not often."

"Lady Radcliffe says it's wrong to lie, though."

Bet rolled his eyes. Of course she did. And no doubt the boys who grew up under her care all thought so as well and grew to be noble knights and lordly companions. Perhaps even just rulers.

"And you should listen to her above me. Come"—Bet rose and offered the boy his hand—"I'll take you back to your rooms."

Roland slipped his hand into Bet's and stared up at him. "Did you kill Lord Jorun? I heard the maid say—" He chewed his lip.

Bet sucked his cheeks between his back teeth and sighed through his nose. The king would not appreciate Bet illuminating the horrors of the world for his son, but though Bet might wish he'd heard more lies to protect his own young heart, he couldn't lie when Roland had complained of the same.

He released Roland's hand and turned to face him. Roland stared up at him, but as Bet crouched, the prince's chin tucked down to meet his gaze squarely.

"Do you remember what happened to Lord Lunden?" Bet asked.

Roland nodded slowly. "He was executed for treason."

Lord Lunden, a close friend and counsellor to the royal family, had been one of the preeminent magicians in Llangard—until he'd been discovered attempting to enchant King Edmund.

Bet licked his lips. "Yes. For the good of the realm, King Edmund had him executed."

The prince swallowed. His head bobbed. "And Lord Jorun tried to kill Tris."

Bet's lips twitched. How like Prince Roland to think Tris's life held the same value as the king's. "He did."

Roland considered him for a moment before he agreed. "Well, sometimes kings must make difficult decisions for the good of the realm. Will I have to kill someone one day?" Roland's eyes were wide enough that Bet could see the whites all around his irises. How much longer would he be able to hold onto that innocence?

"Not with your own hands, Your Highness," Bet promised. "You may always use mine." He stood, and Roland took his hand when Bet offered again. They walked together back through an archway into the Spires.

Though Bet had no business in the royal wing of the palace, he knew every inch of it. As a child, he'd hidden there. Now, knowing the weaknesses of Athelstan's palace was part of his duty.

Outside the door to Roland's rooms, he let the prince go. "Can you make it from here, Your Highness?"

Roland had only begun to nod when a shout echoed down the hall.

"Boy!"

They both turned to see Reynold staggering toward them, his doublet open and his shirt sagging out the middle. His forehead shone with sweat and his eyes were glazed.

"Roland!" the king called.

"Go to bed, Your Highness," Bet said to Roland in a whisper, hardly moving his lips. He gave the boy's shoulder a soft squeeze. The prince was sharp as any nine-year-old. He snuck into his room, while Bet stepped forward to catch the swaying king.

"Let me help you to your rooms, Your Majesty," Bet said.

Reynold sagged against him. "Past the boy's bedtime anyway, 'n't it?" he slurred. "Useless. Can't have just the one. He'll never last on the throne. Too soft."

"He's nine, Your Majesty. It's premature to guess at how your son will turn out. He comes from a strong line." Bet hefted the weight of the king to one side as he reached to open the door.

"And a weak one."

That gave Bet pause. "The late princess was an admirable woman."

"The late princess *died*."

Bet pressed his lips together. He understood the hurt of being the one left behind. But Reynold's wife had not had any choice in the matter. She'd died in childbirth—their daughter with her.

"Come on. It's too late to be wandering the halls railing at ghosts."

"I'll have a woman of power next time," Reynold grumbled. He meant magic, as if that were the simplest thing to come by.

"Of course, Majesty."

Bet had seen the prince's rooms often in his time, but now they belonged to Roland. This was the first time he'd entered the king's quarters. Everything was large and gilt and finely wrought. He shuffled the king toward a sofa, but Reynold shrugged him off.

And before Bet understood the king's quick change of temper, His Majesty had spun and his hand was flying toward Bet's face.

Bet caught his wrist. Unimpressed, he blinked down at his king.

"Better than when you were little," the king said. "I suppose when you were the boy's age, you were a weak, whining, worm of a thing too. Perhaps there's hope for him yet."

Bet sank his teeth into his tongue to keep it still. Beside Prince Roland, Bet had been a pathetic slip of a thing. That he wasn't now was owed entirely to the faith of King Reynold. It would not do to dishonor that faith.

"What is it like to kill a man?" Reynold asked, leaning into him, his breath sharp with liquor. "Did you see the light leave Jorun's eyes before you shoved one into his skull?"

There was a wild smile on the king's face. Bet's lips set into a firm line.

"His back was to my chest, Your Majesty. It was the feel of life leaving his body, and flesh giving way to wire."

Reynold's smile only grew. The king pulled Bet's hand off his arm, and Bet allowed it. With a surprisingly steady grip, he lifted Bet's hand and pressed it to his royal neck, using his own fingers to squeeze Bet's around his throat.

"Would you kill me, Bennet?" the king asked, bright eyes flashing. Bet could feel his pulse, hard and speeding under his fingertips.

When Reynold squeezed harder, Bet fell to his knees and bowed his head, slipping his hand from Reynold's grip as he fell. He crossed his arms behind him. "Never, Your Majesty."

Above him, the king scoffed. He turned away and sank onto the couch.

"Leave, Bennet."

Bet rose, but before he took a step toward the door, Reynold held up a hand to stop him.

"I'm planning to oversee the guards training tomorrow. I'd like you to be there."

THE ONLY REASON for Reynold to include Bet in his guards' training was to make a spectacle. There wasn't one in their number who thought him an honorable man or a noble opponent. The hardy knights of Llangard would take offense to his inclusion, as always. Now, so soon after Jorun's assassination, it was hard to imagine they'd bear the insult gracefully.

But the king had something in mind. He would not just make a spectacle of their dissatisfaction for no reason. As prince of the realm, Reynold's guard had been more impressive even than his father's. He managed this by walking through the sparring matches, culling the knights who performed worst. Nothing like the eyes of the prince—now king—to inspire a strong showing, particularly when one's livelihood was in play.

As he approached the sparring field, walking so lightly on the grass that he hardly bent it, King Edmund's guard stood out gleaming in the sun in their full armor. Lord Gaspar, who had served King Edmund for decades, had his knights train in armor, with weights, as if they were in battle. King Reynold had always insisted his own knights spar in simple cloth, nothing to protect them from the bruising, vicious attacks of their allies. He did not care about the practicalities of battle so much as the familiarity with pain and ability to persevere. Bet could not complain, particularly when Lord Radcliffe joined in training. The sight of Lord Radcliffe's strong, bare arms was always a high point of the day.

Reynold's company stood in a loose group around Sir Sidonie. Sidonie and Gaspar both were breaking people up into sparring partners. Intentionally or not, they kept their parties separate. Neither one was willing to cede ground to the other, and in these early days of King Reynold's rule, there was much to be decided about who would lead and how. Lord Gaspar's animosity with Lord Radcliffe certainly did not weigh in his favor.

Bet felt eyes on him as he approached, but he went to the training weapons and picked up blunt dual short swords. He rolled his wrists, testing the weight and balance in both hands—well made—as he turned around.

And there, an arm's length away, Tristram Radcliffe stood glowering. "You're with me," Tristram said, voice deep and ominous.

Bet glanced toward Sir Sidonie to see her scowling. This, he thought, was not her idea. From head to toe, he took in Lord Radcliffe and shrugged. Despite himself, he failed to keep the tilt of a smirk from his lips. "Oh dear. My lord, am I in *trouble?*"

Tristram glared at him, his fingers stark white around the handle of his practice sword. He jerked his head toward the middle of the yard. Swinging his swords casually, Bet followed.

When Lord Radcliffe rounded on him, his eyes may as well have been molten. As furious as he was, Tristram still raised his sword, swung it out, and bowed formally to Bet. If this had been a real duel, Bet would've used the opportunity to run his sword into the joint between Tristram's shoulder and neck. Now, he only appreciated the strain in it and inclined his own head briefly, never moving his gaze from his opponent.

When Tristram began to move through his first steps, they were formal. Trained. Bet hardly had to shift his weight to avoid the first sweep of his longsword. All the fury that had made Tristram a wild opponent when he'd first come to court had been carefully honed. His style was born of hours of training, consideration, thought; Bet's was all instinct and desperation. He knew what it felt like to get caught by a stronger opponent. The lesson had been beaten into him.

"You signal your every move," Bet accused. Casually, he stalked around the knight. When Tris swung his sword above his head, Bet caught the blade in the cross of both his swords and threw them off.

"You killed Jarl Jorun," Tristram shot back through his teeth, voice low enough that he drew no attention from the knights falling into their own bouts.

"He embarrassed our king," Bet snapped. Tristram came at him again, sweeping toward his chest. Bet ducked. With the weight of his blade, Tristram overcompensated, and Bet sliced his side just under his ribs. A warning, not hard enough to bruise. "And tried to kill you. Don't tell me you mourn the man, Tristram."

The knight bared his teeth at him as he lunged again. "You made it look like I had done it!" he hissed.

At that, Bet laughed. He parried Tris as the broader man advanced on him. "Did I? Anyone who knows you knows you're incapable." Bet used the opening of Tristram's arm to move into his defenses and strike him again—a harmless blow to the thigh. "I heard when you were accused, even the Torndals laughed," Bet said with a sneer. Tristram would let Jorun destroy him before he debased himself with murder. Without Bet's intervention, one day, Jorun might have.

Tristram was mightier than him, but that hardly mattered if he could not land a hit. A hair faster than any man at court, Bet had no intention of letting that happen. Suddenly, Tris had to step back. Bet's blades were a fury. As Bet pushed him across the field, moving into the dueling spaces of other fighters, people had to stop and dodge. They turned to stare at their furious dance. Bet felt the rictus smile on his own face as Tristram began to take more blows than he could block.

And then he saw the sun catch a curl of auburn and the glint of gold on the king's brow. Every knight in the yard knew what happened to those who sparred poorly. If Bet made a fool of Tristram, the lord could lose the king's favor.

His black eyes settled on Tristram, who'd used his momentary distraction to recover. Tristram swept his sword at Bet's chest. He could have jumped back.

He didn't.

❦ 12 ❧

TRISTRAM

The blow knocked Bet back half a pace and was sure to leave a bruise. He'd been distracted; Tristram knew he had. He'd seen the man's gaze slide past to look at something behind him. There was no doubt in his mind that Bet could have dodged the blow if he'd tried, despite the distraction. But he hadn't even tried.

Half of Tris wanted to back down immediately. Something was wrong, and they weren't getting anything out of sparring anyway. The point was sharpening one's skills, and instead, he was acting like a spoiled child, angry that he had been looked on with suspicion for a moment. Bet was right. Most people had not truly believed him capable of the murder, particularly one as grisly as the jarl's had been.

Reynold hadn't even looked at him when the subject had been discussed in court, despite the fact that the injury clearly mimed what Jorun had tried to do to him during the joust. That had confirmed his suspicion: Reynold already knew who had killed Jorun. The only possible answer for that was Bennet Kyston.

No one said out loud that he was Reynold's personal assassin, but that was what the stories about Bet amounted to. He was Reynold's shadow. He was one of the most accomplished fighters in the whole country, but his style didn't lend itself to honorable dueling.

He could stand against Tristram in an entire sparring match and walk away without so much as a touch. Slippery as an eel and twice as mean, some of the knights called him, but mostly because they were jealous of his agility.

The temptation to back down passed quickly when Reynold's voice sounded behind him. "I seem to remember giving you instructions about getting hit, Bet. Do I remember incorrectly?"

Bet's jaw clenched, and he swallowed hard. "No, Your Majesty."

Tristram took a long step back, out of Bet's range, and half turned to look at Reynold. Reynold, who stared at Bet for a long time, then let his own gaze sweep across the field. His mouth pursed in annoyance as he took in Gaspar and his company in full armor, beating against each other like hammer and anvil.

Tris had tried to warn the elder knight, as had Sidonie, that King Reynold wouldn't approve of his methods—there were times to train with armor and weights, but this was not one. Gaspar was set in his ways, though, and determined that they, not he, would displease the king by "acting as though they were defending a mere princeling." As though a prince's guard was made up of toy soldiers or untrained youths.

"I do not believe I've ever heard so many old and creaking joints on this field before," Reynold announced. His gait as he walked over to the old king's guard was casual, but Tris could see the coiled viper in him, waiting to strike.

Gaspar turned to face Reynold, back straight and head up, then bowed as best he could in his heavy armor. "Your . . . Majesty."

Every person on the field stopped moving.

Reynold wouldn't acknowledge the hesitation, but he'd noticed it. Everyone had. Reynold also couldn't allow it to go without response, because such disrespect, intentional or not, was poison to his ability to lead his people.

It was a tiny speck of a mistake, made by a man who had simply taken a moment to remember that his king of more than four decades was gone.

And it was going to be the end of Lord Gaspar.

"Your people seem to be struggling, Gaspar," Reynold said, looking them over. They were actually holding up remarkably well, given the heavy armor and warm, humid afternoon.

Gaspar drew himself up, and Tristram wanted to shake him. Why in the name of common sense was he choosing to be difficult? Perhaps Edmund had allowed him to question the king's decisions, but surely, he realized that things would change with a new king. "My soldiers are always at their best, Majesty."

Reynold smiled. "Excellent. Then you won't mind a little contest."

Gaspar smirked, clearly thinking his guard superior to Sidonie's in every way. He was forgetting that in their armor, his knights were comparatively stationary targets. Armor had weak points, and those were more easily accessible to people not encumbered by their own metal shells—and people whose long service to Reynold had taught them all that was at stake.

He bowed again, and when he came up, he looked over at Sidonie. "Perhaps the heads of the guards can show you who is superior, Your Majesty?"

Reynold chuckled as though it had been an intentional jest. "Oh no, that won't be necessary. I was thinking more along the lines of . . . Bet?"

Bet was at Reynold's side so fast Tris didn't even see him move. He looked unaccountably nervous for a man who could almost certainly take down anyone on the field. "Your Majesty?"

"I want you to fight Lord Gaspar's guards." When Gaspar sputtered, Reynold turned to him. "You don't think it a fair fight? Shall I allow you to join them as well?"

"I assure you, sire, any one of my knights could handle this whelp of a commoner, even if Lord Radcliffe cannot." He sneered at Tristram, as he had since Tris had been a child. He'd been a friend of Tristram's mother's husband—the man the court thought was his father. Tris had always assumed Gaspar knew him to be a bastard, but frankly, he had more important things to worry about.

He wasn't sure why, but he was worried about Bet. The man was dishonorable and infuriatingly smug, but also . . . like Tris, he never hesitated in his duty to his king. Wasn't there a kind of honor in that, when one committed dishonorable acts for a king who could not afford to sully himself? Possibly it was Tristram grasping for excuses because he found Bet beautiful, but it still rung true. Perhaps.

"You question Lord Radcliffe's skill as well?" Reynold asked, pretending to be surprised. He turned to Bet. "Get to it, then. You against Gaspar's men. If you win, you and Tristram stay. If they win, they stay."

He had to be joking. While Tris had every faith in Bet's prowess, it was madness.

But this was no farce. Tristram couldn't even suggest he deserved to have a part in deciding his future. Reynold had announced it, and now Tristram's fate was in the hands of the king's shadow.

Bet rolled his neck and crouched low, waiting for the confused soldiers to come for him. They did their job well, but it was clear that they hadn't been trained to fight something like Bet. He dodged around the first, slamming the hilt of his practice sword into the back of the man's knee and producing a painful crunch. The man howled in pain and dropped, clutching his ruined knee.

Before the next guard reached him, Bet rolled himself up to his feet, planted a foot on her chest, and pushed her down on her back, where it took her a long time to roll onto her side and push up. By that time, he'd kicked her sword halfway across the field and moved on to his next opponent.

The full plate Gaspar put his knights in was unwieldy at the best of times, and now, Bet proved just how much of a limitation it could be. He plowed through them like they were a herd of turtles, incapable of defending themselves. Every time Tris thought one would get in a nasty hit, Bet twisted out of the way and took them out at the knee.

Gaspar stared in dawning horror. "He can't do that. He grabbed the blade of that sword. He'd have lost a hand."

"It's a training sword," Reynold informed him, as though he did not already know it. "They're blunt."

"But—"

"Aren't you glad you didn't choose to fight with them, Gaspar?" Reynold asked, a false, friendly smile on his face. "Do let them clean up before they remove their things from the barracks." And without staying to watch Bet handle the last of them, he turned and went back into the palace.

✣ 13 ✣

RHIANNON

The king had asked Rhiannon to join him in his private chambers for supper. After the commotion of the past few days, he said, he needed a respite and would be honored if she would join him. It was all very formal, and Rhiannon was running out of appropriate clothing.

Her people lived in the high mountains and dressed for it. Between fire, flying, and shifting, there was no sense trying to maintain finery. What small pieces Rhiannon found, she saved for her hoard. Before she blew her candle out for the night, she would run her fingers over the pieces of stained lace, the tarnished jewelry—what small and delicate trappings of humanity she'd been able to collect.

Since coming to the palace, Rhiannon had spent an absurd amount of time befriending ladies, flirting her way into their wardrobes, and asking to borrow clothing. Smiling, she flounced her way out of their rooms in satin. And Hafgan—precious Hafgan, who watched the movement of the courtiers so closely—had quick and clever fingers to help her bend her light gold locks into something fashionable.

"I don't like you being alone with him," Hafgan mumbled as he twisted her last braid into place.

Rhiannon reached back to squeeze his hand. "There's nothing to worry about. If the king had any magic of his own, he'd never have let his sister pay homage to their father at the funeral. Reynold is harmless."

In the smooth silver glass, she watched a frown turn down the corners of his lips. There'd be nothing for his worrying but to prove there was no cause.

She stood and spun toward him. "How do I look?"

"Beautiful. Like a human," he grumbled, crossing his arms.

"Perfect!" She leaned in and kissed his cheeks—a human habit, but one that had its charms. "You should go to the great hall. Have some fun on your own."

In the corridor, a pair of guards waited to escort her to the king's chambers. Rhiannon pressed her lips together to try and keep from smirking. She lasted a single second before her lips tilted.

"Sir Sidonie," she said, narrowing in on the one who mattered most—not merely out of rank, but because Rhiannon found surly men tiresome. Without invitation, she slipped her arm around Sidonie's and rested her hand lightly on the knight's forearm. "Are you here to escort me? What a delight! Surely, the best part of my day."

"Thus far, perhaps, though it sounds a dreary sort of day if you expect me to brighten it," Sidonie said. She did not pull her arm away but turned at once to lead them down the plush carpet that ran the length of the hall.

Rhiannon laughed. "Actually, I've had a lovely day with Lady Elinor. Though she suggested you may have had a trying one. The king must have a great deal of faith in you to halve his retainers in one day."

Sidonie stiffened. "He must."

"I've no doubt his faith is well placed."

Sidonie only hummed. Their walk to Reynold's quarters fell silent after that. Rhiannon bit back a sigh. There was only one lady she'd found at court bold enough to keep her attention, and Sidonie was set on ignoring her.

"You don't like me very much," Rhiannon mused after a minute.

A small line puckered Sidonie's brow. The line of her jaw was firm—the way of warriors who trained hard. Rhiannon watched her swallow. "Why would you think that?"

Rhiannon laughed. "You don't deny it."

Sidonie's skin, fair as light off snowcaps but for her glorious scattering of freckles, began to turn pink. "It's for the king to draw opinions."

"But I'm asking for yours." Rhiannon stared up at her, suspecting that with enough patience and pressure, Sidonie might reveal a measure of her own thoughts.

She only pursed her lips. "I have none."

Rhiannon sighed.

Well, it didn't matter. She was not there to woo ladies.

Outside of Reynold's quarters stood another pair of guards. They knocked before ushering them in. Inside, near a balcony with the doors flung wide to catch the warm breeze, Reynold sat at a table with an impressive spread—maybe even enough to feed a dragon in their natural form.

"Your Highness," Rhiannon said as she released Sidonie and curtsied, "with all this company, I'm beginning to worry you think I'm your enemy."

Reynold rose from his seat and shooed the guards away with a dismissive flap of his hand. "Not at all, my lady. Here—" He took her elbow and led her to the table, even pulled out the chair and prompted her to sit, though she'd scarcely seen anyone seated first in his company.

That moved him a bit higher in her regard. She'd heard lords and ladies bemoaning his capriciousness of late, but perhaps that was just the warbling that always followed change.

The guards retreated, and the food taster followed once he had sampled Reynold's plate, leaving the two of them alone with their supper.

"This all looks delicious," Rhiannon said as she bent over the table, eyeing the spread, weighing where to start.

"Have whatever you like," Reynold offered. And Rhiannon, too starved to care much for human manners, piled her plate full. Happily, she ate, only making small talk, giving compliments to his decor, the food, his most admirable person. He returned them until she was blushing.

"Have you ever been north, sire?" she asked once her stomach was full and his mood seemed pleasant enough to bear hard topics.

"I have, but we didn't linger."

"Too rough?" she teased.

There was a flash of affront in his eyes, but he shook it off quickly.

"No. I saw nothing to recommend it. Had I known you were there, I may have changed my tune." He leaned across the table to refill her goblet.

"Then I don't suspect you've seen the dragons flying over the crags." She took a sip, hoping to mask her attentiveness.

"I have not," he said stiffly.

"Pity." She set her goblet down again. "I think they're fascinating."

"I suppose," he agreed, "if you enjoy slavers."

Rhiannon frowned. "I enjoy beauty," she said. She took a moment to cut a piece of mutton, raise it to her lips with a honeyed date, and chew.

There was no purpose in taking affront, but his quick dismissal pricked her nerves. Once she'd soothed them, she tried again. "Do you not think there are some similarities between how the lords of Llangard treat their vassals, and how dragons once ruled?"

The king scoffed. "Hardly. Any Llangardian vassal may leave their lord's holdings without fear of being eaten. Dragons demanded our subservience in exchange for our lives."

"And protected the humans of their steads from other dangers."

"Other dragons, you mean."

Rhiannon breathed through her nose to cool the heat that rolled in her belly. "Common folk are lost in skirmishes between lords all the time."

"Rarely," King Reynold snipped. "The lords of my realm are loyal to the crown. They're not petty children warring between themselves like the clans of Tornheim."

Rhiannon set down her fork and twisted the silk skirts of Lady Elinor's dress between her fingers, wrinkling the fine cloth. "And dragons rarely eat people," she whispered. She feared, if she were to speak too loud, she would shout. "Not in more than three centuries. Not since Athelstan drove them into the mountains."

"People go missing near the Mawrcraig Mountains all the time," Reynold replied. Smugly, he sat back in his seat and balanced his goblet delicately from his fingers.

"If they're missing, you cannot know how they died. After all, Llangard has had no quarrel with the dragon clans in centuries. You don't think that Tornheim poses the greater threat?"

Reynold finished his wine, set his goblet aside, and crossed his arms.

"The dragons keep Tornheim in check by staying precisely where they are, along the border."

It was common wisdom that dragons could be territorial, that they would not take lightly to gruff soldiers from the north passing through their lands to attack Llangard. Less common was the knowledge of dragons' weaknesses.

"Is that so?" Rhiannon asked. "I heard rumor that Tornheim razed an entire dragon village to the ground two decades ago." She took another bite. As the topic of conversation put Reynold off his appetite, Rhiannon became ravenous.

Reynold cocked a brow. "That would be impressive, but I doubt you've heard right. As magic fades, we have few offensive options against dragons. Even Llangard has only a handful of magicians to keep the lizards at bay."

Skies above, Rhiannon could've eaten a horse. She could've eaten the man in front of her, the way he was talking.

Rhiannon remembered Hafgan's egg, so small and fragile in Halwyn's claws, alone in the rubble of the village.

"Well, assume that it's true. It is only a matter of time before they try again, and then what will keep them from marching on your kingdom?"

"It isn't true, though. If Llangard has little magic, you can be assured that Tornheim has less." He leaned across the table toward her and set what was meant to be a comforting hand on her wrist. "However close your home is to the border, I promise, you are safe from those barbarians."

Before the heat that rose up her neck and the hunger that rumbled in her belly could loosen her tongue and muddle her senses, there was a knock on the door.

A moment later, it burst open and a broad man with gray hair and a square beard marched into the room. Behind him, a guard staggered in to introduce Prince Laurence—Edmund's brother, she surmised from the resemblance between him and Princess Gillian's figure of her father on the stone of his tomb. As the prince approached, Reynold wiped his lips with a cloth and tilted his head toward the interloper.

"Uncle, you seem flustered. Whatever is the matter?" Reynold asked.

The man marched right up to the table and leaned over it, menace in his glare. "The Torndals are leaving."

"Too bad. I'd thought to have one more feast before they returned home."

"They are *leaving*," His Highness clarified, "because they've received no satisfaction in the matter of Jarl Jorun's murder. They think you are not sympathetic to their concerns."

Reynold frowned. "Sympathetic? Of course I am. It was a tragedy. But I don't know what they expect me to do—"

"Find the culprit!"

Prince Laurence's shout set her teeth on edge. She straightened in her seat, finally shifting her chair back from the table.

"If only there were some clue," Reynold lamented with a sigh. "Alas, the guard have found none."

"Reynold—" Prince Laurence said warningly.

The king cocked a brow at him. "Your Majesty," Reynold corrected.

"You cannot begin your reign as king with a war," his uncle hissed. "Not over a single jarl. You must give them the traitor who murdered Jorun."

"If only we could find them," Reynold said mildly, leaning onto his elbow and shrugging.

His uncle sputtered. "We both know—"

With a look, Reynold cut him off. "Know what? Uncle, if you are so concerned about a war, you would do well to call your wife and son back to court where we can protect them."

Rhiannon fought the urge to roll her eyes. Before she could say anything untoward, she set her napkin on her plate. "It sounds like the two of you have much to discuss—"

Before she'd finished standing, Reynold was out of his seat. He reached for her arm again. "I would like to court you," he blurted. Then, remembering the other man in the room, he straightened, glanced at his uncle, and shrugged. "I believe I *can* start my reign with a hunt for a new wife to secure our legacy, or do you think that unwise, Uncle?"

The man in question frowned, but Reynold had posed the question in such a way that even to Rhiannon, to answer in anything but the affirmative seemed dangerous.

"Of course not, if the lady will have you."

They turned their matching blue eyes on her. Her lips twitched. As irksome as that conversation had been, if Rhiannon wanted to open a door to the world of men, she suspected she'd have to deal with more annoy-ances. Perhaps in her efforts, she would change King Reynold's mind.

"I would be honored to see you again, sire. But I'm afraid this poli-ticking has no interest for me. I'll bid you both good night."

She took her leave, and on the other side of the door were two guards, neither of which she particularly wanted to see.

Pity. Rhiannon could use the ear of someone who knew the king better.

14

BET

"Why are you crying?" Reynold demanded of him. The prince was a few years older than Bennet's eight, tall and broad and beautiful with his russet hair and bright blue eyes. Bennet, tucked into a rough stone alcove and cowering behind a thick curtain in the royal wing, was a waif in his shadow. A sliver of onyx and obsidian that faded to nothing in the prince's glow.

He knew he was not allowed in the royal wing of the palace. The Spires stood in jagged points over the city of Atheldinas, hewn with Athelstan's magic. The king and his family lived on middle floors, away from the unwelcoming points where fewer and fewer magicians watched over the realm.

Reynold grabbed his chin, strong fingers digging into his jaw, and turned his head to see the welt on Bennet's cheek from the wooden spoon his father had struck him with. It was summer, the kitchens sweltering, and his father was in a worse mood than usual.

The prince holding him leaned in, his weight pressing Bennet back against the wall as tears streamed down his cheeks. Prince Reynold lifted his hand, and Bennet flinched. But no blow came.

When he opened his eyes again, the prince was staring at him. "What's your name, boy?" he asked in that cultured drawl of the well born—not the sort of voice Bennet heard in the kitchens.

"Bennet Kyston, Your Highness," he whispered, unsure if he were allowed to talk to the prince of the realm at all.

"You don't want to get hit, Bennet?" His hand still hung in the air, fisted and threatening.

Bennet shook his head as best he was able with the prince pressing him back. "No, sire."

A shudder ran through him, but the prince dropped his looming arm.

"Then I'd suggest you not just stand there for it. Get faster. Don't get hit."

❧

DON'T GET HIT. *Don't get hit.*

The words had stuck with Bet. He'd remembered the way his mother moved, how she'd slipped away when his father drank too much and his anger turned to violence. Faster, the prince had said, so Bet got faster.

Don't get hit.

He remembered the words even after the first time he'd dodged the swing of his father's fist and the brute had grabbed him by the front of his shirt and struck him so hard that his vision went black. When it cleared, the whole world had felt uneven.

He remembered them when the prince, haughty despite his youth, dismissed his father from the kitchen staff and told Bennet that he would simply have to try harder next time, to pay him back for the trouble.

And he remembered it now, with the mark of a bruise from Lord Tristram's blade throbbing across his chest.

Taking the blow had no doubt hurt Bet far more than it would've hurt Tristram not to make it—right? Lord Radcliffe was the king's cousin. He was untouchable.

Probably. Bet was not sure enough that he had wanted to make a fool of Tristram in front of the king. Far better to make fools of King Edmund's guard than take the risk. And the only reason for that? Bet would rather look upon Tristram's scowl than upon a smile on any other face at court.

He rubbed his chest as he stood in the receiving room of the finest brothel Bet had visited. After Jorun, Reynold had given him a heavy purse, and Bet decided he had earned the release and luxury while his body still ached and his frayed nerves continued to make him jumpy.

"Lord Kyston," Madame Isobel said softly. He tried not to flinch, knowing she only meant the respect for the weight of his purse, not his person. "Did you come with something in mind?"

His thoughts had begun to wonder to his aching chest and the man who'd struck him. Without thinking better of it, he offered, "Someone fair haired. A man."

A smile spread over her face. She turned to her second. "Send for Ethan, Iskander, dear." She led Bennet to a sofa to wait, offered him wine. "Ethan is our new boy. He's caused a stir among the gentry."

Bet bit his tongue. He knew the game—raise the reputation, raise the price. But he was not so easily swayed, and when Iskander returned with a young blond man with hair to his shoulders, Bet found Ethan to be far too golden, far too lean. Far too . . . Ethan.

He wore a thin robe. Bet could see the contours of his body through the airy white fabric. He was beautiful, but he wasn't—he wasn't sturdy. That was the problem.

"How much?" Bet asked, his eyes on the man while Ethan batted his light lashes.

"Four gold," Isobel said. And though it seemed an egregious sum, Bet was not in a mood to argue.

"Done."

"You won't be sorry, my lord," Ethan said softly, stepping forward to draw Bet to stand.

He led the way to a private room upstairs. No sooner had the door shut than Ethan removed his jerkin and slid his hand over his chest. His teeth grazed Bet's ear. "What is your preference, my lord?"

Bet flinched. "First, that you do not call me lord."

A tiny frown crossed Ethan's face. He fell back onto his heels to stare up at him. "That's uncommon."

"Is it?"

Ethan nodded. "Even peasants like to pretend."

"I'm no good at games," Bet admitted.

"Oh? Has a serious man stumbled into my room?" Ethan grinned as if he were delighted with the prospect. His hand slid down to cup the front of Bet's breeches. "Then I suppose you've no taste for teasing. What am I to call you?"

"Bet."

Ethan frowned. It took him a moment to place the name, but when he did, he tensed like a caged cat. "The king's shadow?" he breathed.

Bet only swallowed. His shoulders inched higher as Ethan's searching fingers stilled.

"You killed the—" Ethan rasped. He paled.

Bet could hardly deny it. If Ethan didn't mean Jorun, he meant *someone*, and in all likelihood, Bet had killed them.

Before Ethan could pull away and the entire night could go sideways, Bet stepped in and grabbed his hands. Halfheartedly, Ethan tried to pull them away.

Suddenly, it was imperative that Bet have this. Ethan may not be perfect—he wasn't exactly what Bet wanted, but Bet would never have what he wanted. And Bet needed to believe he was not so loathsome that not even the sin-stained gold that lined his pockets could buy him some relief from its own weight.

"Calm down," Bet whispered like he was trying to calm an anxious horse. "I am not going to hurt you."

Ethan made a high, tight sound. He didn't believe it, so Bet lifted Ethan's hands to his lips and tried not to notice how the man tensed, how his fingers curled away from him as Bet bent to brush his lips softly over his fingertips. Unable to stomach the fear in Ethan's eyes, Bet closed his own.

"If you can pretend that nothing you've heard about me is true, I will pay you double," he mumbled into the tangle of their fingers.

For a moment, Ethan was completely still. Then, Bet felt the faint shift of his nod. Ethan slipped one hand from his grip and touched Bet's cheek. Gently, he turned his head up and stepped in toward Bet.

Ethan hesitated a few seconds, but when Bet made no move to strike out at him, he pushed up on his toes. The brush of his lips was soft but purposeful. There was no room for Bet to press for more, and he did not have the heart for it.

The young man's arms wound around Bet's neck, fingers tangling in his hair, and even if it was all a show, Bet's breath shook at the gentle touch.

He slipped his arms around Ethan's waist, wishing he were holding someone else. A lord with silvery hair, strong from swinging swords, with eyes so light they nigh glowed. There was more of Tristram Radcliffe to hold, but Bet would never know what that felt like, so he slipped his palm up Ethan's back, tracing the curve of his graceful spine, sliding under the gossamer fabric draped over his warm skin.

Bet imagined the sound Ethan made was in pleasure, not fear, as he bent to kiss Ethan's neck. The man dropped his head back, tugging Bet's hair enough to spur him toward the bed.

As he tumbled Ethan back onto it, he undid his trousers, kicked off his boots. He palmed his cock, stroking it to stand straight as he gazed over Ethan's long limbs, watched the candlelight catch his fair, fluttering eyelashes as Bet reached down to trace his fingertips over the smooth insides of Ethan's thighs, drawing out a gasp.

For a moment, Bet thought his fear might have subsided. But when Bet lowered his weight onto Ethan, he bit his lip and looked away, squeezing his eyes so tight that Bet could not fool himself. He sat back on his ankles, scowling. And at once, Ethan sat up.

"My—Bet, I'm sorry. Are you—" Ethan swallowed. "Do I displease you, sir?"

Bet shook his head. "No, Ethan. No. You're lovely." He could hardly fault Ethan for his fear and distaste. He touched Ethan's cheek. "You don't have to—"

Before he could finish, Ethan shook his head vehemently. "I need this. I cannot—" Already, he was scrambling into Bet's lap, rocking his hips as if Bet were the one who needed further enticement.

But Bet understood desperation, pride, all the complicated notions that would compel Ethan to tolerate this. Even seek it out.

"As you wish," Bet said, stroking his arms soothingly. "If it is your desire, I assent." He turned his cheek against Ethan's temple. "Why don't you just roll over? Do you have anything—"

Ethan nodded, scrambling for the small bottle on the side table. He pressed it into Bet's grasp before turning onto his hands and knees. It must have been a relief to turn away.

Bet was careful, efficient in his preparations. When he slid into Ethan, the pleasure was tight, slick heat that closed up Bet's throat and made him forget to breathe. He thrust. They fell into a rhythm, and in time, Bet reached around to palm Ethan's leaking cock. Ethan threw his head back, panting, braced on the headboard to rock back into him.

He peaked, and Bet used the sounds of his cries, his spasming cock in his hand, the clench of his body to pull him over the edge. He grunted against Ethan's salt-slick shoulder as he spilled inside him, mouthing open kisses against his skin.

Slowly, Bet slid out of him. Ethan collapsed onto the bed. Bet might've imagined Ethan turning toward him, draping his arm across Bet's chest, catching his breath while they were still tangled together. Instead, Ethan rolled onto his side facing away from him. When Bet collapsed beside him and traced a finger over the lithe curves of Ethan's arm, a shiver ran through the man and tension returned to his shoulders.

Bet didn't allow himself a sigh, only dropped his hand. By the time Bet had recovered his breath, all illusions of spending a few comfortable hours skin to skin with another person had dissipated.

He stood, retrieving his clothes, and when he walked around the bed toward the side table, Ethan's eyes were closed. The tension was still there though, and his chest jumped with anxiety as Bet stepped nearer. He wasn't asleep.

Ethan was hardly the only person in the city afraid of him. But guilt crept its way into Bet's mind. He'd clearly caused this innocent man suffering, and for what? A preference for fair-haired men.

He left the whole purse on the table and departed without a word.

15

TRISTRAM

His mother sighed from her place in the doorway of Tristram's private practice room. "It's been so long since you broke down like this, dear. Rumors about what happened in the practice yard have been filtering through the palace all afternoon. Did Reynold truly threaten you?"

Tris turned and tried to use the bulk of his body to hide the wall behind him. "Not exactly," he hedged. "I don't think he believed Bet would lose."

"He really made your place in court contingent on that . . ." A sad look crossed her face as she trailed off, sighing. "Boy?"

He stared at her for a long time. Boy? Tris doubted anyone had called Bet a boy since his own mother, and he didn't know what had happened to the woman, but he'd never met her.

"I'm sure His Majesty knew what he was doing, Mother." It was a lie, but if he could reassure his mother, it didn't matter.

Reynold had always been eccentric, and his moods changed with the breeze, but what he'd done in the courtyard had been the worst Tris had ever seen. Not because he'd personally been involved, but because none of the threatened parties had been the true source of the king's anger. The whole exercise had been intended to shame Gaspar, who'd had no stake in the matter but pride. The knights on their way out of the palace hadn't angered the king, but they suffered for his anger.

He felt his mother's hand against his cheek and realized he'd lost himself in thought. "Sorry."

"There's nothing to be sorry for, dearling." She, in that too-clever-by-half way of hers, peeked around him to look at the new acquisitions hanging there. "You don't use short swords. Haven't since you were a boy."

He couldn't meet her eye, so he turned to look at them: the swords Bet had used against King Edmund's old guard. Against Tris. For practice blades, they were quite fine. Tris would have to pay to have them replaced, but after what had happened, he'd needed them.

"And you haven't made off with anything from the practice field since"—she looked around the room, eyes falling on a battered old practice sword hung on another wall—"the first sword you ever defeated Lord Radcliffe with."

His instincts didn't usually demand things like practice blades. He took in his collection himself, leaning his back against where he'd hung the blunt swords. He had hundreds of them, and those were only the ones he had on the walls. There was a trunk where he kept the odd things that it didn't make sense to display. Knives from the great hall, old rusty daggers no one would use for anything, and even a particularly sharp rock from his earliest years. He should get rid of them, but he couldn't. It was painful to even consider.

Reynold had seen his collection and was pleased by what he saw as an obsession with war. Tristram was at times proud of his collection, and at times ashamed that he couldn't seem to stop gathering every damned pointy thing he found and . . . well, hoarding it.

"Now, dear, don't look like that. You can't help it." His mother came back to his side, sliding her hands into his and leaning up to kiss his cheek. "How many times have I told you about your father? Every time he visited, a book would go missing from the library."

"So you started leaving out ones you wanted him to read," he continued the story. It was as comforting and well worn as the blades in his collection, from all the times she'd told it to him when he'd come to her as a boy, ashamed that he'd stolen someone's dagger.

Just as she always had when he was young, she nudged him out of the way so she could look at the new acquisition, inspected it as though she were an expert in steel, and nodded approvingly. "They're a good addition." Then she turned to him with worry in her eyes. "But, dear, be careful about their owner. I know he looks like an orphaned puppy, but you know very well he isn't."

He nodded but couldn't meet her eye. With another soft kiss to his cheek, she left him alone with his embarrassment.

WHEN HE CAUGHT sight of Bet later that evening as he slipped through the entrance hall, Tris decided he was going to try to act like an adult and talk to the man.

They had unfinished business, and he needed it worked out. He couldn't spend every waking moment thinking about Bennet Kyston, or he'd go mad. His mother had been right; those floppy curls and sad eyes made him look like nothing so much as a puppy, but anyone mistaking the king's shadow for something soft and sweet was in for a rude awakening.

Some of the knights from the courtyard that afternoon, who were both injured and being ejected from the king's guard, had learned that lesson all too well. They hadn't acknowledged him as the threat he was until it was too late.

He turned down the hall and hurried to catch up. "Kyston! You owe me an explanation."

The cold-eyed look Bet turned on him would have been sufficient to stop his heart a dozen years earlier. Or possibly get it pumping hard enough that he was forced to spend the rest of the afternoon in his bedroom alone. That the man had the ability to be terrifying, attractive, and so detached all at once made Tris unaccountably angry.

He'd like to be so unaffected by the events of the day. "What the hell was that in the courtyard?"

"Me doing our king's bidding," Bet answered, voice flat.

Tris glared at him as he closed the distance between them. He supposed it was a bad idea, getting within striking distance, but he couldn't force himself to care. "I don't mean that part, and I'd hope you know it."

Slowly, Bet lifted a single eyebrow at him, challenging. "You'd hope I know what?"

It seemed Tris hadn't calmed down enough to act like an adult, because instead of pausing outside of stabbing distance, or even inside it, he crowded all the way into Bet's space. "I would hope you know I'm not asking about you defeating Gaspar's men. You did what you had to do, distasteful as it might have been."

Bet might have flinched at that—it was hard to tell, but he didn't respond. He didn't move. Tris wasn't even sure he was breathing.

There was a long pause, and Tris realized Bet either genuinely didn't know what had bothered him, or he wasn't going to acknowledge it. "You let me hit you in practice," he practically exploded.

For the first time, a ghost of an expression crossed Bet's face, and his hand twitched, as though to draw a weapon. Or to reach up and touch his chest, right next to his heart, where a huge bruise must have formed after that blow.

Their gazes snagged on each other's and caught. How had Tristram ever thought him expressionless? Those black eyes weren't lacking emotion but overflowing with it. Anger mostly, but also a deep melancholy, and . . . want?

Tris glanced away and spotted a long, golden hair on the front of Bet's stark black tunic. He reached out, and Bet flinched away, but again, he didn't draw a weapon. When Tristram pulled the hair off, holding it between them, Bet turned his eyes to the side, and—was he blushing?

"I didn't realize you had a lady friend," Tris said, and his voice came out calm, cool even, but it was nothing like he felt. No, his gut was churning with jealousy, but why? It weren't as though he and Bet had anything in common. Not as though Bet were interested in other men, let alone him.

"I don't have friends." Bet snatched the hair from Tristram's fingers and flicked it away as though he wanted no part of it. That made him wonder for a second if the hair had been from something other than an assignation. Would they find Jarl Katrien dead in a pool of her own blood in the morning?

He ran a hand down Bet's chest, searching for any sign of blood, and his reward was a gasp. At first he assumed it was pain—from a wound inflicted by a dying Katrien? Or was it the damage Tristram himself had done that afternoon?

When he glanced up to meet Bet's eyes, they were wide, the whites showing all around them. He wondered, for a moment, if he'd earned a stabbing, but then those eyes dropped to his lips, and Bet's own parted a fraction.

As was his most unfortunate habit, Tris dove in head first.

Their mouths crashed together, a clash of tongues and teeth that started out anything but good. Tris tasted blood in his mouth, and he wasn't sure whose it was.

In a flash, Bet turned them so that Tristram was the one with his back to the wall. He wrapped a hand around the side of Tristram's neck, thumb coming up to hold his jaw in place in a grip that felt downright dangerous. Then he turned his head a fraction, opening up a little space between their noses and allowing himself full access.

Not to stab anyone, thankfully, though he pushed his way into Tris's mouth as though convinced he'd be rebuffed and wanted to taste his fill before that. Tris just tilted his head up to meet the onslaught, eyes sliding shut and fingers scrabbling against the tapestry on the wall.

Bet kissed like he fought: hard, fast, and with no intention of taking prisoners. His free hand fell to Tristram's trousers, as though he would strip them off right there in the hall, and slowed to press against his growing arousal. It seemed he appreciated what he found there, because he let out a growl that reminded Tristram of his own nearly inhuman one.

What he'd have done, Tris would never know, because a giggle echoed down the hallway, and Bet pulled back as though he'd been slapped. He turned to see a couple of ladies' maids enter the hall, and before Tristram could so much as say his name, Bet turned and melted into the shadows.

16

SIDONIE

Lady Rhiannon was wearing a blood-red gown, and it shouldn't have looked good on her. It was just like a gown one of the ladies of court regularly wore, and she had the same coloring, but the red made the other lady look sallow and sickly.

Rhiannon looked pink cheeked, healthy, and vibrant as Sidonie took her to dine with the king. Sidonie wasn't sure whether she pitied the other courtly lady more, or herself.

Or possibly, the king.

As much as she wanted to arrange for one of her knights to accompany Rhiannon to and from her quarters for meals with His Majesty, she'd never been one to shirk her own duty in favor of making her people do it.

Especially now, with Lord Gaspar at loose ends and looking for a way to avenge himself for what he saw as Sidonie's wrong. As though she'd had a damn thing to do with him insulting the king or the disaster that followed.

To think she'd been looking forward to increasing the size of the guard. Apparently, she just needed that damned Kyston, and the whole of the king's guard was obsolete.

She closed her eyes and took a deep, bracing breath, and then didn't bang her head against the wall as she awaited Lady Rhiannon's return.

It hadn't been Kyston's fault any more than it had been hers, and the man wasn't nearly as invulnerable as he seemed. He'd simply had the advantage, and his foes hadn't realized it quickly enough to stop him.

He wouldn't have beaten her.

They were the same, she and Bennet Kyston. Both peasant stock, both having spent every free moment of their lives working to become what they were: useful to the king.

Perhaps more than anyone else in the palace, both of them understood the simple fact that they lived and died by the king's pleasure. Certainly, she liked other members of the court more than she did him—but with Kyston, there was understanding.

She wasn't such a high, principled lord that she believed herself incapable of the things he did. If the king ordered her to kill a man, noble or not, honorable or not, the man would die.

Even if it meant her life.

At least, she'd felt that way before Reynold had ascended the throne. Something about the way he'd been acting since his father's death set her teeth on edge. She didn't believe for a second that he'd had anything to do with Edmund's death. On the other hand, she also didn't believe he was heartbroken at the loss.

And the disaster on the field, losing all of those good knights who would have defended him with their lives simply to prove a point to a man who'd shown him the most minor, accidental disrespect . . . well, she wasn't sure Reynold hadn't gone mad somewhere along the line.

If she believed him bothered by his father's death, it would have made more sense. Instead, he seemed like a small child whose rules had been removed. He would do what he wanted, when he wanted, up to and including dismiss half his guard, flaunt his personal assassin, and threaten the members of the delegation from Tornheim.

Rhiannon slipped out of the king's suite, carrying a wilted red rose and looking disappointed. Sidonie raised a brow at her, and she shrugged. "His Majesty fell asleep. Too much wine."

Before she could even react to the notion of her king overindulging at supper with a near stranger, Rhiannon turned that beautiful toothy smile on her and wedged her arm around Sidonie's elbow, gripping tight.

"You're to escort me?"

"Yes, m'lady," she agreed, trying to keep a straight face and even voice. "Did you eat enough?"

"Oh my, yes," Rhiannon gushed. "The king does insist on quite the feast."

Sidonie was well aware. Even when dining alone, Prince Reynold had always had enough food delivered to feed a family of four. Fortunately, the leftovers were always put to good use.

Without requiring Sidonie's input at all, Rhiannon turned the subject from the king. "Have *you* ever been north?"

"I cannot say that I have, m'lady."

Rhiannon sighed and stared off into the middle distance, again disappointed. "The mountains are beautiful. But they're getting so dangerous."

"Dragons?"

"No." Rhiannon smacked Sidonie's arm with her rose, and a few petals dropped off. She frowned at it, as though it were entirely unsatisfactory, and glanced around for somewhere to drop it. Finding nothing, she sighed and turned back to Sidonie. "I mean the Torndals. They want Llangard, you know. And they aren't afraid to come over the mountains to get it."

That was an entirely new and even more disturbing thought. "You don't think the dragons will stop them?"

"I don't think the dragons are invulnerable," Rhiannon answered.

If dragons existed, they were strong; everyone knew that. But stories told that the dragons had once held all humans in Llangard as serfs, until the humans had risen up against them with the help of Athelstan and his magic. That the uprising had worked at all implied that dragons were neither invulnerable nor infallible.

Sidonie nodded thoughtfully, then glanced at Rhiannon. "Excellent point, m'lady. It is something we should perhaps be putting more consideration into. Particularly with what happened during the tournament."

Rhiannon leaned in too close, and her breath fanned across Sidonie's cheek, strangely warm and smelling of sweet, spiced wine. "You mean that jarl trying to kill your knight, and then being killed?"

"Yes. It's more forward than they usually are in their aggressions. Perhaps something in Tornheim has changed."

"Perhaps. It is certainly worth checking up on, don't you think?"

"Of course, m'lady."

A smile broke out on the lady's face bright enough to dwarf the sun. "Finally, someone with sense." Rhiannon drew herself up, chin lifted and high flush in her cheeks.

She knew it was what they both wanted, but Sidonie did not kiss her.

She took a step back, letting the woman's arm fall to her side. "I do, Lady Rhiannon. And I will discuss it with those whose job it is to monitor such things as soon as possible. Thank you for your observations." She held out an arm to indicate the door behind her. "Your quarters."

Rhiannon gave a frustrated sigh that Sidonie felt in her chest, nodded, and went into her rooms.

All Sidonie had to do was figure out who to discuss the problem of Tornheim with. A month earlier, it would have been Lord Gaspar. Oh, how heroes fell.

❧ 17 ❧

BET

Impossible, how a crash of teeth and bruising lips could stay with him the way that laying with Ethan had not. But Tristram had touched him, crowded into his space, brushed his hand down his chest like it was nothing. Like he wasn't afraid. Like there was no reason to be.

It was foolish, and if another man had come at him so aggressively, Bet would've slit him throat to prick. But it was Tristram Radcliffe, who had everything Bet wanted—a title, the mutual respect of the king, a mother.

If Bet were being honest, he wanted more than that. He wanted the hitch of Tristram's breath when he palmed his cock, the sweetness of his tongue mingled with the sharp tang of blood, the thought that, for even one minute in his life, he deserved everything Tristram had to give and more.

But he didn't. Tristram was a lord—Lord Radcliffe of Merrick—and he was destined for a lady and children and comfort. Bet would have none of that. He'd *want* none of that. Pathetic, idling fools, the lot of them.

Despite himself, a coil of vicious jealousy rose at the idea of Tristram at his country estate, smiling indulgently at his pretty wife, swinging a silver-haired slip of a child into his arms. He wanted none of it, but damn it all, he didn't want Tristram to have it either.

All he wanted Lord Radcliffe to have was what Bet gave him, and he'd see the man brought low before he watched him escape to his easy life in Merrick, leaving Bet to . . . to what? To stand behind Reynold and see the worst of politicking through to its bloody end?

Tristram owed Bet nothing; nevertheless, Bet was *owed*.

He had returned to his small chamber with fury blinding him and the feel of Tristram's body the only thing he could think about. Never mind Ethan and his common yellow gold. There was Tris, who pushed him and never flinched. Like tempered steel, shining and silver.

Bet had brought himself to finish with his hand braced against the wall, his eyes squeezed tight, and a curse on his lips for a lord too far above him to consider.

He wouldn't have done it—wouldn't have touched him—if Tristram hadn't moved first. And yet, when Reynold sent for him the next morning, Bet was certain that he'd be punished for attacking Tristram, for lunging so far past his station that there was no choice but to cast him down hard.

When he slipped into Reynold's rooms to find the king perched on a plush chair, considering a letter in his hand, he seemed entirely at ease. If Tris had thrown him to the wolves, Bet doubted Reynold would be so casual in the maiming.

"Bennet, thank you for joining me," he drawled from his seat. With one hand draped over the arm of his chair, he dangled his wine glass. It looked dangerously close to tipping over.

"Your Majesty," Bet replied, bowing low before he stepped nearer.

"The Torndals are leaving Llangard." Reynold folded the letter in half and held it out in the air for Bet to take. As he unfolded it, Reynold continued, "They think not enough is being done to avenge Jarl Jorun."

Bet hummed, skimming the page. They made complaints about disrespect and brutality, but that was awfully hypocritical. He arched a brow at the king. "And?"

Reynold laughed. "Well, you didn't have to make it so gruesome. And public."

The shift in Bet's shoulders might've been a shrug, if he'd ever dare be so flippant toward the king. "Jarl Jorun would've killed Lord Radcliffe. In public. And if you've never seen the inside of a man's skull before, I assure you, it is plenty gruesome. Should I have treated the jarl with more care than he would have treated the peers of your realm, Majesty?"

Reynold beamed at him. Swinging his legs over the side of the chair, he stood and plucked the letter out of Bet's hand. "And for a moment there, I had worried that you cared more for my cousin's well-being than my own."

Bet flinched. He did not think the women in the hallway had seen, but the king had eyes other than Bet's to do his spying. He might've known what happened.

Suddenly, Reynold threw back his head and laughed. "As if you ever would. And I am sure the honorable knight loathes you entirely." Bet's mouth soured. He swallowed, trying to clear the taste, as Reynold stepped in and patted his cheek. "Tristram never did understand why I kept you around, but fear not. There are many reasons that you are my favorite creature, and your peculiar application of logic ranks high. I'd like you to follow the Torndals to the border."

Frowning, Bet lifted his gaze to the king's. "To what end?"

Bet's flat tone did not question the sense of the order, only the intended result. Reynold could've told him to scale a cliff to pick a flower, and he would've done it.

"I do not believe their business with Llangard is finished. I'd like to know their plans. What are the conditions in Tornheim that have made them so bold? Lady Rhiannon is convinced they are a threat."

The barest twitch of his brows betrayed Bet's surprise. Lady Rhiannon was all but a stranger at court. It seemed unwise to weigh her opinion too heavily, though the king risked little in sending Bet on this mission alone.

Recovering himself, Bet inclined his head. "I will leave today."

"And I will miss you every second you're gone, assassin mine," the king joked. "But I suppose having you clear of Lord Gaspar's rage is ideal, at present."

"Yes, Majesty."

Bet took his leave to prepare. The best thing for him would be to get away from court for a while. Clear his head of Lord Radcliffe. Bloody his hands for the good of the realm.

18

RHIANNON

Hafgan was getting nervous, and Rhiannon couldn't blame him.

They were eating supper in the great hall with the king's entire court. He was tense, hunched over his food, eyes darting in every direction in response to each noise and movement.

The humans were . . . well, the truth was that they weren't so different from dragons, in many ways. They liked good food, music, and beautiful things. Some of them had small hoards of their own, though for them it seemed more diversion than compulsion. For the most part, they were decent and spoke or acted as though they wanted to do the right thing.

Almost every one of them, though, turned a disgusted look on her when she mentioned dragons. Almost all of them mentioned slavery. Many expressed the opinion that they were happy to have never seen such a horrific monster. It took everything she had not to raise her arms to her sides and wait for them to comprehend that they were looking at just such a creature.

Most of them didn't seem to find her horrific at all.

The king's uncle, maybe. He looked on her with a calculating gaze, and she didn't like it. She thought if she didn't keep a close eye on her food, she might end up poisoned.

Sir Sidonie certainly acted as though she disliked her, but that was just

Rhiannon's worry talking. No matter how much she bewildered the knight, she fascinated her as well. As long as they had their awkward flirtation, there was a chance Rhiannon could salvage the visit.

That was what it would be, at this point. She certainly could not stay.

The king was not open to reason, but hopefully if she talked to enough of the other courtiers, she could make them see that the Torndals were the threat. Perhaps once, her own people had been a threat to humanity, but no longer. The dragons had little interest in human lands, so long as they had their beloved mountains.

She didn't know what Halwyn would do if Tornheim invaded the mountains, but she suspected that it wouldn't be good for humans from either nation.

"When can we go, Rhiannon?" Hafgan whispered in her direction without even looking up at her.

She rolled her eyes at him. "We came here to do something. It isn't finished yet."

"They don't want us here, and they're—" He broke off and stared across the room, biting his lip.

When she turned to see what had grabbed his attention, she wasn't sure whether to be impressed or jealous. "That's a fine catch, Hafgan. Are you pursuing him?"

She'd noticed the half dragon around court. The king seemed to favor him, which was rather odd, considering the man's rabid hatred of their kind. Maybe half dragons were human enough for him.

Likelier, the little half dragon didn't know what he was. Or maybe he was in hiding. Wasn't that an interesting thought?

She wondered if he would be willing to take their case to the king. Maybe he had a better idea of how to present it so that the infuriating boor would actually listen.

Hafgan was looking back at her, surprised. "You mean Lord Radcliffe? No, nothing like that. We spoke for a moment. There's just something terribly familiar about him."

For the first time in days, Rhiannon laughed. Not that ridiculous courtly tittering that was expected of ladies, but a full-body laugh. She threw her head back and let the amusement take her. It seemed a rare opportunity in the human realm.

Hafgan blushed and glanced around them, not meeting anyone's eye. He wasn't ashamed of her exactly, but very aware of the reactions of the humans. They were important to him in a way they would never be to her.

Once people stopped staring at Rhiannon and went back to their own business, she leaned toward him and whispered, "Of course he looks familiar, sweet song. One of us is probably related to him."

"Rela—" Hafgan's eyes went wide, and he whipped around to stare at the half dragon for a moment before turning back to his food. He was breathing fast, biting his lip, and Rhiannon could practically smell his earnest fascination. It was adorable.

If Hafgan wanted a piece of the half dragon, she decided, he should have one. It wasn't hard to get a man's attention, but a dragon was trickier.

Perhaps he was enough human for her feminine wiles to work. She leaned forward, watching him until he glanced her way.

"Rhiannon," Hafgan hissed, batting at her elbow. "What are you doing? You'll terrify him."

When Radcliffe's eyes met hers, she deliberately let hers shift, going molten gold and metallic, with slitted pupils. Deliberately, she winked at him.

Hafgan let out a wheeze.

Radcliffe's response was more surprising, and unfortunately telling. He looked like she'd gutted him. He stared at her for a second, then turned and left the room as quickly as two feet would carry him.

Next to her, Hafgan's chair made a horrible squeak as he pushed it back and stood. She looked up at him, still surprised about Radcliffe's retreat, to find Hafgan glaring at her.

"That was mean, Rhiannon." And he turned and marched after Radcliffe.

How very strange.

❧ 19 ❧

TRISTRAM

By the time Tristram made it back to his practice room, he was panting. It wasn't that the run was so far, or that he'd gone so fast— though he had—but terror had him firmly in its grip.

His heritage held him in constant worry about his place in the king's good graces. In court. In Llangard. In the entire world.

Surely the dragons wouldn't want him any more than the humans would if they knew what he was. Humanity was obsessed enough with the bad blood in their shared history.

Tristram even believed that the humans had had the right of it. They'd had every right to demand their freedom from servitude. It was a state no one should be forced into; that was one of the basic truths the kingdom of Llangard had been built upon. But when defeated, the dragons had retreated and not attempted to harm anyone. And humanity, in their oh-so-human way, had doggedly pursued the conflict until it had nearly destroyed both races.

Surely this woman, this *dragon*, knew what a horrible idea it was to come to court?

And the young man sitting beside her.

Hafgan, his mind supplied. The young man with the name that had so puzzled him.

There was a small sound from the doorway, and Tristram turned to find that very young man standing in his doorway. He was staring at Tris's collection, mouth hanging open in awe.

"Your hoard is incredible," he whispered as his eyes scanned one wall after another.

Tristram almost choked on his tongue. It wasn't that he hadn't considered his collection that way in the past, but . . . his mother had never acknowledged the word, even as she'd assured him that his compulsion to collect was only natural. Everyone else thought him eccentric, or single minded, or some other thing that didn't amount to "secretly a dragon."

He wanted to deny it. To tell the young man that wasn't what it was. To yell at him, send him away, insist that he and his lady leave the Spires immediately. Instead, pitifully, he asked, "Do you think so?"

Hafgan turned to face him, eyes still wide. "You can't be that old, but you have so many." He bit his lip. "Mine isn't half so impressive. It's harder, though, I suppose. Maddox keeps telling me it's a good hoard, and I've just got a longer road because they're rare."

"What are?" Tristram asked. He felt almost like someone else was having the conversation, but he had to know. Tristram's mother had said his father "collected" books, so it seemed an easy assumption that every dragon hoarded something meaningful to them.

For Tris, learning the sword had been a way to prove himself to the court without leaning on the Radcliffe name, since he knew in his heart that it wasn't his own. So he needed them.

The young man blushed and turned to stare at the floor. He was quiet so long Tris almost thought he wouldn't answer, but finally, he cleared his throat and whispered, "Dragons." For a second, Tris thought he meant actual living dragons, but then the young man reached into the neck of his tunic and pulled out an object at the end of a leather thong. A tiny wooden carving of a dragon in flight.

Given how it had warmed Tristram's entire body when Hafgan had admired his swords, he strode over to the young man and gave the tiny carving his full attention. It was impressively detailed for such a small thing, clearly made with care. "It's beautiful," he said, pleased that he could say it honestly. "I always carry one too. It's easier, since no one expects me to go unarmed, but meeting King Edmund for the first time was excruciating, since one isn't allowed to go into an audience with a dagger."

Hafgan shuddered and dropped the carving back into the neck of his tunic. "I cannot imagine. You must have more willpower than I." He sighed and rolled his eyes. "Rhiannon always says it's because I'm so young."

Tristram made a face thinking about the lady. "Perhaps Lady Rhiannon is not someone to emulate."

The young dragon laughed but didn't seem offended. Instead, he turned to look at the front wall of Tris's collection before stopping himself and looking back for a moment. "Do you mind? Queen Halwyn hates when we gawk at her hoard, and I don't want to offend."

"No! No, I don't mind at all." He followed Hafgan over to the wall, where he proceeded to do as Tristram's mother always did. Inspect a piece, nod his approval, and look to the next. "May I ask why you and Lady Rhiannon are here?"

Hafgan let out his breath on a long, gusty sigh. "The Torndals."

"They're bothering the dragons?" That was disturbing, regardless of whether it was only affecting dragons. Knowing Tornheim, it was only a matter of time before they crossed the mountains and headed into Llangard itself, if they were already invading dragon lands.

Hafgan stopped for a second and cupped his chin in his hand thoughtfully. "Yes and no. They aren't bothering my clan right now, but they've been encroaching, slowly, for years." He dropped his hands limply to his sides. "I believe they're the ones responsible for the destruction of my first clan."

"You believe, but you don't know?" How young would Hafgan have been, to forget entirely? It must have been many years earlier.

"I hatched after the Summer Clan found me. I was all that was left in the wreckage. A damaged, undersized egg whom no one expected to survive." For some reason, the young man looked ashamed.

Tris took a moment to consider. It made sense that dragons laid eggs, though he was sure he'd had a normal, human birth. Perhaps there was some shame in being small. Or more likely, the young man felt guilty for being the only one to survive, and for not having helped, as impossible as that would have been. "I'm sorry about your clan," he said eventually, since it was the only thing he could think of to say.

Hafgan smiled at him shyly. "Thank you." He turned back to the wall, and his breath caught in his throat. Tris looked to see what had caught his attention.

It was an early acquisition. An elderly knight with no living relatives had bequeathed his sword to Tristram. It was shorter than was his preference, so he didn't carry it, but the make was fine. More importantly, the guard was sculpted to look like two brassy wings, and the pommel had the delicate features and curved horns of a dragon. It was understated, for such a thing. No gems in place of eyes or anything so gaudy. Despite the decoration, the sword was no piece of jewelry. It was a fine weapon.

Tristram could feel the longing in Hafgan's eyes in his own gut. He remembered the first time he'd looked at his favorite dagger and simply known that it had to be his. It had been made for him.

Hafgan's fingers drifted up to trace the wings, the hilt, and the sinuous lines of the dragon's head. With a start, he jerked away and turned to Tris. "I am so sorry. I meant no disrespect. I—" He glanced back at the sword and quickly away. "It's just very beautiful."

That was when Tris realized, truly realized, what the hoard was about. He collected swords because they had freed him from his mother's wretched husband and given him his own name in court.

Hafgan collected dragons because he'd lost so many before he'd even been born.

Though his belly recoiled in horror, every instinct screaming for him to stop—think, please, *what was he doing?*—he reached up and grasped the sword by the top of its scabbard and pulled it out of its setting. Without giving himself time to truly think about it, he shoved the still-sheathed sword into the boy's chest, almost too hard. He had to force himself to let go, and it felt like every muscle in his hand had gone rigid.

Hafgan reached up to grab the sword, clearly more from instinct than conscious awareness, because it was only after Tristram let go that his eyes went wide, and he looked up to stare in shock.

"You—"

"Need the space," Tris told him, though it was a struggle to tear his gaze away from the sword. When he finally looked up into Hafgan's eyes, they were watery, and the younger man was biting his lip again.

Instead of answering, Hafgan nodded, and Tristram was grateful. He had a feeling the man knew how hard it had been, and that discussing it was unnecessary.

He turned away. "The Lady Rhiannon has come hoping to convince the king to help fight Tornheim?"

"In a manner of speaking, yes. She thinks Llangard and dragonkind have been at odds for too long. She wants us to work together to defend our lands." Hafgan sounded so young, so hopeful, that Tris didn't want to express his opinion on how unlikely that was.

Llangard hated dragons and everything they stood for in the histories. Perhaps dragons had moved forward, but men were still emotionally trapped in a time when they had been forced into servitude.

"They don't know, do they?" Hafgan asked, surprisingly perceptive.

Tris shook his head. "They would banish me." *At best*, he thought, but he didn't dare say it aloud. The young man was worried enough.

Hafgan sighed heavily. "I see. I'm sorry."

"So am I." He turned to look at the young man, who had cleverly moved to hold the sword behind himself. "I will try to help if I can. I might not be able to convince the king to help dragons, but he's already aligned against Tornheim. Incursions they make into the mountains threaten Llangard. He'll be concerned about that even if he isn't concerned about y—" He stopped, took a deep breath, and met Hafgan's eye. "Even if he isn't concerned about us."

20

GILLIAN

There wasn't much that Gillian Cavendish could do with her magic —draw her father's image from stone, coax a breeze on a muggy day, care for the plants in the gardens—and all of it exhausted her. She was not born for the earthquakes and tempests of old. Some said that Athelstan Cavendish had lifted an entire mountain. Frankly, it sounded impossible.

But caring for the gardens was nice. There were servants who could have managed just fine without her, but it was something to do—something that felt productive. And something that her brother cared nothing for, so she could keep it for herself.

Carrying a handwoven basket with her tools into the courtyard built into the space between stone towers, Gillian was delighted to find it already occupied. Lord Radcliffe was sitting on a low stone bench, his leg bouncing up and down with the twitch of his heel.

"Tristram!" Gillian practically threw herself at him across the rose-bushes, ignoring the paving stones arranged for the very purpose of moving gracefully through the courtyard.

At once, Tristram was on his feet. With a hand on her elbow, he helped her past the bushes. The thorns caught on her dress, but she didn't care. The lord's strong hand remained on her arm, steadying her.

"I'm so glad you're here," she breathed. Heat had flooded her cheeks. "I've been meaning to talk to you since the Penrose Festival."

He looked pale, a little tired, but she could hardly blame him. Between her father's death, then Jarl Jorun's, no one at court felt particularly at ease. If she'd been so close to Jorun's death, she would not have been able to sleep either.

"Is there something I can do for you, Your Highness?" he asked. His kind smile made his handsome features even more striking.

The appropriate thing would have been to open her mouth and tell him what she wanted. He was a good, honorable, kind man, and she would be happy to let go her courtly responsibilities and care for him instead. But at that moment, her mouth had dried out, her tongue felt clumsy, and she forgot every word she knew.

Rather than stammer her way through her confession, Gillian used the anchor of his steadying hand to propel herself forward. She closed her eyes and brushed her lips across his.

For one blissful second, Tristram kissed her back. Then, his hands were on her upper arms, and he pushed her away. Startled, he blinked at her with eyes so wide she could see the ring of white around his honey-brown irises.

"Your Highness, this is not appropriate—"

"I am of an age to decide that for myself," she informed him with a scowl. No longer in the immediate line of succession, her marriage was completely her own choice—barring the king's dissent—and at twenty, she was old enough to decide on her own. Surely, Reynold would not question Tristram's worthiness.

Something was wrong. Tristram did not agree. Was it her age? There was nearly a decade between them, but she'd seen ladies she'd played with as children married to men her father's age. Perhaps he simply did not like her, but then why bother being so kind? He must think her frivolous or— she did not know!

When he continued to hold her away from him, her eyes narrowed and jaw clenched. "Is there something wrong with me? Some feature unbecoming, some—"

"Highness," he whispered, cutting her off. "There is nothing wrong with your formidable and lovely person. I am certain you are precisely as anyone would want a wife to be. It is simply . . . that I am looking for the same qualities in a spouse as you yourself."

She blinked at him for a moment, confused, before understanding dawned on her.

"You prefer men," she said. When he blanched and looked away, she swatted his chest lightly. "Why did you never say before?" She huffed a sigh. "Now I've made a fool of myself."

He smiled and shook his head. "On the contrary, Your Highness. You flatter me, that an intelligent and beautiful person could hold me in such high regard."

"Now who is the flatterer?" She was trying, and failing, to hold back her smile. "I do wish I had spent less time swooning over you." Gillian sighed. "Was it terribly awkward?"

"Not at all. I assure you, Highness, if I sought a lady for a wife, you would be my first choice. Not that I would think myself worthy of such an honor."

She rolled her eyes, then met his anxious look. "I can hardly fault you for finding men beautiful. It has always been my opinion, after all." For a moment, she worried her lip with her teeth. "Can you forgive me for throwing myself at you?"

Her face was burning, but she didn't let herself duck her head.

"Of course. It's forgotten already. Though I'd appreciate if you wouldn't tell the king about it."

Gillian laughed. "Reynold? Oh, Tristram, he is the last person I would talk to about kissing."

For a moment, she considered how odd it was to find Tristram alone. Well, perhaps at the training grounds, but she didn't know him for one to sit alone amongst flowers.

"What were you doing out here, anyway?" she asked.

Like all the energy had leeched out of him at once, Tristram slumped his shoulders. "Nothing, Your Highness." Nevertheless, he looked pale and listless as he shifted his weight, folding his arms over his chest.

"Oh yes, you seem like everything is going just wonderfully." Gillian shifted the basket on her arm and reached inside for the blanket. "Would you like to sit with me? I know, it must be tempting to run off and recover from my thoughtless advances, but if you have need of an ear, I am in possession of two."

Tristram glanced around, frowning. "Highness, are you sure that's appropriate?"

Lord Gaspar had not been so attentive in his duties since Reynold had made a fool of him and dismissed his men. Gillian had no escort, but in the Spires, she hardly needed one. "We're friends, are we not? I am perfectly safe in your company. And I promise, you are perfectly safe in mine. Well, now."

When he still hesitated, she said, "Tris, I command you to sit with me. I need company while I prune the rosebushes." The words came with a smile and no weight at all—he could have walked away and she wouldn't have said a thing—but instead his brow smoothed. He helped her spread the blanket near the bushes where she could work, and when he sat, he crossed his legs. His hands were on his elbows, and he seemed to be chewing his cheeks. She set to her work and allowed him to gather his thoughts.

"What do you know about our visitors from the north?" he asked after a few minutes.

Gillian started. "The Torndals?" She had attended the tournament enough to show support and no more. Since then, the Torndals had kept to themselves. "I heard they intend to leave soon."

"No, Lady Rhiannon and Hafgan."

"Oh." Gillian blinked. "Well, not much. I know Reynold is taken with her, but we've only spoken a few times. She seems perfectly pleasant, if a little, um . . . forward? Perhaps that isn't the right word. I mean she's not easily cowed. That might be good for Reynold. Why? Do you not like her? Oh! Do you like *him?*" She leaned away from the bushes to grin at him.

Tristram blushed. "Hafgan? No. Nothing like that. I gave him my sword."

Gillian cocked a brow at him. "And you realize what that sounds like?"

"An actual sword." He scowled.

Gillian chuckled. "Well, you have enough of them." She didn't understand the vaguely ill look on his face when he spoke of giving one away. "Was he in need of a weapon?"

"This one, I think."

"Then it was kind of you to give it to him. You are sure there's nothing there?"

"Completely." He said it with such certainty. Was there someone else? Hard to imagine. Reynold did not usually afford his knights—even his friends—much time to let their eyes wander. If he had, perhaps Gillian wouldn't have spent so much time thinking Tristram's decency toward her was anything more than that.

"Too bad." As much as Gillian might've liked the idea of a life with Tris, a chance to escape to the wild northern country, as soon as he'd expressed his preference for men, Gillian was happy to drop it. Tris was dear to her; she'd hardly push him in a direction that would make neither of them happy. And she did wish them both to be happy.

"Here," she said, leaning over to cut a rose off the bush.

"Highness—" He seemed ready to refuse her, but she held the stem out to him. He scowled at the flower. "You didn't have to cut your rose."

"Don't think on that. It's getting colder. They are all going to wilt soon, and it looks better in your hand than on any old bush. Just enjoy it."

Rather than lean in to sniff the blossom, Tristram frowned and ran his thumb over one of its thorns. It puckered his thumb but did not cut it.

"I can tell something is bothering you, Tristram. Is it the jarl?"

He flinched but shook his head.

"You don't have to tell me what's on your mind," she said, "but I am sorry that you're bothered." She squeezed his knee. "I hope you'll tell me if there is anything I can do."

And then he opened his mouth, closed it, and when he opened it again, he spoke to the thorn digging into his palm. "They are dragons."

Gillian stiffened. "Lady Rhiannon?"

He nodded.

There wasn't a human in Llangard who hadn't heard the worst things about dragons. For centuries before Athelstan had come up from the southern mountains to free them, humans had served dragons. He had been the first magician, and the best Llangard had ever had. And Gillian, with her pitiful magic, shared his bloodline.

He'd marched on the beasts, used the wind to pierce their soft places with enormous steel bolts, and when they'd retreated, he had made the mountain fly. He'd crushed dragons the size of manor houses, and his people had been free to build their own kingdom.

Since then, dragons had been banished from Llangard. But Gillian had always assumed when they came, they'd come with fire and claws and gnashing teeth, not brocade and clever smirks and flaxen hair like strands of sunlight—far too bright to be usual. There was only one other person she'd seen who looked anything like her—

Before Tristram said another word, her eyes flicked up toward his own hair, so blond it was nearly white. A line puckered her brows. "Oh, Tris . . ."

When she met his eyes again, he swallowed hard. "Yes, Highness."

She never would've put it together. Never would have thought. But knowing what they were, there was nothing else for Tristram to be. And he, too, was from the north.

Without thought, she set her pruning knife aside, pushed up onto her knees, and wrapped her arms around his neck. He stiffened, but only until she combed her fingers through his short hair. Then, he buried his head against her shoulder. "I had no idea," she whispered.

The thought that he had kept this secret and it had weighed on him all this time settled heavily in her own chest. He couldn't have told anyone, or he'd have been in danger. Even she was willing to discount Lady Rhiannon and her ward the second Tristram revealed them.

If Gillian had known him less well, he would've scared her too. But rather than change her perception of Tristram, she adjusted her ideas about dragons. Whatever he was, he would continue to be all things good and decent in the world.

"All will be well," she whispered as she leaned back and cupped his cheek. Her thumb brushed his skin. "No one will find out."

B et had spent days on the road trailing after the Torndals, all the way to Windy Pass. Legend said that once, a mountain had stood right in the middle of it, but when Athelstan had chased the dragons into the mountains, he had lifted rock and dirt and tree and boulder out of his way to follow them. It was one of the few easy routes between the kingdom of Llangard and the harsh clan lands of Tornheim.

The company did not make any suspicious stops. Their caravan rode hard, only stopping for short spurts to change out their horses and eat. They moved directly toward the mountains. Seemingly, their affront at the jarl's fate made them disinclined to linger in such an inhospitable kingdom as Llangard.

Good.

Bet would be glad when they were back in the stony north.

After they'd been two days on the road from Atheldinas, they stopped at the base of the Mawrcraig Mountains to make camp. Even with Windy Pass, it was not the sort of trek one wanted to start at the end of the day. They'd go in the morning, and Bet would return to court with nothing to show for his time away.

He followed them into a forested curve set into a cliff. With their backs to stone, some of the Torndals moved to watch the open plains behind them, alert, like they knew he was there. Rather than risk getting caught, Bet tied his horse four furlongs away and moved in a wide arc around the trees through their camp. When he came to a bluff, he began to climb. From above, he'd be able to see everything. Hear everything.

The rocks weren't too steep, but when his hand clutched one and it came loose, tumbling a few down the side, he froze. To him, the sound was deafening, but he was focused on his own folly. None of the Torndals noticed, so he pulled himself up the last stretch onto a flat midway up where he could sit back from the very edge and watch from the shadows.

For more than an hour, they watched the path behind them, the hands of some busy with erecting tents or preparing food. Still, they waited. It wasn't for Bet but for something else.

He cursed his shortsightedness as a rider approached their camp. Bet had not seen him on the road. Now, he had trapped himself against the rock with no way to intercept the messenger that did not give his own position away. He cursed and inched toward the edge of the rocks.

The rider was not carrying any sigil that Bet could see, but despite the dark, he trusted his own sight. The horse was too fine by half to belong to anyone but a noble.

Bet had seen the man before. He was no noble but worked in the kitchens at the Spires—he had since Bet's own father had been dismissed by Prince Reynold. Dylan, his name was.

He carried no distinguishing marks. Bet narrowed his eyes. With enough concentration, he hoped to see the seal that closed the missive, but it was flat. Whoever had sent him, they didn't want to be found communicating with the enemy.

And though no war had been declared, Bet had no doubt that the Torndals were the king's enemies. Tornheim had never posed much of a threat, disjointed as their clans were. They spent so much time fighting amongst themselves that when a zealous jarl tested the border, they worked alone and were put down quickly.

In recent years, something had changed. They were bolder. Showed more consideration in planning.

In the past, Jarl Katrien wouldn't have cared a lick for Jarl Jorun. She might have even considered his death an opportunity for her own clan. And now, she acted as if his murder were a personal affront. They were working together, and the only things that ever brought people together were a shared purpose or a shared enemy.

From the cliff where Bet had hidden in the shadows, he watched Jarl Katrien burn the letter the moment she was finished reading it. His annoyance flared, but there was nothing to be done to save it.

If he had hoped to extract some information from the messenger himself, that thought was lost in a spray of blood as Jarl Katrien flicked her arm efficiently. The moon caught the steel of her dagger for one second before Dylan clutched his neck and fell to his knees. The Torndals left him to bleed out in the dirt.

There was nothing for Bet to do but sit and wait. The Torndals gave nothing away, and bitterly, Bet thought there was little left for Dylan to reveal either.

When the Torndals marched for the pass the next morning, leaving the body behind and uncovered, Bet climbed down from his perch to search it.

Dylan had nothing in his jacket to give him away. His skin was sallow and cold, dewy in the early morning. His limbs were stiff, but Bet left no inch of him unchecked. If he wanted to make an accusation, he needed proof. The Torndals had taken Dylan's horse—worth more than the man's life, no doubt. At his belt was a small purse, but he seemed to have nothing else of value. Bet took that and left the rest, returning to his mount and setting a path home.

On his own, he could move far quicker than the Torndals had moved with their carts. He rode hard back to the capital, whispering words in his mother's tongue into the velvet ear of his horse to keep it from tiring. The words of elves carried special weight for living things.

When he returned home, what he wanted first was sleep. Then drink. Then, perhaps, something to hit. He'd been gone nigh on four days and had little to show for it but suspicion and a dead man's purse.

There was no guild of assassins, no company with which to train. No doubt if there had been, Bet would have been at their throats. Normally, he didn't lament his solitude, but right then, he wanted to hit something, and a practice dummy wouldn't do.

In the course of getting a drink, maybe he could pick a fight with a man broader then he was. Lay his opponent low. First, he had to see the king.

"You're certain the messenger came from Atheldinas?" His Majesty asked.

"I am certain he came from this very palace, Majesty," Bet confirmed. "His name was Dylan—a kitchen boy. No one important. He had this on him." He dropped the small purse between them on the enormous table spread with wooden figurines of troops and supply lines for wars King Edmund had never fought. "A small amount of coin for the price of his life."

A curl twisted Reynold's lip. "A small amount of coin to betray his king."

Bet frowned. "He died a traitor's death."

When Bet had returned to the Spires, he'd found the king in his war chamber, alone. Now, His Majesty glanced out the window at the sunny spread of grass below. With a twirl of his hand, Reynold waved him on.

"The horse he rode was fine," Bet explained. "But Dylan wasn't well dressed. He carried no sigil and came from the direction of Atheldinas. Katrien burnt the letter, so whatever evidence he carried went up in ash. Whoever sent him didn't want to be found out, but no one outside of this castle would've had such a clear idea of the Torndal's route or when they would leave."

His jaw tight, the king nodded.

"Is there anything you would like me to do about it?" Bet asked. If Reynold had an inkling about who might betray him—he had to have an inkling—Bet would gladly put them out of their misery before they could put the king out of his.

"Not presently, no." King Reynold's tone was deceptively mild, but Bet decided to let it pass. No sense trying to spark a reaction to a threat that had yet to reveal itself. The king was definitely not the right outlet for Bet's frustrations. "You may go."

Though the king had not turned to look at him since their conversation started, Bet bowed before he left him to his thoughts.

To save time, he cut through the courtyard between the royal wing and the far side of the palace. He'd slip into the city, spend the night drinking and brawling, and by the end of it, he'd feel in control of his circumstance again. What did it matter that he could not pin down the villain plotting against the king? No harm would come to Reynold while Bet was at court.

As he stepped onto the grass, he froze and leaned back into the shadow of the door. There, on a blanket with their legs folded cozily toward each other, sat Princess Gillian and Lord Radcliffe. Radcliffe, who kissed Bet like he wanted to devour him whole.

They were speaking in voices far too low for Bet to hear, and sitting very close to one another. Bet watched as the princess lunged in and wrapped her arms around Tristram. Her fingers curled in his short hair, combing through it. Lord Radcliffe buried his face in the curve of her neck. To kiss it no doubt.

Bile soured the back of Bet's throat. Perhaps Lord Radcliffe made a habit of putting his mouth on everyone who let him near enough. Bet hadn't realized, but why should he be surprised? Tristram would hardly be the only lascivious lord at court.

Bet had seen enough. He stepped back into the corridor. He'd go the long way. And he'd damn well find someone to put the fear of his fists into.

22

SIDONIE

If Sidonie had mentioned her unease toward the king to anyone, she would assume they had informed on her to him. It wasn't that she disliked looking after Prince Roland, but the king specifically ordering her to look after his son could be little other than a demotion.

If he were concerned for the boy's safety, her reassignment was the only sign he'd given. One might think he would have given her a warning if the prince were under threat.

And of course, as though the universe were frowning upon her, on the second day at the assignment, Rhiannon came to visit the princeling.

Their meeting strengthened Sidonie's resolve to keep her distance from Lady Rhiannon. Not because she was cruel or inappropriate, oh no.

She was perfect.

Instead of inviting the young prince to go inside and do something she would enjoy, she went right out into his private stretch of garden and sat down in the dirt with him, silk dress and all.

He gave her one of the brightest smiles Sidonie had ever seen on the boy, and held out a bit of wood, vaguely carved in the shape of a person. "This one is me, and that one is Lord Radcliffe." He pointed over at a bigger block lying on the floor a few feet away. "And he's the evil dragon king, and we have to fight him."

Rhiannon listened earnestly, not a sign of amusement in sight. She scooted over to the bigger block, painted black, and it did indeed have the lines of a dragon. It was no masterpiece, but it was far more impressive than anything Sidonie's siblings had played with.

After a second, Rhiannon sat up with a frown. "That is not a dragon king!" Roland looked confused, but the lady immediately continued. "She is a dragon queen."

"Oh," he said, nodding agreeably, leaning over to inspect the dragon as though he'd missed some sign of femininity.

"She doesn't want to fight you either," Rhiannon added.

Roland shot up, staring at her, eyes wide. "But if she doesn't want to fight, what do we play?"

Sidonie had to fight down a laugh. Trust a child to ask such a sad truth about humanity.

Rhiannon leaned toward him and pointed toward a trail of rocks that lined the path through the garden. "Look at that. The Torndals are coming, and they're going to attack all of us. She thinks we should work together."

The king would not approve of such play. He preferred the uncomplicated villainy of dragons to the much more difficult situation with the clansmen to the north. For her part, Sidonie wished that such a fantasy were possible. The dragons were intimidating, certainly, but during her lifetime, she hadn't heard of a dragon attack. For much of her childhood, she'd believed them pure fantasy.

Who ever heard of hill-sized lizards?

Until she saw one for herself, in fact, Sidonie still was not sure if she believed in them. They seemed like convenient bogeymen to blame for childhood fears.

Meanwhile, Tornheim was a real and ever-present threat. Sidonie had met too many of its people to think otherwise.

The prince was staring suspiciously at the row of rocks, and he narrowed his eyes and nodded. "We'll hold them off together. Tris is good at fighting, and he taught me."

Radcliffe had done no such thing. He had suggested it once, and Reynold dismissed the notion, saying that the boy was "too weak" for the sword. Sidonie had always found that learning the sword improved the constitution, but no one had been willing to press the matter.

They had barely started lining up their forces when a throat cleared to one side. For a moment, Sidonie worried it was the king, come to check on them and finding his son allying himself with toy dragons. Instead, it was his old nurse. She inclined her head respectfully to Sidonie, and then to Rhiannon, though she eyed the place where her dress met the dirt path. "The prince needs to eat," she announced.

Roland scowled and hugged his toy to his chest. "I'm not hungry."

The nurse's expression didn't change. Apparently, it was an argument they had often, and as was usually the case with royals, the nurse simply waited until the prince realized for himself that he was better off eating and coming back. He was a well-behaved young man, so it didn't take long.

Eyes downcast, he turned to Rhiannon. "I suppose you need to go."

"Not in the least. You go eat, and then we can defend the north from the clan warriors." Her smile was breathtaking, and it made Sidonie long for a world where she could have such a life: a beautiful wife, a sweet son, and a warm afternoon in the garden. But her duties left little time for such things, and her duties had always come first.

Roland followed his nurse, glancing back at Rhiannon to make sure she didn't disappear. When Sidonie went to follow, the lady sprang to her feet as quick as a blink and put herself between Sidonie and the door.

"He's fine."

"The king ordered me to watch him," Sidonie countered.

Rhiannon looked toward the door, where it was easy enough to see Prince Roland seating himself at his small table, staring unhappily at whatever the nurse fed him.

"I wouldn't be able to react quickly enough if—"

And then Rhiannon's lips were on hers. They were soft and warm, and tasted of dates and honey. For a few seconds, Sidonie let herself fall into that perfect embrace. The reality of their situation came back quickly, however, and she put a hand on Rhiannon's chest to push her back, though it took a surprising amount of her strength.

There was a tiny giggle, and Sidonie's gaze snapped to where Roland sat, turned toward them, one hand over his mouth. Her first thought was the most selfish possible. She rushed to the door to locate the nurse.

"She left," Roland announced, knowing somehow what Sidonie was looking for. "She doesn't stay long now that I'm older. She has other things to do. That's why it's mean for me to make her wait."

Sidonie looked back at him, and his bright blue eyes, so like and unlike his father's, were sparkling with amusement.

"I'd rather kiss you than Father too. Or Tris. Or Millicent from the kitchens."

Sidonie had to cover her mouth to hold the hysterical laughter in. Millicent spent most of her hours filthy—cleaning up in the kitchen was hard, dirty work. She was lovely though; Sidonie had to concede that to the princeling.

Still, King Reynold would probably have all three of them killed at the idea that any of them would be preferable to him.

"Your dashing knight isn't for me," Rhiannon said as she sat herself in one of the small chairs at the prince's personal table.

It seemed a cruelty that there were four of them, but Sidonie never saw other children in the royal wing of the palace.

Rhiannon didn't seem to have the slightest issue sitting in one. Sidonie did not try.

"This is disgusting," Rhiannon said, picking at the prince's dinner. After a second, she grabbed a small purse she had, opened it, and dumped a pile of sugared almonds out onto the table. "There. Much better."

The prince stared at the nuts and then the lady.

After a moment, she rolled her eyes and waved at them. "Not for me. I already ate my dinner." She looked at Sidonie, who shook her head and demurred. "There we are. All yours."

He bit his lip thoughtfully. "You don't have to. I don't tell Father things."

Rhiannon snorted. "Tell him. Don't tell him. It's not a bribe. They're just things. I like giving people things."

And there was his bright smile back. "Me too."

"I don't doubt it. You must be like your mother," Rhiannon said, as though it weren't a horrible insult to His Majesty.

Roland, of course, didn't notice. "Everyone says so." He sighed and looked down at his hands. "They say I have Father's eyes and nothing else." He fidgeted for a moment, then stood and ran out into the garden, coming back with one of his toy soldiers. "There's something else, but I think it's from Aunt Gillian."

He looked up at Sidonie with huge, nervous eyes, and she melted. She still didn't sit in the damn child-sized chair. She preferred not to break fine things.

Finally, he set the wooden soldier on the table in front of him and closed his eyes. Barely a second passed before the wood shifted without so much as a touch, turning into the fine features of Tristram Radcliffe.

Sidonie's breath caught. Regularly, the king had been heard to lament his son's utter lack of magic, but there the boy was, proving him wrong. He was looking from Rhiannon to Sidonie, biting his lip. "Please don't tell Father though. I'm not very good at it. He'd just tell me not to try, because I'm too weak."

And indeed, the boy slumped into his little chair, taking a few deep breaths.

Rhiannon shoved the nuts in front of him and edged his goblet closer too. "Eat. You need to keep up your strength. Learning magic takes a strong constitution." The boy's face fell. Clearly, he thought it an insurmountable obstacle. But then Rhiannon leaned into him and whispered. "But you'll get there. It takes work, but you can be as big and strong as anyone else. You're magic, after all."

Strangely enough, even Sidonie believed it.

❧ 23 ❧

TRISTRAM

Tristram passed the nurse in the hallway and assumed Roland was eating dinner. He didn't think much of it, until he stepped into the prince's doorway and saw Lady Rhiannon throw herself at Sir Sidonie, pressing their lips together in a passionate embrace.

He was never one to begrudge other people any chance at happiness, but he could not be present for such a thing. He only hoped Roland didn't notice and cause them trouble. And that Rhiannon left soon without turning the entire court on its head.

Sir Sidonie was a strong, beautiful woman whom he considered his equal and possibly his friend. He did not want to see her suffer for Rhiannon's folly.

He ran directly into a person and backed away a step, already stammering out an apology when he realized he was looking into Bennet Kyston's glittering black eyes. He only wished they weren't glittering with barely suppressed rage.

Perhaps he shouldn't be surprised. As much as he thought he'd read the man's expression right, Tristram could be slow to understand people. Maybe the intense looks Bet had been giving him were sheer hatred for some reason that Tris could not guess.

Before he'd gotten more than two words of an apology out, Bet reached out and shoved him in the chest. "You should not be in the royal wing of the palace. It's not appropriate."

That stopped him dead. "Appropriate?"

Bet glared. "Unless you're on the king's business, you don't belong here."

Naturally, Bet was always on the king's business, and Tristram was a mere lackey. Just a cousin who had won the king's favor. Still, before Bet had always at least tolerated his presence. Had his attention the other day been so unwelcome? Or perhaps he'd been disappointingly unskilled. In the aftermath, Bet had disappeared. He might have been avoiding Tris all that time.

"I belong here as much as you do," he said, narrowing his eyes and setting his feet apart as though for a fight. Perhaps kissing the man had been a mistake and now they would forever be at odds, but Tris refused to be ashamed. If Bet hadn't wanted him, he should have done what Tris did with Princess Gillian and told him so.

Bet gave that low rumble of a growl, and it made Tristram's breath catch in his chest.

Perhaps it would be best if, in the future, Tristram avoided the man altogether. If he struggled to control his reactions when Bet was angry with him, who knew what he would do when the man showed him the slightest bit of—

Bet grabbed one of Tristram's shoulders and pushed the other, swinging him around to press his back against the wall. He muttered something under his breath about Tris not "sowing his seed," but it was hard to hear and cut off when warm, dry lips crashed against his.

The man's whole body was a warm line against him, hands still planted on his shoulders as though he could hold him against the wall. Tris was stronger than any human he'd ever known, but something in the idea of Bet holding him down sent a jolt through his whole body, making his cock strain against his hose. It pressed obscenely into Bet's own groin, and they both groaned aloud at the pressure.

Bet pulled away, eyes even blacker than usual, and stared at him. "What is it you want, Lord Radcliffe? Perhaps this peasant on his knees for you?"

On . . . his . . . Tris's eyes went wide with understanding, and his mouth fell open. He'd heard about such things, but—peasant, Bet had said. He thought Tristram was trying to demean him. Could he offer the opposite? To get on his knees for Bennet Kyston?

To take his cock, like—

"Bet!" came the excited cry from halfway down the hall, and Tris let his head fall back, thumping against the wooden support beam. He had to find a way to drag the man into a room somewhere. Kissing in hallways was dangerous, and apparently little more than a good way to get himself worked up with no release in sight.

Calmly, Bet shifted his tunic to be certain the bulge in his hose was covered and turned his back to Tris. For a moment he thought it plain insulting, then he realized Bet was standing between himself and the approaching Prince Roland. Shielding him, in a way.

"Your Highness," Bet said, voice dry as dust.

"You were gone so long," the prince told him.

Bet chuckled, crouching down to meet the prince's eye directly. "A few days, Highness."

The boy sighed. "Forever." Then he looked up and spotted Tristram. "Tris! I didn't see you there."

"I was just coming to see you," Tris only half lied. "But I saw the nurse leaving, and didn't want to interrupt your dinner."

Roland's eyes sparkled. "You both have to come see my new toys." He grabbed Bet's hand and turned to drag him away. "Lady Rhiannon had to go, so one of you can play the dragon queen, and we'll force the Torndals to leave us in peace."

Tris's blood ran cold.

Was she trying to force the prince to her way of thinking? Make him believe dragons were harmless, so she could hurt him somehow?

He didn't doubt Hafgan's word, that the dragons were worried about encroachment from Tornheim, but he had less faith in Rhiannon's good intentions.

Bet was also looking at the prince curiously. "The dragon queen, is it?"

Roland nodded furiously. "Wait till you see her. She's huge and scary. She'll help us protect Llangard."

All thoughts of heading back to his rooms to, um, take matters into his own hands were set aside for the moment. He needed to speak to Rhiannon. Whatever her intentions, she was not allowed to drag Roland into them. He was a sweet boy, and he deserved to keep his innocence for as long as possible.

❦ 24 ❦

RHIANNON

That night, Rhiannon refused King Reynold's invitation to dine again in his private quarters. One thing she could say for humans was that their tastes were varied and their feasts delightful. She suspected that was simply the difference between living in a mountain village and a lavish palace. Nevertheless, small pleasures would keep her sane in this place.

She passed Hafgan a plate of thinly sliced beef, eyebrows raised as she chewed an entire folded piece and nodded enthusiastically. "Try," she mumbled around her mouthful.

It seemed a struggle for him not to roll his eyes, but he gave in. He had watched the humans carefully these past days, and rather than fold the slice up and stuff it in his mouth, he cut a piece off with knife and fork. "It's good," he said once he'd swallowed. Rhiannon grinned and nodded.

"We need to talk," a man said on the other side of the table. Rhiannon looked up to see the serious scowl of Tristram Radcliffe.

"Well, hello, my lord. Whatever can I do for you?" Rhiannon asked with a smile, licking pink blood from the rare meat from her fingertips. He looked aghast at the display.

"Not here," he grunted.

With a sigh, she heaved to her feet. "I'll be back," she said to Hafgan. "Mind your manners."

"I don't think I am the one to worry about here," he muttered.

All she could do was shrug. Then she turned on the balls of her feet to follow Tristram out of the great hall. He did not slow until they'd rounded a corner into a more private corridor.

Then, he turned on her. "Are you trying to sway the prince?"

Rhiannon started, blinking. "Excuse me?"

"Turn his mind. Convince him dragons are good company."

"Well, I am sorry, but I think he already keeps company with at least one." Rhiannon looked him over head to foot. Tristram glared at her.

"Prince Roland is not an appropriate target for your machinations."

"You'd keep the truth from your leaders?"

"The truth? The truth is that your kind are dangerous," Tristram accused.

She had thought that he might be keeping secrets from the rest of court, but she'd never considered that Tristram was so ill informed himself. She stuck her jaw out.

"Hafgan showed me the sword you gave him. He's had a hard time growing his hoard. That was a kind gesture." Rhiannon pursed her lips. Swaying forward into Tristram's space, she put a finger in the center of his chest and stared up at him directly. "Why did you do it?"

His mouth snapped shut, a muscle in his jaw twitched, and Rhiannon began to smirk.

"I know why you did it," she continued when he offered no explanation. "He needed that sword more than you. You saw that, and you know, dragon or not, Hafgan is a good person."

Tristram pursed his lips and crossed his arms. "Is that why you brought him here? Because he's kind and decent and tempers your . . . personality." What came out of his mouth was practically a sneer.

Rhiannon laughed. "Actually, no. Surprising as it may be, not everything in the world revolves around your king, or even this court. I brought Hafgan because I wanted him to see that humans are not like what he's heard. Well, and because he is one of few dragons willing to give humankind a chance."

Tristram flinched. He straightened as if affronted. Rhiannon rolled her eyes. Seven hells, she rolled her whole head with them.

"Do you honestly think that these people are the only ones who huddle together and tell stories of monsters? I know what you've heard from them, but what do you think my people—*your* people—tell around their fires?" she asked.

Tristram grimaced. She was beginning to wonder if he'd ever met a dragon before she and Hafgan had come to Atheldinas.

"They speak of a mighty king who, when we fled to the mountains, hunted us there," she said. "And when we hid between rocks and in caves, he lifted whole mountains to crush us alive. And we tell stories of Tegan gan Carryl, who was sent to kill the king but fell so deeply in love with a man that she wished instead to end the war. Do you know what Athelstan did to her lover?"

Tristram's lips pressed into a thin white line. Slowly, he shook his head.

"Your mighty king dragged him to the western pass and tied him down. One by one, he dropped pebbles onto the man's chest. No one knew what he was doing, until the man began to scream. They were only pebbles—no bigger than a fingertip. They couldn't have hurt anyone. Not unless he wanted them to. But he built them tall enough that the weight crushed the man while Tegan listened from the mountains. When she flew to save him, he threw sharp stone through the air that tattered her wings and brought her crashing to the ground, so she'd never fly again."

Rhiannon had visited the place once, seen the stone between the mountains where Athelstan had pinned the man and crushed him. He'd been the king's advisor, but Athelstan considered his love for Tegan an unforgivable betrayal. There was no hint of his body left, no bloodied stones that had torn through Tegan's wings. Only a heavy foreboding.

When Rhiannon took a breath, her chest jumped. "My people have sinned, but we are not the only ones who need to prove our good intentions. Luckily, our queen has no interest in you, though I suspect that might change if she learned Athelstan's line had been reduced to parlor tricks. If she saw your dear princess, she'd raze this palace of daggers to the ground in a night."

Tristram bristled at that, his hand twitching toward the pommel of his sword. "Princess Gillian is not a warrior."

"No, she is not," Rhiannon agreed. "And more's the pity for that. I will not tell Queen Halwyn how the power of the Cavendish line has waned —*if* you agree to help me turn the king's ear."

"You seem to do that well enough on your own."

Rhiannon scoffed. "Hardly."

"What you're speaking of is treason." Tristram said, like there wasn't a thing he could do for her.

"And apparently, I'm speaking to a coward."

Rhiannon turned away, determined that the closest thing she would find to an ally here was a boy prince whose father didn't love him well enough by half.

25

BET

et didn't know what he was doing. Halfway down the corridor where
lords and ladies slept, he thought his purpose was to punish himself.
He'd slip into Tristram's room to find the lord's arms locked around the
princess.

Of course, he should know better. Neither one of them were fool
enough to have their tryst in the Spires. If Reynold heard about it, it could
ruin them both. Still, as Bet slipped through the quiet halls, over thick
wool carpets and past striking paintings of peers of old, he was looking to
get hurt.

He snuck through the door to Tristram's rooms. The receiving room
was empty—hardly uncommon for the hour—and he could see a flicker of
a fire under a door. The nights were growing colder, though the days were
still warm.

He opened the door not to find Tristram asleep in his bed but sitting
beside the fire scowling. At the sound of the door, his head popped up. He
scowled at Bet.

"What are you doing here?" Tristram demanded.

Bet glared right back. He had no words for this, but did he need them?
They could hardly pass in the hall without one or the other lunging in for a

kiss. So as Tristram rose, ready to defend himself in nothing but a night-shirt, Bet did just that.

In three long strides, he closed the distance between them and crashed into Tristram. He slipped his arm around the lord's waist to keep him from toppling back into the mantel and curled his hand around the back of Tristram's head. Bet's lips closed over Tristram's, and his tongue delved into his mouth, intent on driving thoughts of anyone else from his mind.

Tristram gasped, hands fisting on Bet's shoulders, pulling at his sleeves. He did not push Bet away—did not hit him. He should have hit him.

"I will not bend for you," Bet growled against his lips.

"I have not asked you to."

"Good," Bet spun him and walked him back toward his bed. It had a high canopy and was more than twice as big as Bet's own. Everything about it was lovely and luxurious and soft. Bet had seen beds like it before, but he'd never been in one. It seemed impossible, but not as impossible as the man who fell back onto the silken sheets and reached for him.

Bet crawled up after him, relieved to find him yielding. Wanting. It was a far cry from a brothel and a man who could barely look at him. Seven hells, Bet could almost imagine Tristram wanted him personally.

As Bet kissed the man's neck, Tristram's fingers slid through his hair. It fell in curls around his ears. Princess Gillian's was a similar shade of onyx, but straight and smooth as silk.

Bet pulled back. "How do I compare?" he asked coldly.

As ever, Bet was looking for the words sharp enough to slip between his ribs and pierce him through. If he was going to be hurt, he would rather see it coming. Invite it, even. But Tristram only blinked up at him.

"I'm sorry?"

"To Princess Gillian. How do I compare?" He kept his voice even, intent on proving he did not care. To both of them.

A small frown puckered Tristram's brow as his thumb found the shell of Bet's ear. He traced its point, the flicker of something crossing his features, but it was quickly dismissed in favor of answering the question at hand.

"You don't." There was none of the biting harshness in Tristram's reply that Bet had expected. Still, his throat tightened. Bet nodded, and when he ducked his head—in part to hide, and in part to kiss Tristram's neck—the man fisted his fingers in Bet's curls and pulled him up to look at him again. "I have not been with Princess Gillian," he clarified. "She is lovely, but not to my tastes."

Bet stared. Lord Radcliffe could've done far worse for a wife. So what if Tristram preferred to shove his tongue past men's lips? Very few people married for love, and fewer still held onto it once they had.

But there Tristram was, lips parted, cheeks flushed, and the words tumbled out of Bet's mouth before he could catch them. "And what is to your tastes, my lord?"

Tristram slid his hands down Bet's sides, over his shirt and down to the tops of his thighs. He gripped Bet's ass, hauling him in and flexing his hips. Bet bit back a moan at the pressure. "This," Tristram whispered.

The way the lord's breath hitched gave Bet pause. He pushed up, hands braced on either side of Tristram's head on a pillow so soft he'd had no context to imagine it before that night. Keenly, he watched Tris flush and chew his lip until his gaze slid away. He was shy. Given their exploits in the hall and his formidable strength on the battlefield, that was unexpected.

The corner of his jaw, stubbled with fair hair, stood out from his neck beautifully. Bet bent to kiss the hollow just below it. "Have you ever done this before?" Bet asked.

"Done what?" Tristram continued to look away, and Bet's stomach began to twist.

"Fucked a man. Been fucked by one."

Tristram's grimace was faint, but it was enough to shatter Bet's nerves. He was not the kind of man who should show anyone the way of the bed chamber. Tristram deserved someone kind, who would care for him.

Bet sat back on his heels. Tris's head snapped up, and he glared at him. "What?" Tristram demanded. "Are you going to treat me like a wilting flower now?"

"I mistook your intentions." Those kisses, the heat of his lips—Bet had thought, since Tristram had initiated the first, that he knew something of what he was doing. Perhaps he did, or perhaps Bet had taken the hint of something he wanted so desperately and pushed and pushed until he wound up in Lord Radcliffe's bed, pinning the hard muscles of his body down with his hips.

Tristram laughed sardonically. "I assure you, you did not."

"To my credit, you do not kiss like an innocent." Excuses—they both knew it.

With a curse, Tristram dropped his head back. It seemed to take effort not to roll his eyes. Then, he grabbed Bet's wrist and pulled him in. He pressed Bet's palm over his rigid cock. The heat of it passed through the fine linen of his nightshirt, hotter than anything Bet had ever felt, and hard as steel. Maybe the lord was feverish, or maybe Bet was losing his mind.

On his own, Bet curled his fingers around the thick shaft and stroked.

"Is it that you think I don't desire you, Bennet?" Tristram asked as his fingers brushed up Bet's forearm to circle the bend in his elbow, a coaxing, feather's tickle of a touch.

The fire was beginning to dim, but even in that light, Tristram's eyes gleamed.

"I can feel that you do," Bet rasped, his hand moving in a slow, easy stroke.

Tristram's hand slipped up to his forearm, his shoulder. When pleasure hitched his breath, his fingers squeezed. His heels pressed into the mattress, and he lifted his hips toward Bet's touch. It struck Bet that he could have this. Could be the first. Tristram would never be able to deny him that.

"I will not bend," Bet repeated.

"I know," Tris said, and the way he licked his lips said he hardly minded that thought.

"And I won't fuck you."

Bet was a thrice damned fool for saying it, but it wasn't to protect Tris's virtue. Already, he could feel how easy it would be to lose himself in the man. Fall into distraction. Harbor ideas of something soft and sweet of his own—something he would never have. The king wouldn't allow it.

"I believe you'll do what I tell you to, Kyston."

A growl tore its way out of Bet's chest and he lunged on top of Tris, pressing him down with his weight. His free hand clutched Tris's throat.

"You do not command me, Tristram," he snarled. There would not be another lord—not one in all of Llangard—who could pull his strings. He could not stand the entanglements. If he allowed it, they'd tear him apart without a thought. But while Bet held his throat, his other hand gripped

Tristram's cock. The man under him thrust into that grip, unafraid. "Do you understand?" Bet asked.

Tristram only nodded, but it was enough. Bet released his throat, and free to move again, Tris didn't flinch away or shove him off. Instead, he shifted his nightshirt up, pulling it over his legs, curling up to shrug it off. And then, Lord Radcliffe was naked under him.

Even on the fresh, finely woven sheets in gentry chambers, Tristram was luminous. Maybe it was the way his fair hair caught the light. Perhaps it was the mere thought that this moment was sure to be one of the few gifts Bet received. Whatever the cause, he was beautiful.

Tristram ruined it by sitting up and reaching for Bet's own shirt. Bet only wanted a moment to admire him. He grunted and allowed Tristram to tug it off, but when Tris reached for him again, Bet put his hand in the middle of his chest and shoved him down on the bed.

"I want—" Tristram protested.

Bet clicked his tongue. "Quiet."

"But—"

Bet cocked a brow, and for once, that was enough to get Tristram to shut his mouth.

With the hand resting over his heart, Bet traced his fingers down the muscles of Tristram's chest, down his stomach. There, between his legs, his cock stood out, flushed pink, from a thatch of silvery blond curls. Bet smiled.

"Keep looking at it like that, I'll think you like my cock more than me," Tristram said.

"I do."

To prove his point, he stroked his hand down the shaft, sliding skin back to reveal his tip. With his thumb, he smeared a glistening drop to slick the head. Tristram's lips parted on a moan.

"Please, Bet. I need—" Tris didn't seem entirely sure what he needed, but he grappled for Bet's shoulders and pulled, so Bet slid up his body. He sat on his heels long enough to untie his hose and slide them down his hips. At that exact moment, he couldn't be bothered to shed his clothes entirely, but when he pressed his weight onto Tris, slotting their cocks side by side and thrusting, that was enough to sate both of them.

Tristram moaned, arching off the bed. His fingers dug into Bet's back, so Bet thrust again, setting a smooth, unrelenting pace. Tristram's sounds grew louder. A tingle of pleasure lit the back of Bet's neck to think that he —a cook's whelp, low and loathsome as he was—could take Tristram Radcliffe apart.

Rapt, Bet forgot to chase his own pleasure as he watched Tristram's play out on his beautiful features. His full lips fell apart, trembling over words he never managed to speak. His eyes fluttered shut so that his silvery lashes brushed his golden cheeks. Rather than let Bet do the work alone, his body rolled to meet him, strong and sure and flexing impressive muscles. Finally, his breath hitched and caught. And far too soon for Bet's liking, the man shuddered and spilled between their bellies.

Bet slowed as Tristram shook. It took a moment for Tristram to blink his eyes open again, and when he did, they were hazy.

"Are you all right?" Bet asked.

Tris nodded. That was enough.

And Bet had served his purpose. He drew back, intent on finding his relief elsewhere. Alone, where he could imagine sinking into Tristram and being welcome, a smile on the lord's face when he looked up and saw him there. But he hadn't even managed to pull his hose up before Tristram lunged on him with a growl, pushing him back onto the bed, his head at the foot of it. Tristram grabbed his arms and held them above his head, all that strength that Bet had dodged on the practice field coming to bear in a vise grip that held him down.

"I said I would not bend," Bet gritted out.

Tristram leaned down and buried his face against Bet's neck. He breathed in deep, like one would smell a flower. "I heard you."

Under Tristram's weight, Bet struggled. For one horrifying second, Bet's only solace was that Tristram would need some time to recover, and in those passing moments, he would make a mistake and Bet would slip away.

But Tristram kissed his neck sweetly, dragging his teeth over his flushed skin until Bet shivered. "I heard you," he whispered again in Bet's ear. "I don't want that. I just want—" Tris pulled back to look in his eyes and licked his lips in nervousness. "May I touch you? I've not—"

Bet bit his tongue. Hard. Of course Tristram wouldn't force him. He hadn't ever fucked anyone at all. And he was so damnably noble.

Clenching his jaw, Bet nodded.

At first, Tristram continued to hold his wrists above his head, though he shifted them together so he could manage with one hand. With the other, he touched Bet's cheek. His fingertips brushed across his lips, but when Bet frowned and turned his head, Tristram gently turned it back. "If you want me to stop—"

"I don't."

"Then I would very much like to see you."

Bet's heart gave a hard pound, just the one, but it punched air out of his lips. Tristram's answering smile was resplendent.

As his touches traced lower, Tristram found use for both hands and let him go. Tempting as it was to use the opportunity to shove him back and make his escape, Bet relaxed his arms by his sides, swallowed, and stared up at the canopy above him.

He could not allow himself to get swept up in this. Lord Radcliffe was not for him, and imagining one night might sprinkle water on some deep buried seed of affection was useless.

"Bet," Tristram whispered, his hand frozen in its circle around his navel. "You are very quiet." He laughed, but it sounded nervous.

Frowning, Bet glanced down at him. The lord sat, pretty and shining, beside Bet. His legs were folded under him, and Bet could not help reaching down to touch his strong thigh. "I am always quiet."

Tristram smiled. His shrug was sheepish. "Yes, but right now I cannot tell if you like this."

Bet blinked. That it had been a consideration for Tristram when it was hardly one for himself was . . . startling. "I do," he said after a moment. "Continue."

Tristram took his time touching Bet—brushing his hands down the insides of his arms, his sides, his thighs. Bet half thought he'd remove the rest of his clothes, but Tristram only shifted one knee between Bet's. Frustratingly, that pinned the cloth of his hose to the bed and trapped him, stopping his squirming as Tris's fingers inched up between his legs.

He weighed his balls and rolled them in his palm, assessing. When a low growl rumbled in Tristram's throat and he leaned in to press his nose to the bend where Bet's leg met his groin, Bet flushed. It almost seemed that Tristram liked it. Him. His body. The way he smelled.

"Get on with it," Bet grunted.

Tris's eyes flashed toward him and a wicked smirk tilted his lips. "You don't order me, Bet," he teased.

Nevertheless, his attention converged at the crux of Bet's legs. Tris stroked him—tip to root and back. He moved slow, testing, and Bet stifled his moans with his tongue pressed to the roof of his mouth. Nevertheless, Tristram was keen enough to learn. He moved faster, stroking toward the tip. And when Bet came apart, white spots flashed behind his eyelids.

As he recovered, Tris bent to dart his tongue over their mingled seed. He crawled up Bet's body and kissed him, shoving the bitter taste into his mouth with his tongue.

"I think you're to my taste," Tristram muttered against his lips.

But without the man gripping his wrists or pinning him down with a cleverly placed knee, Bet was free to slip out from under him. He could not stay and flirt. He'd never survive it.

He rolled to the side, pulled up his hose, and shrugged. "That only proves you have none."

Bet grabbed his shirt and headed for the door before he could get any more absurd ideas about soft sheets and sweet nothings whispered by a peer of the realm into his own pointed ear.

❧ 26 ❧

TRISTRAM

Tristram didn't enjoy the boxing matches Reynold held for entertainment on occasion. Tourneys that mimicked honorable battle were bad enough, pointless violence that they were. Outright fisticuffs? It was like two cutthroats fighting in an alley, not two honorable members of the king's court.

He especially did not like that this match had been staged simply to please Lady Rhiannon. Every moment she sat at Reynold's side, the king shooting occasional glances at her to make certain she was watching his spectacle, put everything Tristram cared about at risk.

Reynold's increasing fear of everyone could only grow tenfold if he found out the lady he was courting was a dragon in disguise.

Still, watching Bet fight in the round council chamber was like watching a snake strike. His motions were swift and sudden, and the fact that the bout managed to last as long as it did was almost certainly a choice on Bet's part. The man was better in a fight than anyone else Tristram knew, and just as vicious unarmed as he was with his swords.

His poor opponent didn't manage to land a single blow, despite his apparent skill, and it made the fight seem entirely pointless. Wearying, even, but for the continuing display of Bet's speed and accuracy.

Tristram couldn't help but turn his mind back to the night before, to

Bet hovering over him, lying beneath him, stripping him naked. The man's pearly skin had been painted gold by firelight, his black eyes even darker in the shadows. The way he'd moved in Tristram's bed had been more masterful than his work on the field of combat.

His pride wouldn't allow him to ask, but he wondered if the man would return. Perhaps it had been a passing fancy, and now that his lust was slaked, he had no further use for Tristram.

Bet's gaze met his over the shoulder of his opponent and locked. Perhaps he wasn't done with Tristram after all. Without even glancing away, Bet struck the man in the belly and jaw. The opponent, whose name Tristram couldn't remember, crumpled to the floor, and the people of the court cheered.

It was horrible how they enjoyed the spectacle of violence without purpose. They cheered Bet in this when they all feared him in private. Not a one of them would agree to be alone with him.

Excepting Tristram. He wondered if his lust was blatantly obvious to everyone who watched them. He felt so.

"Perhaps the loser's life should be forfeit?" Reynold suggested, as though such a thing were to be considered. Something commonplace, that a decent nation like Llangard did.

Tris looked away from Bet finally to stare at Reynold. His Majesty had one corner of his lips turned down, and he was staring at Rhiannon, who looked vaguely disinterested.

Moons above, was he trying to impress her by offering to have a man murdered?

The crowd had gone deathly silent, waiting for someone, anyone, to respond. Laurence Cavendish leaned forward on his knees to stare at his nephew. Tristram had the ugly feeling many would enjoy seeing the man die, but perhaps that was ungenerous of him. He couldn't allow the speculation to continue, no matter if it made Reynold angry with him.

"That is a Torndal custom, Your Majesty," Tris said, trying to keep his voice as even as possible. Surely that comparison would make Reynold rethink the suggestion.

Reynold looked over at him, expression bland, and shrugged. "Perhaps there are things to admire in the customs of Tornheim."

"Their brutality?" Laurence asked mildly.

The look that crossed Rhiannon's face was nothing short of furious, but she mastered herself in the space of a blink. A few in the crowd gasped, and Tristram turned to look, only to find that somewhere in his exchange with the king, Bet had slipped away. Perhaps, despite his bloody reputation, he felt as Tristram did about pointless violence.

He almost laughed at himself, such a ridiculous fancy, but kept his face blank. He couldn't give the appearance of mocking the king, and that was how laughter would be interpreted.

Reynold huffed and waved his hand. "Music, I suppose. I do hope that isn't too common for your tastes, my dear lady."

Rhiannon gave the king a bright smile and shook her head. "Of course not."

Thank goodness.

Quietly, Tris called over a servant and gave orders to have Bet's opponent taken away and given aid and healing. Reynold did not seem much interested in it.

When Tristram had imagined Reynold taking over at his father's death, he hadn't imagined that it would be quite so exhausting.

27

BET

For years, Bet had been the king's shadow, his sharpened blade, his weapon. It was not the first time that Reynold had called upon his servants and lesser men to brawl for the sport of the nobles. When he'd been younger, Bet had fought ferociously, never realizing that the entire purpose was entertainment—that he ought to draw the spectacle out. He hadn't wanted to lose.

He'd learned better. But there ought not be murder in sport where lords sat drinking, placing bets on which common man would come out worse for it. As Bet glanced down at his opponent, his shallow breaths, his reddened jaw, he felt no desire to kill him.

Yet if the king ordered it, he would have no choice. He'd killed without desire to do it before. Rarely did he get to mete out his own revenge on a mark like he had on Jarl Jorun.

When Lord Radcliffe interceded, Bet used the opportunity to slip away. The king might be willing to order his opponent's death, but he wouldn't bloody his own hands. All Bet had to do to ensure the man's survival was make himself scarce.

As he walked away from the boisterous chamber where they had held the match, Bet rolled his shoulders, flexed his sore hands, and tried to convince himself that he was no longer sparring, despite his racing heart.

It was always hard to calm his nerves after a fight. More anxious than usual, he picked up every sound in the hallway and beyond, so when he heard another set of steps following from the chamber, he hastened toward the nondescript servants' hall.

Those narrow passages wound around the castle, keeping servants out of the sight of nobles whenever possible. Bet made his way quickly through to the private quarters and into his own room.

Somehow, it wasn't a surprise when, a moment later, a knock sounded on his door.

No one opened it—of course Radcliffe would respect his privacy, despite the thin walls and the narrow door that did not quite fit in its frame, its lack of a lock, or the fact that Radcliffe was a lord and could do as he damn well pleased.

It only took two strides across the room before Bet gripped the door and yanked it open. Radcliffe stood on the other side, his soft lips pursed, a scowl on his gratingly handsome face.

"Sniffed me out?" Bet challenged.

"Or maybe you aren't as slippery as you like to think."

Bet stepped back to allow Tristram into the small space. The only thing worse than having Tristram in his tiny, barren room was leaving him to linger in the hall for any passerby to see. Bet shut the door behind him.

All at once, Lord Radcliffe crowded him back against the rough wooden door. Bet narrowed his eyes at him.

"What?" Bet snapped.

"You didn't kill that man," Tristram whispered. He leaned in, his broad shoulders and strong arms trapping Bet against the door. Had he a blade or real cause to think Tristram meant him harm, Bet would have been well justified to run him through. Instead, all Bet could think of was Tristram in the corridor, dragging him in, his lips parted and warm breath falling over Bet's skin as they tangled together out of sight.

This was out of sight, and disagreeable nonetheless. There was something far too intimate about having Lord Radcliffe here when his pulse was already racing. Bet didn't take company into his own quarters and bristled at the imposition, as if the lord might be startled to find out that the commoner he'd trapped was, in fact, a commoner.

"I did not," he agreed, turning up his chin so he could glare down his nose at the lord.

"You've killed before."

Bet only narrowed his eyes further. So what if he had?

"Why not this man?" Tristram asked. A slow smirk began to slide over his lips, making Bet's stomach twist. "Because I dissented?"

Bet rolled his eyes. "If you're determined to play this game, my lord, you will lose. I take my orders from the king, not Your Grace."

Tristram was undeterred by his sneering. "I think you care for me," he teased.

Sweaty, his fists aching from the blows he'd thrown that night already, he thought about knocking the air out of Tristram in the narrow chamber.

"I work in the best interest of His Majesty," he ground out. "That man's death did not serve His Majesty's interest. Llangard has had brutal kings before, and its people do not remember them fondly."

"Mmhmm," Tristram hummed.

He lifted his hand then and cupped Bet's cheek. With the pad of his thumb, he traced the dark line of Bet's brow, the outer curve of his eye, his sharp cheekbone.

Tristram was thinking about Jorun—should have been horrified by his murder—but he just stroked Bet's cheek until there was nothing left for Bet to do but swallow hard and drop his eyes.

"I do only as the king commands."

Tristram scoffed. It was a soft breath of air, completely lacking in theatrics. He leaned close enough to brush his nose against the tip of Bet's. "If you had, that man back there would be dead."

"King Reynold did not order—"

"You did not stay long enough to find out what he ordered."

Bet huffed. "His Highness loves you." He'd often had reason to be jealous of the bond between the pair—first he'd been jealous of Tristram for being a true friend to the king and not an instrument, then of the king for—for things he could not allow himself to want. "He would not have moved against you. You, m'lord, are weaving wishes from air. There is nothing here for you."

He planted his hand in the middle of Tristram's chest and pushed him back a step or two. Far enough for Bet to sweep his arm around at his barren room, his lumpy cot, the unvarnished table with his wash basin. Perhaps the lord *had* forgotten his status.

But Tristram didn't look away. His glinting eyes bore into Bet's, and he shook his head. "There's one thing."

Suddenly, Tris was on him again. His arm wound around Bet's waist. He yanked him in, the stone hardness of his muscles pressing their contours into Bet's body. There could be no doubt, when their hips met, what Lord Radcliffe wanted.

It was all too tempting to melt for the lord. If Tristram could forget his status for a night, couldn't Bet?

Bet cupped his face in both hands, felt the movement of Tristram's broad jaw as he leaned into the kiss. His tongue plundered Bet's mouth, sweet with the honeyed wine the king had offered his guests at the bout.

A moan tore out of Bet, escaping at the corners of their locked mouths. His fingers, in firm curls, dragged Tristram in like there was space yet for them to be closer.

He could get used to this—the lord's short stubble under his fingers and his soft lips, his teasing, the way he spoke to Bet as if he were a person and not a monster. That, alone, was terrifying.

Bet could fall for the idea of a lord and all the gentility and pleasure that he'd never found elsewhere. But he could not afford the distraction or the heartbreak that would follow when Tristram, inevitably, returned to his duty. He would find himself a lord or lady and return to Merrick to sire children or—

He wrenched his lips from Tristram's and turned away. "I cannot."

"Why?" Tristram demanded, pressing into Bet with a fluid motion that had blood rushing out of his head and protests dying on his tongue. "You're the only one who can sneak into my room in the night? I am not allowed to turn the tables?"

Bet flinched. When he snuck into Tristram's room, they could preserve the illusion that it was proper, their liaison swathed in silk sheets and surrounded by candles that had only been burnt once. Here, in his own room, the absurdity of this tryst was in the full light of candles burnt down to stubs and remade from those fine ones burnt first in noble rooms.

"No."

Tristram scoffed. "Come now, Kyston. You're being melodramatic. I don't mind your room. Or we can go to mine. I'm not asking for anything more than a—"

Bet shoved him back. Somehow, that was worse. His mind was full of soft thoughts and longing, and Tris only wanted—well, he didn't get to hear what he wanted. Shocked, the lord blinked at him.

"Leave," Bet snarled before Tris could get his bearings. "There is nothing for you here, so go."

"Bet . . ." Tristram's bright eyes glimmered with something that looked far too much like pity.

Bet swallowed roughly and shook his head. He was tired. His limbs were heavy. And he needed to be alone. "Please, my lord. My position is not so secure as your own. I am asking, for both our sakes, that you leave. If you are half as noble as—"

Before he could finish, Tristram nodded. Bet should have known that bringing his honor into it would do the trick.

"Apologies if I misunderstood or pressed you to . . ." Tristram trailed off, looking utterly at a loss.

Bet shook his head. "It's fine. Just—"

"Leave?"

Sharply, Bet nodded.

With his brow pinched, his plush lips turned into a frown that still, miraculously, managed to be gorgeous, Tristram bowed his head. "As you wish."

He had to bite his tongue as he watched Tristram slip out of his room. He'd go back to his own, sleep in a soft bed, and if he had any damned sense, he'd forget about this by morning.

Bet sat down on his cot, where he could've tipped Tristram Radcliffe onto his roughly woven blanket and stripped him of all his fineries. He could have taken a moment, an hour, and had Tristram to himself. But there was no room for either of them in the other's life, and Bet couldn't live with only a taste.

He curled over his knees, fisted his hands in his hair, and once, his breath shook with the thought of all he could not have. Then he let it go, steeled his nerves, and reminded himself that he had not been made for the likes of Tristram Radcliffe. His duty was to his king alone. When he sat up, letting the air out in a slow, even flow, his eyes were hard and his heart was harder.

✸ 28 ✸

RHIANNON

The guard who arrived to take her to dinner in the king's rooms wasn't Sidonie, and it seemed like a sign. Rhiannon had pushed too far, and Sidonie would avoid her moving forward.

The only person in the palace she knew would listen to her was a child. Roland was a lovely youngling, but by the time he came into power, it would be far, far too late.

She could try to follow through with her mess and marry Reynold, see if she could get the man to fall in love with her and try again, but she didn't think either of them had the patience for that. One of them was bound to kill the other if she didn't give up and leave soon, and he was the one with the rooms full of armored guards, so it didn't bode well for her. At least she'd been eating well. Maintaining her dragon form for the flight home would not be so difficult.

Even with all the trinkets that she'd picked up for her hoard, Rhiannon was beginning to long for home. She could practically feel her wings outstretched, carrying her higher through the cool air. Her village would smell delicious with all the meat Rhoswyn would be smoking. Older dragons would gather furs in their caves to last out the winter. Young couples would pair off, seeking their own amusements to stave off the winter tedium. If she were determined to change anything in Llangard, she would have to winter in Atheldinas. She was not sure she had the fortitude.

It didn't help her mood that Hafgan was barely speaking to her. He said she'd been unfair to Radcliffe after she'd taken to calling him the half human and said he wasn't worthy of being called any kind of dragon. Poor Hafgan was loyal to a fault, and he couldn't see past the coward's single kindness to a traitor who ignored the plight of both of his races just to preserve himself.

No, it was time to give up on the hope that any human—half or otherwise—could be reasoned with. They were ridiculous, illogical creatures, and Rhiannon struggled to imagine why her ancestors even wanted them as servants. Perhaps Queen Halwyn would decide to move their people somewhere else when the Torndals moved into the mountains—somewhere not caught in the middle of a war. Rhiannon would miss her home, but she would miss her people more if the humans were allowed to slaughter them all, as they had the wind dragons of Hafgan's first clan.

Something about the king's stance when she walked into his receiving room put her on edge. He was too loose, too casual. He waved her over to the table, motioning for her to sit down, so she did, but even that made her unaccountably irritated.

They spoke of unimportant things. The weather. The growth of crops. Rhiannon's meeting with the young prince, though at least that was something that interested her.

"He's a clever child," she told him, pleased to be able to compliment someone at court and tell the truth.

He smiled blandly at her, but at least he listened and seemed to pay attention. "Would you mind very much having him about? You needn't bother yourself with him terribly, but he is my heir."

Needn't bother herself? What kind of thing was that to say? In her clan, if a child lost a parent, the entire clan stepped in to help.

"Children are a gift," she told him, parroting what every dragon in her clan would say when speaking of hatchlings. "We hardly deserve them at all. One can hardly imagine grudging them their very existence. Your own is especially precious, Majesty."

He waved it away, as though the words had been mere lip-service. "Indeed, that should be perfectly serviceable then."

Serviceable? What in the seven hells was that supposed to mean?

"The only thing left is a certain . . . compatibility." He let his eyes fall from her hair, down the front of her gown, to the table, as though he could see what was beneath it.

Had she been in her scales, she might have roasted him for the sheer disrespect.

"Does your family breed well?" he asked casually. Was that such a common question among humans? Among dragons it was a taboo subject, since so many struggled to reproduce.

As it happened, her mother had been blessed with two hatchlings, which was enough to please any dragon. She doubted the king would be pleased to hear that she had a single sister, Rhoswyn, and that both of her parents had been the sole issue of their families.

The fact was that it mattered little to him, since she wasn't going to marry him, let alone bear his hatchlings—even though, by some miracle, Roland was vastly more charming than his father. Reynold's late wife must have been an exceptional woman.

"Well enough," she answered, setting her napkin aside. "I believe I should go, Your Majesty. I feel suddenly unwell." She thought that was something the fading flowers of humankind said. They feigned illness in the face of awkward conversations and later pretended nothing had happened at all. Well, Rhiannon would do the same, and she and Hafgan would leave this place, never to be seen again.

"What about magic?" Reynold asked, setting his napkin aside as well. He watched her intently. It would have taken more patience than Rhiannon had not to glare back at him. "Do your people have power?"

"Oh, sire, yes," she breathed. She could practically feel the sharpening of her teeth. "We have power enough." She'd have been better served lying on that front, but her pride would not allow her to belittle herself in front of this pale, sharp-eyed man. "Perhaps I will tell you about it when next we see each other."

When she stood, he did as well and crossed to intercept her. "Now, Lady Rhiannon, there's little need for concern. I'm hardly a rogue who goes about deflowering ladies."

Deflowering? What did that even mean?

She must have made a confused face, because he gave her that awful patient look, as though she were a child who needed everything explained to her. She wondered if he would give her the same look if she told him she'd pleasured more women in her life than he ever would. Not likely.

Then he grabbed her around the waist.

She shoved him back, taking a step to one side to keep him from trapping her against the table. "Your Majesty, this is entirely inappropriate."

He rolled his eyes and grabbed her again, this time the grip on her upper arm was positively bruising. She suspected if she were a human woman, he might have done her real injury.

No entitled ass of a man was going to push himself on her, king or not. She bared her teeth at him and shoved him away again, using more of her own strength. He stumbled back a few paces, backside hitting the table and sending food scattering across the floor. Wine goblets tipped and spilled their contents over the fine cloth.

His eyes were round and huge, the whites showed on all sides. "Dragon," he whispered. Then, raising his voice, he screamed it, shrill and irritating. "Dragon!"

She must have shown quite more than she'd intended. She ran her tongue along the inside of her teeth, and indeed, they had grown sharp. She had no doubt that her eyes had flashed, and the edges of scales were raising on her skin. Damn it all.

She had to get to Hafgan. They had to run.

As she turned, there was motion from the corner of her eye, and something crashed down on the back of her head. Everything went black.

❦ 29 ❧

HAFGAN

Rhiannon hadn't even been gone long enough to finish dinner when a cry went up through the castle. Hafgan opened the door a crack and poked his head out to find the hall empty.

He paced the room, worrying for no reason he could lay a finger on. Rhiannon could take care of herself. There was no reason to assume things would go any more wrong than they already had.

Then, through the window, he heard a group of men with heavy strides. Guards, no doubt. "A dragon?" one of them was muttering to another. "How could such a creature sneak past everyone?"

His stomach flipped.

Rhiannon.

It had to be.

He turned and grabbed the sword Tristram had given him, but then thought better of it. If he tried to fight the king's men with it, he might get the knight into trouble. And how did one fight with a sword anyway? He certainly had no skill with the object.

He was still staring at it, undecided, when the sound of booted foot-steps approached. The same men, no doubt. They weren't after Rhiannon; they were coming for him.

When he opened the door again, there were half a dozen men with swords drawn storming down the hall. "There it is—the other one. Get it!"

They rushed at him, and Hafgan did the only thing he could think to do in that moment. Later, he would be ashamed of himself for leaving Rhiannon when she needed him, but he ran.

He let the wind take him as he went, faster than any human could go, and more agile than most. He dodged people who tried to get in his way, people who tried to get out of his way, and when he got into the garden, he kept running.

Even after he couldn't hear humans behind him anymore, he ran over rocks at the back of the Spires, away from the city on the other side. They gave way to grass beyond the city's edge.

Finally, alone in a field of blue flowers, he pulled the tiny dragon from around his neck and wrapped its leather thong around the hilt of the sword, still in his hand. He wasn't sure how much of a lead he'd managed on the guards who had come to kill him, so he didn't bother taking off his tunic and hose—he just shifted, blessing the hearty meals he'd eaten at court and letting his bulk as a dragon do what it would with the irrelevant scraps of cloth.

Snatching up the sword in his claws, he bunched his leg muscles and leapt up into the air, letting the wind fill his wings and take him aloft.

He glanced back at the palace only once.

Rhiannon had been right—even at twenty, he was still a child. He couldn't help her himself. He needed to go home. The queen would know what to do.

30

BET

Bet spent the next day doing everything he could to avoid Tristram Radcliffe. He skirted through the great hall and only grabbed something for breakfast before heading out. On the way past a long table, he accidentally caught Tristram's eye. His throat closed up and he rushed on. He skipped the midday meal entirely.

And still, every whisper of wind sounded like Tristram's sigh. Every shine—off a coin, off the river that ran through the city—reminded him of the way Tristram's eyes had gleamed in the dark.

For so much of his life, Bet had counted his worth in small victories. Through Reynold's grace, he'd escaped his father. Through training and effort and the skills of his mother's people, Bet had become someone useful to the king. His loyalty, his brutality, had made him an indispensable addition to the prince's retinue, if not a public part of it.

And now, that prince was king.

Bet had risen by his grace. The cost was the whispers of dark magic that followed wherever he went. But he had enough. He was comfortable. Safe. No one could hurt him.

He knew better than to think there was any further to rise or any chance that Tristram Radcliffe—a lord of the realm with his own manor in the north—would want anything to do with him other than a tumble. Bet had done his part already. He flattered himself to think that Tristram had not come out the worse for it. After all, the lord had found his pleasure and had not had to sacrifice even a measure of himself in the bargain.

But thinking so much about him was a dangerous distraction for Bet—one that would surely come to nothing.

He went about his business in the days that followed, sticking to the shadows, avoiding the finer parts of the Spires where the lords and ladies slept in feather beds. With the Torndals gone and the tourney over, all was quiet. Bet was starting to get twitchy.

It was a relief when the king called him to the war room three days after the boxing match. More and more, the king spent his time there. Bet hardly minded the setting, though he might question the state of a king whose first thought was a violent one. It hardly mattered; the king would have some task for Bet to complete, some vicious deed that would wipe softer thoughts from his mind entirely.

"Majesty," Bet said, bowing lowly once he'd entered.

"There's been a traitor in our midst," the king said. His lips pressed into a thin line as he glared down at the map of the realm spread out over the table. Tiny figurines of dragons spread their wings above the mountain ranges. "A dragon."

Bet straightened. "Who?"

"Rhiannon," the king spat. "She tried to kill me."

Bet blanched. The lady had been bolder than most at court, but Bet had only thought she was reaching above her station, using all that brazen energy to catch the king's eye. She was a threat Bet should have dealt with before she had ever been in a position to threaten the king. "Majesty—"

"No need to apologize." He waved Bet off. "She has been dealt with. But the dragons are up to something. The younger one, Hafgan, escaped before the guards were able to apprehend him. We need more information. I would have you accompany me."

"Of course, sire," Bet said without missing a beat.

Normally, he would have questioned why the task did not fall to Sir Sidonie, but Bet knew—the king would not ask the knight to do something as distasteful as what he'd ask of Bet, not because he cared for her finer sentiments but because she would not be as quick to act on the king's behalf if she were in shock.

Bet followed him to the dungeons. They were dark and dank, filled with the scent of trapped bodies and the soft sounds of life languishing. It was here, at the base of the Spires, that one could see the skeletal remains Athelstan had dragged from the deep earth when he'd called forth his palace. Prisoners had been known to speak to the old dragons trapped in stone.

The dungeon's cells had mostly been empty during King Edmund's reign. There weren't other prisoners now. The king led him to the end of the hall where there was a chamber used for torturing traitors.

Inside, Bet's eyes fell on the king's executioner, Walden, standing before a beautiful woman in green silk, her wrists chained above her, hatred gleaming in her bright blue eyes behind a curtain of gold hair.

In the weeks she had been at court, Rhiannon had seemed lovely, if strange. She was curious and engaged in court in a way Bet hadn't expected —not merely interested in turning the king's head. But he hadn't seen anything insidious about her. Perhaps Tristram, the press of his lips in the hallway time and again, had distracted Bet from critical evidence of her foul intentions. He glared at her.

Blood trickled from the side of her mouth and bruises from the days of torture had turned her tanned skin purple, and still, she grinned at them. "Your Majesty," she said, "how lovely to see you again. And you've brought company."

"What has she said?" the king demanded of Walden.

"Nothing, Your Majesty."

"I'll have her spill her song. More," King Reynold commanded.

Rhiannon's wrists were locked into cuffs, her arms stretched out at her sides. The thumb of her right hand was trapped in a vise, and at the king's command, Walden began to tighten it.

Once, when he was very small, his father had caught him sneaking bread from the kitchen, he'd held Bet's hand down and hit it with a meat mallet. He'd broken bones, and his mother had sung softly as she'd set them back in place. He did not envy Rhiannon as pain etched her brow. That she did not cry out at once was impressive.

But she did eventually cry out. Bet heard the crunch of bones, saw her face pale and sweat sheen on her forehead in the dim light of the cell. She sagged forward, panting.

"You want to know something?" Rhiannon asked to the floor beneath her feet, so lowly that Bet almost couldn't hear her. She lifted her head and stared directly at Reynold. "You have another dragon at court."

"I know," the king sneered, his lips curling at the foul idea. "Your companion escaped before we could apprehend him."

Rhiannon laughed. "No, sire. Lord Tristram."

Beside Bet, Reynold stiffened.

The lady smirked. "You've been beset by monsters, Reynold. Or befriended by them."

Mouth dry, mind reeling, Bet thought every twisting organ in his body had frozen and atrophied. Tristram couldn't be what she said. He stared at the king, unsure what Reynold had in mind, until fury twisted His Majesty's features. "I want him questioned."

❧ 31 ❧

TRISTRAM

Tris didn't wait up to see if Bet would come back the next night, or even the one after. There were too many other reasons to lose sleep —he didn't need that excuse.

Something had happened, and the palace had been unusually subdued for days. No one seemed to know what was going on, which was unusual in a place where everyone sought out everyone else's business, and dozens of ears were pressed to half the walls. The only reasons Tris managed to keep secrets were the Radcliffe money and the fact that he had a private suite of rooms.

That first afternoon, he had heard tell of some commotion in the royal wing, but when he'd checked on Reynold, the man had dismissed him. He was busy, everything was fine, and Tristram didn't need to worry.

He hadn't looked fine, but pushing him would not change his mind, so Tristram had retreated. Reynold had not dined in the main hall, and the servants whispered that the king's guard was on high alert.

While he considered going to Sir Sidonie, that felt inappropriate. They were friendly acquaintances, not bosom companions. Using her that way would be dishonorable.

When nothing had changed the next day, he went to check on Hafgan and found no one in the room he shared with Rhiannon. Their belongings

147

WM. FAWKES & SAM BURNS

were still there, but he saw no sign of them at dinner that night. Or the day after.

So hours later, he sat up in his quarters still fully dressed from the day, instincts telling him that something was wrong. Something.

But what?

There was a rap on the door to his suite, metallic and loud. He jumped to his feet and rushed to answer it. A pale-faced Sidonie waited outside, and she seemed downright disappointed to see him. She sighed and looked at the floor between them.

"Sir Tristram Radcliffe, I've come on behalf of the king to take you into custody." She drew herself up and glanced over her shoulder to where half a dozen knights stood, then back to him, her gaze pleading. "Please don't fight us."

Her eyes flicked behind him to the window next to his bed. He glanced at it as well, but they were on the third floor. Did she think he could fly?

Oh.

Oh gods.

She did.

He nodded to her. He started to turn for his things, but what could he bring? His sword? They wouldn't allow it. His gut churned. He couldn't take any of his things, in fact.

He put his hands out to show himself as harmless—not that anyone would ever believe that again—and leaned over to pull his dagger from his boot. It felt as though he were removing a finger, just hacking it off right there in the doorway.

"May I leave this here?" he asked her softly.

She nodded and stepped back into the sitting room to give him a moment. Instead of leaving the dagger on his bed, he followed her in and lay it on the small table halfway between his mother's room and his own.

His mother knew that it was the one thing he would never willingly leave behind, and she would see it for the sign it was. He only hoped that Reynold left her alone. Perhaps he thought Tristram a snake who had hatched in a bird's nest, and his mother a complete innocent. Whatever happened, Tristram would never say otherwise.

Just looking at the dagger sitting there, everything in him screamed to snatch it back up, to fight every person in the room over it if need be. But

Tristram knew these knights. They had been his friends, his compatriots. Perhaps he'd not been a member of the king's guard, but he had trained with them, befriended them. He would not harm them.

He wondered if they even knew why they were arresting him. Considering the sympathy in their eyes, and the downright dissatisfaction on at least one of them, he doubted it.

And yet, Sidonie seemed to know.

She was frowning at him, looking again at the window, and then at him, in confusion and annoyance. In the end, she took a deep breath and motioned ahead of her. "Shall we, my lord?"

He nodded to her and followed the other knights out.

"Don't know why he's listening to that damned lizard," one of the men muttered. "As though it weren't obvious Lord Radcliffe is an honorable knight and nothing like her."

Rhiannon, then. He spared a moment of worry for Hafgan, but he supposed that perhaps this once, he should be worried for himself. Would they execute him this very night? Tell everyone what he'd been? Shame his mother?

He turned to look at Sidonie, who followed behind him, head down. "My mother," he whispered to her. "Please do what you can to protect her."

When she looked into his eyes, she seemed caught between confusion and sadness. "Just tell him it isn't true, and—"

"And?"

She sighed and looked away. "And it won't matter even if it isn't. Something is"—she glanced up at the others, who were still muttering to each other a few feet ahead—"something is wrong, and I don't think it's you or Rhiannon." She lowered her voice to a breathy whisper, and he wasn't sure she intended him to hear it. "Even if she is a dragon."

As much as he wanted to give her any reassurance, particularly given the kiss he'd witnessed between Sidonie and the dragoness, he had none to give.

The dungeon was dank and musty, as he supposed all such places were, but he'd never before gone into one with the understanding that he was never coming out again.

A feminine scream echoed through the hall as a door opened. Reynold came out, accompanied by Bet. Oh gods, Bet. His black eyes were intense but unreadable as usual, while Reynold looked at Tristram as though he were mud on the bottom of his favorite shoe.

"Put it in the cell and let it consider what it's done," he told the guard in front. "We will get to its questioning soon enough."

The guard in front tensed, and Tristram wanted to throw himself at the man to shut him up, because whatever he was planning to say was beyond inadvisable.

"Of course, Your Majesty," Sidonie said aloud, then cleared her throat and turned to the men. "On you go."

Without so much as a second of regret or concern, Reynold turned away from him. Reynold, his cousin and friend of nearly fifteen years, had not only ceased to love him. He had ceased to acknowledge that Tris existed.

Bet left with him, but he turned his head to watch Tris, even as they left. He supposed anything other than hatred that might have been there before was gone now.

"Why did you not just say?" one of the guards asked, giving Tris's arm a little shove. "Just tell him the truth. That woman is mad."

His partner, a woman in her forties, shoved him back. "No point in saying. His Majesty believes what he believes, and words won't convince him." She glanced after the king, dissatisfaction in her eyes.

"I don't even believe *she's* a dragon," one of the others muttered. "A mad mage, maybe, but if she were a dragon, she'd have turned and eaten us all."

"Enough," Sidonie announced, loud enough for her voice to reverberate through the hall. "Who believes what is of no consequence, except for the king. If—" She stopped and looked at Tristram, for the first time cocking her head in confusion, doubt in her eyes. "When the king determines that Lord Radcliffe is no danger to Llangard, he'll release him. Everything will be fine."

She gave Tris a decisive nod, though her certainty didn't reach her eyes. They hustled him into a room that he knew was the biggest miserable cell in the place. It was a kind gesture, even if it simply meant he'd be able to pace four steps instead of three. Laughably, they all still bowed and called him "my lord" on their way out.

Sidonie stopped next to the cell. "I don't know if you're a dragon. For

Athelstan's sake, don't damn well tell me if you are. But she is. I saw it with my own eyes." She was still looking in his direction, but her gaze went through him instead of at him. "She had scales and claws and pointed teeth. And the boy who was with her escaped. Turned into a dragon and flew away."

Thank goodness. Tris stifled a sigh of relief at that. He didn't want to imagine the innocent young man being tortured. Not that he wanted to imagine anyone being tortured, even Rhiannon. She hadn't exactly been wrong when she'd called him a coward, and look where it had landed him.

The same place it would have landed him if he'd told the king the truth to begin with, apparently.

"It doesn't matter," he told her. "There's nothing I can tell the king that will convince him of anything. You saw the way he looked at me."

She nodded but stared at the floor. He could hardly blame her. He was already dead. All she could do was try to protect her own from the coming storm.

He leaned against the cold stone wall and watched as she locked the door from outside. She didn't look at him again.

32

BET

"Sire . . ."

Bet had escorted King Reynold back to his private chambers. He had kept his mouth shut as Walden had tortured Rhiannon, and it'd stayed shut until they were in private.

He had never made a habit of questioning the king. In fact, he could not remember a single time that he had dared. But this . . . it had gone too far.

"Yes?" the king said impatiently, jerking the cuff looser around his neck. A servant stepped forward to help him, but His Majesty dismissed him with a flick of his hand.

"You have known Lord Radcliffe for fifteen years—" Bet had been there, standing in the shadows near the castle's outer wall when Lord Radcliffe, Tristram's father, brought his family to the Spires. Tristram had been taller than Bet then. Haughty and clearly dissatisfied, he'd glared around the courtyard, but he'd waited to take his mother's arm before marching off. The sun had caught his hair and glinted so brightly that Bet had stared, stunned, after the pair of them.

In the years that followed, Tristram had caught more than Bet's eye alone. It was impossible to look at him and think he was average. The child of a minor lord, he had nevertheless impressed the king, not only because they were cousins but because Tristram stood out. He was handsome and strong and righteous. There were days that Tristram had seemed every bit as regal as His Majesty—some more so, if Bet allowed himself to think it.

He had hated Tristram for all that—his easy friendship with Reynold, their equal footing, the jokes they shot back and forth without care. Bet was not fool enough to think he had ever been Reynold's friend. Or Tristram's, for that matter.

But it startled Bet to think that Reynold could throw away a long friendship with the man he had grown up beside without a thought.

"It seems . . ." Bet weighed his words as he continued. "It seems premature to mark him an enemy of the realm when you have such a long and loving friendship between you."

"Radcliffe is a liar and a traitor," the king spat. "All those years, built on lies. Who knows! Those lizards from the northern reaches might've placed him in our path for this very moment, thinking to catch me unaware. That damned dagger he carries could have been the end of me."

Bet scowled. Lord Tristram was not capable of such duplicity. If Bet had missed the signs that he was not entirely human, he would not have missed his foul intentions, had he any. And His Majesty had long admired that dagger and Tristram's attachment to it.

His mother, Lady Radcliffe, cared for young Prince Roland as well. She would not betray the realm. Nor would her son who'd fought for it. If they had meant Llangard harm, they would have harmed it already.

"I do not think—"

"I do not ask you to think!" the king snapped, rounding on Bet with narrowed eyes. "I will not have inhuman filth slithering around my castle."

Bet dropped his head in a bow. "Sire," he said, for what else was there to say?

Reynold stepped into his space. "Dear Bennet," he said softly. Reynold shifted his fingers under Bet's curls to touch his ear. Swallowing hard, Bet closed his eyes. "Don't fret. You know I'm not talking about *you*."

Bet had not always had long black curls, but once his father had left court and he was free to make his own decisions, Bet had wanted to hide his ears. Now, Reynold traced it so gently it made Bet's breath catch.

There'd been a time when Bet was younger that he'd desired Prince

Reynold. The prince had given him everything—a place to live, a life without fear, the strength to keep himself safe, a way to be of service. He'd seen sixteen summers—the prince, twenty—and Bet had wanted Reynold to give him just a little bit more.

But he hadn't been foolish enough to press, and the prince showed no real interest. In time, he lost the illusion and turned his sights toward more attainable conquests—people he could pay.

It wasn't desire that stilled his breath as Reynold stroked the shell of his ear, but tension. The king's thumb flicked the pointed tip.

"I know what you are, Bennet. I know everything about you." The low rumble of his voice sent a barely suppressed shudder down Bet's spine. It was hard to imagine a single secret he had from the king—there were none but the press of Tristram Radcliffe's warm body under his, the yielding of his lips. And that was a secret he would keep clutched tight to his chest.

"I know you'd never lie to me," Reynold mumbled.

Bet swallowed, dipping his head in a nod. "No, sire."

"Good!" His grin returned, and Reynold stepped back. "Then you are precisely what I need you to be—useful. You're hardly the only person with elven blood at court. And without your mother's lineage, you wouldn't be as useful by half."

Biting his lip, Bet nodded to the floor. He didn't think his situation was common, but there was no sense in arguing. Once, humans had sought out elvish partners for their fine features, quick wits, and skill in battle. But a person could either have magic or be magic. Elves were magic incarnate; when the practice of casting rose in the kingdoms of men, interest in elves waned. There might be a few members of court with particularly high cheekbones, but none who shared blood with a full elf.

Bet's thoughts drifted to Tristram, alone in his cell.

"What do you plan to do to Lord Radcliffe, sire?"

The king's scowl hardened. "He will receive the same treatment as every traitor to the realm."

Walden would break him. Bet considered his ferocious brutality toward Rhiannon, the things he might do to Tristram. The way he'd make him scream. Bet could not stand the thought of it. Someone else putting his hands on Tristram's smooth skin and breaking it.

"It's too soon," Bet blurted out.

Reynold's frown deepened. "Why?"

"Lord Radcliffe is, well, a lord. Get what information you can out of the woman first. He'll break quickly. Faster still if you leave him alone in his cell to stew."

"You think so?" Reynold asked.

Bet nodded. "As much can be done with darkness and silence as with pain, sire."

"Then we will let him drown in both."

༒ 33 ༒

TRISTRAM

It took Tris about an hour to break down and start looking for a way out of the cell. It was one thing to refuse to fight his friends, possibly kill them, in a selfish bid for escape. It was entirely another to sit there and wait to be executed.

His only crime was being born a dragon. Was that a crime? He had not chosen it, but neither could he say that he wouldn't if given another chance.

He liked who and what he was, damn it all, and if Reynold couldn't see past the dragon in his ancestry, he had to be shown. Tristram would never hurt Llangard. His country was his life, and he would protect it as such, even if Reynold was being stubborn and making his charge difficult.

Clearly the king's fear was coloring his judgment.

Tris should have noticed it before, tried to find out what was happening. Perhaps there was some threat Tristram didn't know about, or there was substance to the rumors that King Edmund had been poisoned.

Tristram shuddered. If that were true, it was no wonder Reynold had become more reclusive in the short time since he'd taken the throne.

Either way, Tristram was doing no good locked in the dungeon. He examined the hinges of the cell. They were surprisingly sturdy. He didn't have lock picks or, more importantly, the skill required to pick a lock. He sighed and sat down on the cot opposite the door.

Even if he knew how, breaking out of the dungeon would hardly serve his purpose—just the opposite, in fact. It would prove him guilty.

Truth told, he could probably break the door down, sturdy hinges or no. He might not be able to fly, but he was certainly stronger and more resilient than the average human. But again, that did not help his position.

Shamefully, the only way he could see out was to not only lie, but lie incredibly well. Convince the king that he was no dragon, that Rhiannon had besmirched his honor to weaken Llangard. It was shameful and horrible, but he saw no other way.

He could do his best to prove Rhiannon a liar and condemn her, or he could admit the truth. If he did the latter, they would both die, and who knew where such a conclusion would lead Reynold? A bloody and pointless conflict with the dragons at a time when they should be preparing for attack from Tornheim, likely.

One of the guards came to feed him some time later. He didn't know how many hours it had been and thought it best not to try to count them. The guard was a young man, nervous, whom Tristram had beaten in practice dozens of times. Tris looked around and raised an eyebrow at him. "No torture, Ewan?"

The boy shrugged, but he wouldn't meet Tristram's eye. It mattered little enough. He had made his decision. He would not hurt the guards, and he would make no escape attempt.

He would lie and hurt Rhiannon.

It sat ill with him, and he suspected it always would, but honor be damned, Llangard was more important. The opposite conclusion did not bear contemplation, since there was no option that allowed him to retain his honor. Perhaps he had lost any right to it the first time he'd implicitly lied about his parentage, and his high-minded morality had been a mask all along.

A door slammed open at the end of the hall, and the young guard flinched.

A moment later, the king's executioner, Walden, led a pair of guards, dragging a barely conscious Rhiannon along with them. Her beautiful face was covered in blood, hair matted with it. Tris recognized the locked metal collar around her neck; a magical thing that would not break if she turned into a dragon, and as such, would kill her if she tried. He wondered why he hadn't been fitted with such a device. Probably precisely because he hadn't made that leap for his window.

Tristram couldn't become a dragon. It was not that he hadn't tried on occasion during his childhood. Before they had left the border, on days when Lord Radcliffe had been particularly drunk or angry, Tristram had gone out into the hills and tried.

And tried and tried.

But he didn't know the first thing about being a dragon. He had figured out how to grow claws accidentally, and most of his time after that had been learning how *not* to grow them.

That was Tristram's true specialty in life: *not* being a dragon.

As the group passed by Tristram's cell, Walden curled up his nose in distaste. "Lizard," he sneered, then spat at him.

It missed and hit the door, but the young guard stepped forward, hand to the hilt of his sword. "Keep to your business, old man."

Tris had to hide a smile. Whatever else was true, Sidonie trained her guard well. He could not help but be grateful that the guard hadn't precisely defended him when a few moments later, Reynold strolled up to the cell door.

"Your Majesty," Tris said, but Reynold didn't even glance his way.

"I do not recall giving an order to feed this creature," he said to the young guard.

Ewan glanced at Tris and then quickly away. "I was ordered to feed all the prisoners, Your Majesty."

Reynold smiled indulgently at him and patted him on the shoulder. "Of course. And your kindness does you credit. In future, however, know that you need only feed human prisoners." He looked at where the guards were dumping Rhiannon on the cot in the cell across from Tristram and waved at her as though illustrating a point. "If the snakes die, they die." And with that, he waved for the young man to leave them alone.

Yes, there was something very much wrong in Reynold's mind. Tristram couldn't imagine why Reynold hadn't come to him, confided his worries in him. They could have figured things out before it came to this madness.

He took a breath and tried again. "Majesty, there's been a mistake—"

"Shut it up, guard," Reynold ordered, looking to the guard he had brought with him. It was one of the newer men, who hadn't come with the guards sent to retrieve Tristram. He smiled at Reynold and bowed, then unlocked and entered the cell.

As soon as he'd passed the key back to Reynold, he lifted his mailed arm and swung at Tristram's face. Instead of trying to mitigate the blow, Tris leaned into it. It was difficult working against everything he'd ever learned, but hopefully it was a step in convincing the king he was just a man.

His lip split spectacularly, dripping blood down his chin and onto his tunic. The guard looked smug.

The king inspected him, then turned, for the first time, to Tristram. "I believe you actually injured the creature. Well done."

"I do as His Majesty commands," the young knight agreed. Clearly, he was enjoying the opportunity to beat a lord with no chance of retribution.

Reynold looked Tris over as though he were a hunk of meat and not his cousin, finally settling on his eyes. "What did the lizards send you here to do, monster?"

"No one sent me here, cousin," Tris answered.

Reynold motioned to the guard, who hit him again, this time a blow to the soft part of his belly. Fortunately, the young guard wasn't subtle about his intentions, and Tristram had a moment to brace for the blow. It still hurt, but he wasn't brought low by it.

"Who are the other dragons in my court?"

Tris sighed and shook his head. "I know no dragons."

"What treachery do you have planned?" Reynold demanded.

Tris looked up at his cousin, meeting his eye again. "I have no treason planned. I seek, as I have always sought, to serve Llangard and its king with my life."

Reynold's lip curled in disdain. "Consider telling the truth, or you shall best serve Llangard with your head on a pike, monster." He motioned the guard out, and without another word, they left.

✤ 34 ✤

HAFGAN

By the time Hafgan landed, he was ready to pass out from exhaustion. He shifted to use less of his remaining energy hauling around the massive bulk of his dragon form.

Sword still gripped tight in his clawed hands, he ran, not even bothering to shift fully or stop for clothes. He ignored everyone and everything he passed, until someone stepped right out in front of him.

"Hey now," a soft, deep voice said. Relief shuddered through him, and Hafgan wanted to bury his face in the neck of the broad dragon before him and cry. On two legs, Maddox was still the tallest man on Brynaf. His long, dark hair was thrown back over his shoulder. "What's the problem, little song? How can I help?"

"Have to—" He panted for a breath and tried again. "Halwyn. Have to talk to the queen."

The wall of a dragon, Maddox, gave him a soft smile and nodded. "Let's get you to see Mother, then." Without another word, he swept Hafgan into his arms and carried him toward the queen's lair.

Under normal circumstances, he'd have been terrified to bother Her Majesty, but Rhiannon's life was at stake.

"What have you got there?" Maddox asked, pointing with his chin at the sword.

Hafgan blushed and clutched it tighter. "I would have left it, I swear, but it was already in my hands—" Maddox lifted one brow, and the gesture was so like his mother that Hafgan could hardly look at him. He hadn't been asking why Hafgan had the sword. He would never begrudge him a new dragon. "A dragon at court gave it to me."

At that, Maddox finally looked dubious. "A dragon at the humans' court? What clan? Whose song?"

Hafgan shrugged helplessly. "I don't know. His name was Radcliffe, but I think it was a human one."

At the name, Maddox's eyes narrowed, displeased.

"We only spoke twice, but he was kind. This was part of his hoard, but he gave it to me." Hafgan held out the sword so Maddox could inspect it, which he did, grudgingly.

After a moment, he nodded. "It's beautiful. How like a human dragon, to hoard objects made for killing."

"I didn't say he did."

With a dry look, another borrowed from his mother, Maddox asked, "Does he?"

Hafgan frowned and looked away. "He keeps them on the wall. He's a good man. I liked him."

"Probably as useless as his father," Maddox answered with a snort, but before Hafgan could ask more, they walked into the queen's lair. It was a thing of splendid beauty, Her Majesty's hoard, but she didn't like people looking at it, so he kept his eyes up, looking for her sleek black form.

Two enormous sleepy gold eyes blinked open, narrowing on them. Her Majesty lifted the front of her top lip, to bare the row of sharp teeth there, and snorted a puff of smoke in their direction. "It's the middle of the night. What is it?"

Maddox set Hafgan down, letting him retain the tiniest portion of his dignity, and Hafgan pretended he didn't see the other dragon palm a few stray coins from his mother's hoard as he straightened.

Hafgan moved to bow to Halwyn. She rolled her whole head to one side, looking at him like he'd gone mad.

"Ah, sorry. I'd gotten into the habit."

She snorted again but waited for him to get on with it.

He wrapped his arms around himself and tried to scrub away the chill.

"It's Rhiannon, Majesty. She went to have dinner with the king, and only guards came back. They called me dragon and tried to capture me."

The queen let out a sigh through her nostrils that warmed the whole room. "I told her humans weren't to be trusted."

"But we have to—"

"Have to nothing," Her Majesty interrupted. "I told Rhiannon that if she insisted on this nonsense, she did it alone. Bad enough she talked you into going. We could have lost you!"

"Mother—" Maddox tried, but she turned a glare on him. He returned the stare full force, and Hafgan wanted nothing more than to slink away into the shadows.

He looked down at his sword, thought of how he'd left Rhiannon there instead of fighting, and strengthened his resolve. "This isn't fixing anything! Rhiannon is one of our own, and we need to help her."

Halwyn looked away from Maddox to Hafgan and sighed. "I would love to, little one, even as much as I am angry with her for leading you into danger. But we have other things to worry about. The Stone Clan is on the move, and we know nothing of their motives. Their queen has refused to speak to me for more than a year." She reached out with one clawed hand and petted him. "We shall look to ourselves, and when the danger has passed, then we can concern ourselves with unruly children."

Hafgan was hardly appeased, but there was little he could do in the face of the queen's determination. He turned to see if Maddox was as dispirited as himself and found the space beside him empty.

❧ 35 ❧

ROLAND

Father didn't know that Roland still played in his mother's empty room sometimes. He wasn't a silly child, he did not think her ghost watched over him, the room just reminded him of her. She had been soft and gentle, and he missed her.

Father didn't know he cried about her death sometimes either. He would not approve. He hadn't always been as he was. Father had never been as caring as Gillian, as kind as Bet, or as honest as Tris, but if he thought about it very hard, sometimes Roland could remember a time when Father hadn't hated him.

Even a year earlier, before the illness that took his grandfather had started, Father had not been so angry all the time. It made everyone angry, too, or frightened. Like Roland. He was frightened a lot.

He was having his wooden soldier that looked like Bet ride the dragon queen over his mother's old spinning wheel when there was a noise in the other room that caught his attention.

Aunt Elinor's voice.

He dropped the toys on his mother's bed and ran to the door to see if he could get a look. He hadn't seen her much since the funeral; maybe she would stay to talk to him.

The door was open a little, so he peeked through the gap and found her easily. She was still wearing mourning black for Grandfather. Or maybe for her husband. Aunt Elinor often wore black.

". . . not like him to simply disappear," she was saying to Father.

Father gave her that empty smile he'd started giving everyone and waved his hand in the air. "I assure you, Elinor, there is nothing to worry about. I sent him on an errand, and he'll be gone a few days. I shall send him to you first thing when he gets back."

He turned away from her and picked up some papers. Roland was pretty sure that meant she was supposed to leave, even though he also knew those papers had been sitting on the table for days and weren't important.

He knew because he'd spilled wine on them and Father hadn't yelled at him.

Aunt Elinor sighed and looked down at her hands. In one, she had a dagger. For a second, Roland thought she meant to stab Father, which was a surprise, but then he recognized the knife.

It was the one Tris always kept in his boot. It was shiny and silver, and Tris had let him see it once. He'd said he got it when he was about Roland's age, but when Roland had asked Father for a dagger, the king had said he was too young.

Aunt Elinor turned away, and the look on her face wasn't like anything he'd ever seen before. She was sad, but she was also angry. Father was lying to her, and she knew it.

And Roland knew it too.

But if Father was lying about where Tris was, then where was he really?

Still in the palace, surely, since he never would have left without his dagger. The palace was big, though, and Roland wasn't allowed out alone.

But his nurse didn't watch him at night anymore, and Roland knew the palace as well as almost anyone. He could find Tris. He would find him and make Aunt Elinor stop worrying.

Maybe then everyone would stop thinking he was weak and useless.

❧ 36 ❧

RHIANNON

R hiannon was vulnerable in this pale pink flesh. The skin was too soft. All the important parts too exposed. And there was nothing she could do for it. The collar around her neck would kill her if she tried to transform.

She'd been horrified the first time she'd seen one in a market north of the mountains. The vendor had proudly told her it's purpose—to subdue a dragon the way they had subdued humankind. She'd been horrified. It was the first piece of jewelry she'd ever picked up that she put down without buying.

Now, there was one looped around her throat, and she was sure it would be the death of her.

Midway through the second day of Walden's ministrations, her nature had won out. Scales had rippled over her skin in an effort to protect herself. He'd liked that too well and reached for his knives. One by one, he removed her scales until she was bloody and shivering, and she gave up trying to protect herself at all.

She must've fainted at some point, because she didn't remember how she'd gotten back to her cell. She woke up to the rusty creak of the cell door opening.

Sidonie locked it behind herself. When she rounded on Rhiannon, there was only a flicker of shock on her face—Rhiannon must have looked nightmarish to get any reaction at all—before her expression turned neutral again.

"I thought you might like a drink," Sidonie said. She carried the water to where Rhiannon sat up on the bed, but as soon as she'd passed it over, retreated out of reach.

"Thank you." Rhiannon took a large gulp and held it in her mouth, swishing it around to get rid of the taste of blood. The water was fresh, not that stale swill they had in the dungeons. She poured the last of it into her hand and splashed her face, using her skirt to wipe away the worst of the blood. The silk had been long since ruined by Walden's attentions.

When she looked up again, Sidonie was staring. "You lied," she said mildly.

Rhiannon sighed through her nose. "I simply did not say I was a dragon."

"A lie by omission is still a lie," Sidonie replied, as if the world were black and white and there had been a way for Rhiannon to be frank from the start that would not have landed her in this cell.

"If you're determined to always be unsatisfied by everything, certainly. I'd like to think of this as a merry surprise."

Rhiannon took another sip of water. She'd have killed for venison, but this—clean and cool—was good too. Bracing. She may not have survived the wary look in Sidonie's eyes without the cup between her hands and the feel of something other than bile in her belly.

Sidonie scoffed. "How can you look like us? Is it some enchantment?" Her eyes swept over Rhiannon like she was looking for the charm that had enchanted the king.

That had enchanted her as well.

"How do you look like you do?" Rhiannon challenged.

The knight only scowled at her, unimpressed. Skies above, it was asking too much to expect her to maintain her patience at a time like this. But with no allies, no one else who would even listen to her, Rhiannon relented first.

"This is just how I look," Rhiannon said. "You know that dragons have two forms?" Rhiannon would have assumed everyone knew that much, but everything she'd seen and heard of dragons since she had gotten to court had been so outlandish that she could have been wrong.

"Some of the stories speak of dragons as if they're people"—Sidonie flinched—"humans, I mean. Two legs, arms, all that."

Rhiannon laughed. "I assure you, in any form, I have the appropriate number of legs. But I understand your meaning. Being a dragon, in the sense that you're thinking—large, scaled, fire breathing—requires a tremendous amount of energy. If we were to try and sustain that all the time, we would ravage the countryside. A full-grown dragon can eat a cow and keep going. But we have another form—this one, like yours—that allows us to move freely. Without decimating entire villages and eating every cow in the country."

"You don't *want* to attack our villages?"

"There is not enough magic left in Llangard to stop us if we did, is there?" Sidonie's lips pressed into a thin, unimpressed line. Rhiannon shrugged. "I've no doubt you'd be a formidable obstacle, Sir Sidonie, but no, we do not."

"Then why are you here?"

Rhiannon took a deep breath. "I don't know. I thought I did . . ." For most of her life, she'd collected trinkets from humans. She'd been late to discover her hoard, but when she'd found a locket half buried in the dirt in Hafgan's village, she'd known it was hers. Now, she thought her hoard, rather than give her a unique connection to humankind, had steered her wrong.

Sidonie blinked at her. When she uncrossed her arms, it seemed as much out of shock as anything. "Meaning?" she said stiffly.

"Meaning I should have kept my distance." Rhiannon stared down at her thumb, swollen and red. It would turn darker, but it was too soon. "I thought our peoples weren't so different or that we could work together. Hafgan's clan was wiped out by bandits from the north. If the Torndals roll through the mountains, they'll be here next."

"You wanted to work together?" Sidonie asked.

Rhiannon shrugged. "A dream and nothing more. The king has shown me my folly." She smiled wryly and could not bear the sympathy in Sidonie's eyes, so she changed the subject. "Your hair is the precise orange of the first rays of sunlight cresting the horizon. I wonder . . . may I have a lock of it?"

Sidonie stared at her like she'd gone mad. Rhiannon didn't have the wherewithal to refuse it.

In her days wandering the market in Atheldinas, she'd seen a locket—oh, she liked lockets best of all—that was made of crystal on both sides. In the middle, someone had lovingly twisted a lock of hair into a decorative knot. She'd asked the vendor why. He had said it was a token from a loved one, but a family line had ended. This was from their estate. When she'd bought it, he'd looked vaguely ill. Perhaps the whole thing was a bit morose, but the idea of keeping a piece of a person and carrying them around? It was so much better than the static paintings in her lockets—a cold reflection to the real touch of a person.

She had not cried when the torturer had broken her fingers, or when he'd wedged his knife under her scales to pry them off, but now, at Sidonie's blank stare, her lips began to tremble.

"What would it hurt?" Rhiannon's voice broke. She pinched her shackled hands between her knees, ignoring the sharp ache, and curled her shoulders in. "I have no magic. I can't curse you with it."

Tears began to well in her eyes. No sooner had the first fallen than Sidonie blurted out, "I have nothing to cut it with."

Rhiannon blinked. "Oh . . ." She'd never taken time to consider how inefficient it was to have blunt fingers, weak nails, to always have to rely on tools. Rhiannon looked down at her own fingers, bloodied and soft, her claws gone. She had nothing useful either. "Your sword would not do?"

"It's too long. I cannot hold it myself and—"

"I could hold it?" Rhiannon suggested.

Sidonie hesitated. Under other circumstances, Rhiannon would have rolled her eyes. Now, she was so tired that she only leaned onto her sore knees with her sore elbows and smiled weakly. "What benefit is there in hurting you? Even if I could—and you are right to worry—hurting you wouldn't get me out of this cell, would it? You don't have the key to this?" Rhiannon tapped one finger on the collar around her neck.

The collar was spelled to never break. And however strong a dragon's scales were, they would give way first. Even if she got out of this cell, she would never fly again. It was no kind of life.

Sidonie shook her head. Maybe she was lying, but Rhiannon didn't intend to check. Not now. She wanted to grow her hoard—it was one small thing that felt possible, so it became the only important thing left. She would find comfort in that.

"Please?" Rhiannon whispered. And lest she cry again, Sidonie gave in.

With the clink of armor, she stepped forward, removed her sword from its scabbard, and dropped onto one knee in front of Rhiannon's cot. Rhiannon sat forward and reached out to touch her—not the long braid of wondrous copper hair over her shoulder, but her smooth cheek. Sidonie's hands were calloused and strong, but her cheek was curved and feminine. She was all things at once: strong and beautiful, stalwart and kind. Humans weren't all bad; Rhiannon refused to think they were, north and south and on all sides.

She allowed herself the briefest touch before she reached for Sidonie's braid and undid the leather tie at the end. When she took the sword, she held it where the knight could see. Sidonie's eyes only flicked that way for a second before they met Rhiannon's again.

So she cut a lock. Perhaps she overindulged and it was longer than she ought to have allowed herself, but given her predicament, she deserved a little overindulgence.

With the lock of hair on her lap, Rhiannon leaned in, closed her stinging eyes, and set her forehead against Sidonie's. "Meeting you has been a singular pleasure, Sir Sidonie. Thank you," Rhiannon muttered.

She sat up to cut a ribbon from her own dress to tie around the copper strands. It was a messy job, with her broken thumb, but she was unwilling to risk losing even one of them in this dank place.

"You are welcome," Sidonie whispered back, her voice thick. When Rhiannon looked at her again, Sidonie's brow was furrowed. Perhaps this cost her something, though Rhiannon couldn't imagine what.

"Would you—" Rhiannon flinched and stared down at the lock in her lap. Humans didn't have hoards, but they did take trinkets from people they loved. Rhiannon was not so childish to think that Sidonie loved her, but she seemed to care a little, and that was a comfort in a place where no one else did. "Would you like to trade? Perhaps, when I'm gone, you would rather pretend I'd never been here at all—"

Already, Sidonie was shaking her head. Tearily, Rhiannon smiled. "Will you braid a piece?" Rhiannon asked. "I can't—"

"Of course."

Rhiannon sat still while she worked, and when there was a small braid just behind her ear, Sidonie sliced it off and put her sword away. Before the ends could fray, Rhiannon wrapped it around Sidonie's wrist. With some awkwardness, they managed to wrap the leather from Sidonie's hair around the ends so it didn't come apart. "There. Now you'll remember me. At least for a while."

Before Rhiannon knew what was happening, Sidonie leaned to kiss her. It was not a passionate kiss—only a brush of her lips offered in comfort—but Rhiannon flinched back nonetheless. She couldn't stomach kissing her captor, even Sidonie.

"Good night, my lady," Rhiannon whispered.

Sidonie sat back. Her eyes were wide, but in a moment, she pushed to stand. "Good night, my lady," Sidonie replied.

Before Sidonie had left the cell, Rhiannon turned over to curl toward the wall, a lock of copper hair clutched in the fist of her unbroken hand.

❄ 37 ❄

BET

"I want answers," the king snarled, pacing up and down the line of his receiving room. "That horrid cow has told us nothing."

Rhiannon gan Derys had proven especially adept at withstanding pain. Bet knew nothing about dragons, but it sounded as if she healed faster than a human ought to have. Even Walden was having trouble finding the right method of torture.

It had been two days since they'd taken Tristram to the dungeon. Bet had avoided going down there since he'd watched the guard lock him away. The situation was too perilous. Tristram wasn't human, and neither was Bet. The differences between them were threadbare and easily dismissed. What kept Bet in the king's good graces was his loyalty.

But Tristram Radcliffe had that too.

For days, Bet had tried to convince himself that it was the similarities in their precarious positions that made him hesitate to discount the "traitor." But really, it was the sound of Tristram's sigh, the light of his eyes in the dark, the way he'd smiled at him. Soft and brief and impossible, Lord Radcliffe's smiles weren't for Bet, but he couldn't shake the memory of them.

And the king shouldn't have been able to either.

Lord Tristram was the king's cousin. King Edmund's first wife had been

Lady Elinor's sister. Tristram's father—was Lord Radcliffe Tristram's father at all?—had risen in station to marry so well, but Bet had heard that when Lady Elinor was young, her family had been keen to send her away from court. Polite company called her passionate, but with a stark look that said that she had taken it too far.

The king had known Tristram for most of his life. They were close companions—had been long enough for Bet to be wildly jealous of one, then the other, as they stood shoulder to shoulder, played their games, swung their swords. King Reynold should not have been able to discount Tristram so easily—it was for Bet to make those hard calls. He was the sword at the end of Reynold's long reach.

"I'm sending Walden to Tristram tomorrow," the king said.

"No," Bet snapped before he thought better of it.

Reynold stopped his pacing and turned to glare at him. "Excuse me?"

The sound of his voice carried a dangerous thread that made the hair on Bet's arms stand on end.

Bet pressed his dry tongue against the roof of his mouth. His Majesty could not think him disloyal. He had always known his position at court existed at His Majesty's mercy, but that even Tristram Radcliffe could lose his favor made Bet weigh his words before he dared open his mouth again.

He dropped to one knee, set his elbow upon it. "I would make my failure up to you, sire. I should have seen Lord Radcliffe's deceit. Let me oversee Tristram's interrogation."

"That is not your job," Reynold said dismissively. He seemed satisfied by Bet's explanation

Bet stared up at him hard eyed. "Isn't it? It would not be the first time you've had me resort to such measures."

With pursed lips, Reynold considered him.

"And I know Tristram Radcliffe far better than Walden ever could. I've watched you together for years. I know where to push. Let me see to him. Make my mistake up to you. Walden has his hands full with the woman."

The king sucked in his cheeks. Hardly shifting, he shrugged his shoulders. "I suppose you could," he mused, rubbing his hand across his lips. "See this is dealt with quickly."

"Yes, sire," Bet said. He rose to his feet, and finally, the king allowed a servant to step in and assist him in preparing for bed. "I'll see it done," Bet swore and took his leave.

Bet returned to his room, and by the time he got there, he was sweaty and panicked. In the course of minutes, he was doubting every reason he had thought this was a good idea. He could not stomach the idea of Walden having his way with Tristram; he could get answers of his own; he owed the king for failing to notice Tristram's deceit.

Bet could kill a man. He'd heard men scream. Interrogation, even torture, should be nothing. Maybe if it weren't Tristram, this wouldn't bother him. He could have found some pleasure in hearing Jarl Jorun scream.

Bet could try to do it gently—make every effort to make Tristram's condition look worse than it was. His insistence on being the one to do the deed would cast him in the only role left to him: monster. But if that were his path, perhaps he could be the lesser beast.

He bent over his wash table, splashed water on his face. When he inhaled, his chest shook. But this was fine. He could handle himself.

Let Tristram hate him; he'd do his duty.

Try as he might, as he squeezed his eyes shut and pressed thumb and forefinger to his closed lids, he could not fool himself into thinking that this was the king's fault. His Majesty had given the order, but he wouldn't be there to see Tristram hurt.

There was a soft knock on the doorframe. With his small window, he often left the door open to try and catch a thin breeze. A young maid held a tray in her hand. "His Majesty said that you had missed dinner," she squeaked.

At the shadows of his scowl, she scrunched back toward the outside wall. He grabbed the side of the water basin and sent it flying through the door where she stood. It splattered water in a wide arc and hit the far wall with a clatter.

"Get out!" he shouted.

She dropped the tray there in the hallway and scampered away.

Chest heaving, he leaned back against the wall. At this rate, he'd eat his dinner with his fingers from the floor, or he could drink the bottle of wine he had hidden under his bed and try to sleep. With the next day looming before him, Bet chose the wine.

38

GILLIAN

Something was wrong in the Spires. In the course of a few days, her brother's scowl had turned darker, his words sharper, and there were people missing.

Lady Elinor seemed entirely convinced that something was wrong with Tristram despite the king's assurances to the contrary. When she'd shown Gillian the dagger he kept in his boot, Gillian had a sinking feeling that she was right. Even at her father's funeral, she'd seen the glint of the hilt hidden against his calf. He wouldn't leave court without it.

Perhaps Reynold was just upset that Lady Rhiannon had returned to the north. Her brother had been smitten, but only because she was pretty and clever and capable. Frankly, there were plenty of pretty, clever, and capable women in Llangard. He'd recover.

One afternoon, a few days after Lady Rhiannon left with her young ward, Gillian found her brother in the library. He was engrossed in a book, so she was able to tiptoe across the carpets to peer over his shoulder. He was thumbing through an illuminated manuscript, replete with dragons flying across the tops of the pages.

"Hello," she whispered in his ear.

Reynold started and snapped the book shut. "What are you doing here? You cannot sneak up on me like that!"

He rounded on her, glaring, so she straightened and frowned down at him.

"I only came to get something to read and saw my studious brother, sitting here reading. What has so captured your attention, Your Majesty?" A smile tugged up the corners of her lips. She had never managed to address her father appropriately without a teasing glimmer in her eyes, and she was doing no better with Reynold. "Are you reading about dragons?"

He continued scowling at her. "They live all along our border, Gillian, and we have no way to defend ourselves—"

"Brother, a dragon hasn't flown down from the mountains to attack us in centuries."

"Because they think we have magic," he hissed, gripping her hand so hard he might crush her bones.

Gillian frowned. "There are the mages who trained at the Hudoliaeth. We're not entirely without protection."

Even Reynold had gone to study magic at the monastery in the western mountains. The Hudoliaeth only existed because the magicians there were powerful enough to hold off the dragons who surrounded them. But Reynold had left home with no magic to start, and he'd returned without any more. After his failure there, Gillian had not been allowed to study. Just as well—she did not have such stores of power that they were worth developing.

"No, but *we* have none," Reynold whispered, wide eyed.

"Ah." That was it then—the waning power of the Cavendish line was what bothered him. "Reynold, a leader can be great without moving mountains. Our father never had need of magic of his own."

Reynold scoffed. "What business is it of yours what I study, anyway?"

"I suppose it's not, but I think it's nice," she offered with a small shrug, slipping her fingers out of his bruising grip and folding her hands behind her back. "I have hardly seen you here since you took the throne. I've missed you here."

He grunted, setting his book on top of a stack of them and shoving them to the side, turning them so that she could not see the spines.

"So why are you reading about dragons now?" she asked.

"I'm reading up on the enemy, Gillian. You wouldn't understand."

Gillian rolled her eyes. "Yes, you're right. You are the only person in the world who has any worries at all, aren't you?"

He was still frowning, so she shoved his shoulder lightly. "You have counsellors and an entire army of knights—when you don't send them packing—and a sister who loves you. What are you worried about? Perhaps you should talk to Tristram about it."

Reynold blanched. "That man is a traitor."

Before she could help herself, Gillian let out a short bark of laughter. "Tristram? He's your dearest friend."

"He is a liar and a snake," Reynold spat.

She could not imagine what Tristram had done to turn Reynold's mood against him. When they'd been boys, they had only ever fought as young men did—who would be the noblest and that sort of thing. Most often, they fell on the same side if there were quarrels between the young nobles at court. On the rare occasions that they did not, Tristram was always first to bend. He had never looked to belittle the prince.

It took Gillian far too long to realize that Reynold meant "snake" literally.

"Oh, Reynold," she breathed, unfolding her hands to squeeze his shoulder. "He isn't."

Fury crossed his features in a single second. He spun out of his chair, grabbing her upper arms roughly before she understood what was happening. "Do you know?" he demanded.

"Let go," she said, jerking back. His fingers dug in harder. "You're hurting me, Reynold!"

She struggled before he shoved her back. When she stumbled into the table, he was on her. He fisted his hand in her hair and jerked her head up.

"You know, and you've kept this from me," he hissed.

Given Reynold's violent reaction, all she could do was lie. If Reynold believed Tris a dragon, and believed that Gillian had known about it, his anger would only grow. "I don't know what you're talking about! You've known him almost all your life. Lord Tristram is loyal." His fist tightened. She winced as he pulled her hair. "I am loyal. Reynold, please."

Tears had begun to sting her eyes before he stepped away.

"Where is Tristram?" Gillian wheezed. "You didn't—"

Reynold could have had him killed. Bet Kyston could have slipped into his rooms in the dead of night, slit his throat, dumped his body in the river.

"In the dungeons with the other one."

"The other *what*, Reynold?" she demanded.

"It's none of your concern! Go," he growled.

Stunned, her fingers gripping the edge of the table where he'd been studying moments before, she couldn't move.

"Go!" he shouted.

Then, she couldn't scramble out of the library fast enough. Tears streaming down her cheeks, she rushed to the royal wing of the Spires. She wasn't looking where she was going, and a hand shot out to grab her arm from the rooms that neighbored hers.

She shrieked, but her uncle caught her and held her. "Whatever is the matter, Your Highness?" Laurence asked, scowling. He had a broad face and a silvery gray beard. And he was staring at her with concern.

In that moment, her uncle looked so much like her father that there was nothing for Gillian to do but fall into his arms. She sobbed into his broad chest. "Reynold. He's—he's . . . Oh, Uncle," she cried while he smoothed his broad hands over her back.

"What happened?"

"He's unwell. He must be. He's thrown Lord Radcliffe in the dungeons—"

"Why?"

He seemed far too interested in Tristram's fall. Gillian's brow puckered. "I don't know," she lied. "He turned his anger on me as well. I thought for a moment he might throw me from the window of the library he was so angry. I don't know what to do."

"I could handle your brother," Laurence said softly.

Biting her lip, Gillian nodded. "If there's some recourse . . . Reynold needs help."

"And I will help him," Laurence swore. Gillian could not place why that made her feel no better.

39

TRISTRAM

Tristram let his head fall back against the cell wall behind his cot and sighed. It was horrible, but he was listless and in want of something to do. He hadn't been allowed out of his cell, and his stomach was starting to rumble loudly, but he hadn't been dragged out to suffer at Walden's hands or even assaulted in the cell again.

"Sounds like you've had a hard day, king's dragon," a rough voice whispered from the shadows. It was so pained and gritty it took Tris a moment to realize it was Rhiannon.

He listened for the hint of anyone else in the area. Movement, shuffling, even breathing, but there was nothing. Now that he was paying attention, he could hear her labored breaths from across the hall, but there was no one else.

He felt a stab of guilt. She was mocking him, of course, but what she'd been through over the last few days, while he sat on his cot and stared at the wall, had been horrendous. Having nothing to do was awful, but it was unimportant by comparison.

"You've had a little rougher, I'd wager," he whispered back, and it wasn't hard to feel sympathy for her. She had done this to him, but truth told, he could not be sure he wouldn't have done the same, had he been in her position.

She croaked out a laugh that turned into a sob. After a moment, though, her voice returned. "I'm sorry. I shouldn't have. I don't—"

"Don't." He had no idea why he wasn't angry with her, but he wasn't. She had known he was a dragon. He didn't know how she was still even coherent. It would have been madness to blame her for telling people about him. "You owe me nothing."

"Did they kill Hafgan?" she asked, the words cracking this time for a different reason. "They said he escaped, but—"

It was a strange surge of pleasure, that while he could give her nothing real, he could give her this one thing: "No. They told me he escaped as well, and they would have had no reason to hold that back on my account. They don't know I'm also fond of him." Tris snorted in realization. "I suppose I've been lying about that too, without even realizing."

"What?" she sounded confused, but interested, unlike the previous time they had spoken.

"I said I do not know any dragons, but I know Hafgan, at least a little." He wondered if that was the information Reynold was searching for—if by his forgetting all about it, they had realized that he was a liar. But he hadn't even thought of it. Hafgan was just a sweet kid who happened to be a dragon.

"He's stopped asking me questions," Rhiannon whispered, more quietly than before.

Tristram had never known Walden, but he promised himself that if he made it through this, the man would no longer have work anywhere in Llangard. If he had stopped questioning but was still tormenting, then he was doing it for his own pleasure.

The fact that the questions had stopped for her meant something else as well.

"They're going to kill me."

That she understood didn't make it any better. Tris hadn't liked her from the start, but he didn't understand. Why not just send her back to the mountains with the rest of her kind? Their kind.

"I suppose I'll be for the same fate when they've finished with me," he whispered back, the words feeling as though they came from someone else's lips. Reynold was going to have him killed for being a dragon.

There was no way for that to make sense.

She gave a tiny sob from her cell, and Tristram turned his mind inward, searching for some topic of conversation less horrifying.

"What is it like being a dragon?" he finally asked. He might be one, but he had little enough idea. He was strong, tough, able to grow sharp claws, and that was about it. Surely, that could not be the entire draconic experience.

She took a deep, shaky breath. "It is the most wonderful thing in the world. I can't imagine how you lot live like this, down in the clearing, no mountains in sight. Not able to fly."

Tris had fantasized, as a child, about being able to fly away, but it had always been more about escape than the actual act of flight. "Sidonie thought I could fly. At least, I think she did. She kept looking at the window as though she expected me to jump out of it."

Rhiannon gave a weak, hoarse laugh at that. "Wish there were a window here. Not that it would do me much good in this collar."

She was silent for a long time before muttering, almost to herself, "This is madness. They're going to kill me for being a dragon who wouldn't let your lord paw her, and you for . . . existing."

Paw her? Tristram wanted to ask, but more than that, he didn't. It wasn't difficult to imagine what she meant, and if this entire disaster had started because Reynold had made unwanted advances—

No. He wasn't a child, or an innocent to be coddled. This was his life, and if he were going to die for it, he would know.

"He acted inappropriately?"

"Assuming that by inappropriately, you mean he grabbed me, and when I told him to stop, he grabbed harder, then yes." There was venom in her voice, and he could hardly blame her for it. If anyone put their hands on Tristram without permission, his instinct would have been to draw his dagger and stab them.

He reached down and caressed his calf, where the dagger should be, but there was only the smooth leather of his boot. "They didn't collar me," he told her absently. "I don't know why, if they truly think me a dragon."

She paused for a long time, and Tris thought perhaps she'd fallen asleep. He was about to mark it a minor miracle and leave her to it when she spoke again. "Why don't you shift and leave? You could be gone from this nightmare in an instant."

"Isn't it obvious?" he asked. Those hours trying to shift as a child came back to him, in all their bitter, angry misery. "I can't. I'm no kind of dragon, and I can't shift into one."

She went quiet again, and this time instead of the slow, deep breaths of possible sleep, her breathing degenerated into soft sobs.

The notion that she might be crying for him felt unjust, but he didn't know what to say to her. When she finally drifted into a restless sleep, tossing and turning, Tristram was grateful for it.

He wasn't sure how long after that he heard someone creeping down the hallway. For a moment, he feared it was some miscreant come to hurt one of them or mock his misfortune, but instead, after a moment, the door to his cell inched open and the guard from earlier peeked in. He glanced back behind himself surreptitiously, and then met Tristram's eye as he held out a small loaf of bread.

"I am sorry it's all I could manage, m'lord, but Walden is watching us." His eyes narrowed to slits. "He'd best hope he never meet a decent member of the guard on a moonless night."

Tris blinked at the northern phrase suggesting future violence against the headsman. He had discovered a newfound hatred for the man, but he did not expect the guards to share his distaste. Slowly, he leaned forward and took the bread—the young man showed no mistrust, but there was no reason to test him.

"Thank you, Ewan," he said. He didn't want to fall on the food like a slavering beast, but his stomach growled its displeasure at the wait. Still, he dismissed it for the moment. There were more important things to discuss. "Walden seems nearly finished with the lady. Am I intended to replace her soon in his tender care?"

Ewan blanched and stared at the floor instead of meeting his eye. "I am sorry, my lord, but no."

"No? Am I simply to be executed without question?"

The tragic look on the young man's face when he looked up gave Tristram a chill. "I cannot wish for your death, sir, but it might have been better. They're sending the king's shadow for you."

Tristram almost laughed, but nothing was amusing. Perhaps not for the reason he thought, but Ewan had indeed brought the worst news imaginable. Pain, he could have handled. Looking into Bet's frozen black eyes as he tortured Tris at Reynold's bidding?

He hadn't been foolish enough to think them friends, but he had thought . . . It did not matter. It was over, and Tristram needed to plan for next, not wallow in never.

❧ 40 ❧

BET

By the time the sun rose, Bet had not slept, but he'd finished off his bottle of wine. His head was only just beginning to ache when he splashed water on his face, rinsed his mouth out, and shrugged into his black doublet. Before he left his room, he grabbed a bundle from under his bed.

First thing in the morning, the dungeons were especially cold.

"Nice of you to visit, Bennet," Tristram said, sitting forward on the edge of his cot, staring at him. Somehow, it was worse that Tristram was determined to treat him like a person when the bundle under Bet's arm held instruments meant for torture.

Lord Radcliffe looked peaked but generally unharmed, saving his split lip. Hells, he looked a good deal better than Lady Rhiannon in the cell across from his. His skin was sallower than Bet had ever seen it, like they hadn't been feeding him well. Hard to imagine that a lord of the realm could be brought so low so fast.

"Get up," Bet snapped.

Perhaps it was all that training, but Tristram seemed used to following a commanding tone. He did as Bet said, and with a rough grip on his arm, Bet took him to the chamber at the far end of the hall—where Walden had taken and tortured Rhiannon. His mouth soured.

A guard stood outside the door, scowling. When they approached, his glare landed not on Lord Radcliffe, supposed traitor, but on Bet.

"Lock the door behind us," Bet said to the guard as he opened the door. "And leave. I need two hours with Lord Radcliffe."

The guard spared an uncomfortable grimace to Tristram, as if seeking out his confirmation.

"King's orders," Bet snipped. Finally, the guard bowed.

Bet shoved Tristram ahead of him into the dank room. There were torches on the wall and the smell of burning pitch covered the stink of blood and worse. Lord Radcliffe stood there, still as a statue, and took in the place. It didn't occur to Bet until then how little horror Radcliffe must have seen in his life.

Under King Edmund, there had been few wars, and what there were had been easily suppressed—skirmishes more than battles. And the lord of Merrick would have little reason to see the kind of vicious, directed violence that took place in a room like this.

"I was wondering when I would wind up here," Tristram commented once the lock had clicked behind them, like he was only talking about the weather even as his gaze swept over stains of blood on the floor near where they had locked Rhiannon.

"Traitors usually end up here," Bet said.

Tristram laughed. His eyes caught on Bet's. "Is that what I am—a traitor?"

Bet swallowed. The king said that was the case, and the only truth that mattered was the one that spilled from Reynold's lips.

"Take off your doublet," Bet ordered as he set his bundle aside on a nearby table. Tristram raised a brow at him, so he clarified, "Unless you'd like me to ruin your fancy garment."

Biting his tongue, Bet unrolled his bundle. He turned the hilts of his knives over in their places. Then again.

"Do you honestly think that matters now?" Tristram asked, but he shrugged out of it and set it to the side, on the platform of the rack. For a moment, Bet thought he saw fear in Tristram's eyes, but the lord covered it quickly.

Bet was not sure what to say to that. Tristram would need his fineries again, surely.

"Go over there." Without meeting Tristram's eyes, Bet jerked his head toward the far wall, where chains were driven into the stones. "Face the wall."

Only once Tristram set his hands against the stones, his face turned away so Bet couldn't see his open expression, did Bet follow. He locked the shackles around the lord's wrists.

"Are you going to whip me, Kyston?"

Bet frowned. "That's a thought, but no. Knives are my preference."

Tristram let out a single laugh. "Mine too."

This was no time to question what he meant. Bet's palms were beginning to sweat. He flexed his fingers and returned to the bundle he'd left on the table. All he had to do was pick one. Any one. All that mattered was that it was sharp.

He looked up at Tristram's broad back. The lord faced the wall with his hands cuffed to the stone by short chains. He smelled like a man who'd been locked in a small room for days, but there were servants who regularly smelled far worse. He was still damnably handsome.

Bet wished that Tristram would fight this—shout at him, throw a punch, anything to give Bet justification in subduing him. Unsurprisingly, Tristram bore this as honorably as he'd borne anything. If Bet could hate him for it, that would make this easier.

As he hesitated, Tristram twisted as well as he was able to watch as Bet pulled the knives out one by one. He laid them on the cloth, fingering each one as if he didn't already know his favorite.

"You are wasting time, Bennet," Tristram accused on a breath.

Bet glared at him, only able to catch the corner of Tristram's one eye and the very edge of his smirk. "Would you like me to move faster?"

"Walden accomplished with Rhiannon in half an hour more than you are likely to get through with me all day, at this rate," Tristram shot back at him. "One might think you're less loyal to our king than Walden is."

Bet gritted his teeth, snatching up the silver handle of one of his thin knives. He moved to stand directly behind Tristram, bit his lip, and considered where to start.

"Or that you do not really want to do this," Tristram added a moment later. Bet's resolve wavered. But King Reynold had saved him. Bet owed His Majesty his life. What was a bit of pain in the bargain?

"You cannot even look me in the eye," Tristram taunted. And that was enough.

Bet cut the back of his tunic. The soft whir of split fabric followed his sharp blade down. He could've dragged it across Tristram's skin in the motion; he didn't.

Rather, Bet leaned in, pressing the cold steel flat to Tristram's side. His flesh was surprisingly warm in the dank dungeon. "Are you saying you would rather turn around and watch me carve your flesh?" Bet asked, growling low in his ear. "There are more tender places on your front, but if you insist—"

Bet pressed against Tristram's back and slipped his blade around where Tristram could see it. He dragged the very point down the lord's chest, leaning over his shoulder so Bet, too, could see the swell of red that trailed in a thin stream from the cut. Tristram gasped and shuddered against him.

"I thought I could not order you, Bet," he whispered.

All at once, Bet was back in Tristram's dark bedroom, between silk sheets, tangled together while Tristram held him down and said that he could not order him either. He had given Tristram pleasure, and now he meant to hurt him.

Bet flinched. The knife fell from his grasp and clattered on the floor. Without thinking, he pressed his palm flat on the thin cut he'd carved into Tristram's smooth skin. Blood stained his hand, but that was hardly new. With his eyes squeezed shut, he gritted his teeth and pressed his nose into Tristram's white-blond hair.

"You're right," he mouthed against Tristram's stubbled beard, "I can't—"

Before Bet could finish, Tristram turned his head and caught his lips. The kiss was like their first—a clash of teeth, violent and demanding. Then, Bet heard the crumbling of stone.

Tristram wrenched the chain from the wall, freeing his hand. Bet shifted his foot, kicking the knife away. He thought Tristram would go for it first, but Tristram didn't look its way. Instead, he fisted his hand in Bet's hair and jerked him in.

If there'd ever been any doubt what Tristram was, it disappeared when he yanked Bet between the wall and his body. Bet scrambled to touch him —one hand cupping his neck, his thumb stretching across it, ready to squeeze or shove him back. Bet's other hand still pressed over the thin cut on Tristram's chest. It wasn't bleeding much, but it had stained the tattered white linen ruby. He rubbed like he could make the cut disappear, like touching it wouldn't hurt him worse.

A shudder ran down his spine when Tristram growled at him. The lord pressed forward, pinning Bet against the stone far better than the cuffs had managed to keep him there.

Bet's hands began to roam. The door to the cell was locked. If Tristram killed him—well, there was nothing for it. With a dragon's strength, Tristram could grab his head and crush it against the stones behind him. Bet was caught, but if he were going to die, he'd have this first.

"So you are what he says," Bet whispered when Tristram drew back for breath. His full lips were flushed and ruddy, his eyes flashing dangerously. Bet's hand slid up his neck; his thumb brushed Tristram's jaw.

Lord Radcliffe glared. He yanked Bet's head back by his dark curls, exposing his neck, his ear. Bet's throat bobbed as he swallowed, fear giving a sharp, sweet edge to the pressure of Tristram's body against his.

"I am no traitor," Tristram growled. "But what are you?"

Bet could feel the chill air on the tip of his ear. He smiled, resigned to whatever came next. "Nothing more than a shadow." With both hands, he dragged Tristram back to his lips.

❧ 41 ❧

TRISTRAM

Damn Bennet Kyston.

Damn him for not being Walden.

Tristram had prepared himself for pain. He had known it would be worse than any injury from the practice field, or the month in his teens when he'd grown a full handspan, or even the time a drunken Lord Radcliffe had pushed him down a flight of stairs and he'd broken his leg. It would be worse, but Tristram could handle pain. Pain was a daily occurrence.

Bennet Kyston was something else, and every time Tristram was in his presence, his careful manners and plans crumbled, and one or the other of them ended up shoved against a wall.

In moments, he'd already given away the single most important thing he'd needed to hide. He'd destroyed any chance he had of coming away from this situation with his life intact, all for a kiss.

Well, Athelstan damn them both, if Tristram were going to lose everything, he was going to get more than one kiss.

His free hand tangled in those shiny, dark curls, Tristram devoured Bet's mouth. His hunger alone would be able to convince the man that he was a dragon, because he was going to take everything Bet could give. He thrust his tongue past Bet's lips, as though he could conquer the man by kiss alone. For once, Bet offered no resistance.

When Tris retreated a moment later, Bet surged forward into the gap, twisting them around so Tristram's back was to the wall. He filled Tristram's mouth with his own questing tongue, pushing forward so hard that he almost knocked his head against the wall. Presciently, Bet's hand was already there to catch and cradle it, as though he were a precious thing and not a monster he'd come to torture.

Tris loosed his hold on Bet's hair to run a hand down his back and squeeze the rounded curve of his ass.

When Bet pulled back to breathe, Tris opened his mouth to say something, anything. To demand what he wanted, to insist again that he was no traitor to his people, even just Bet's name, but nothing came out.

It was just as well, because Bet turned away, rummaging through a table of Walden's implements laid out beside the bundle Bet had carried in himself.

Had it all been a trick? A trap? Convince him to show his draconic nature and use it against him somehow? Or did Bet mean to collar him as they had Rhiannon? It made little enough difference.

"I cannot shift into a dragon," he confessed. Obviously, Bet had been the correct choice to interrogate him, since he was already spilling his paltry secrets into the space between them. A space he greatly wished were smaller.

He looked up at the remaining chain in the wall and considered it. It was his left arm, perhaps not as strong as his right. He could pull it down if he tried though.

"I don't care if you can change into a chicken," Bet muttered right next to Tristram's ear. There was a tiny click, and the lock that attached the useless chain to his right hand fell away.

Tris turned to stare at him as he unlocked the left hand as well. When Tristram was free, he stood there, at a loss, until Bet pushed him over to a low table. Something he was supposed to be tied to for more insidious torture, no doubt, but there was no bloodlust in those black eyes.

Only lust.

"It was a mistake not to fuck you before," Bet told him as he pushed him back against the table and reached for his hose. They tangled in his boots, and Bet muttered a curse, quickly bending down to shove them away and strip Tristram bare below his ruined tunic.

When he came back up, Tris curled a hand into Bet's tunic and pulled him forward for another bruising kiss. "I'm sorry it's treason to do it now."

Bet snorted but didn't answer. Instead, he opened his palm and let Tristram see what he'd searched out among Walden's implements earlier. A small bottle of some kind of oil. Tris did not want to imagine what its initial purpose was, but the realization of what Bet intended to use it for now made his breath hitch.

Treason or not, Bet was going to fuck him.

Tristram let himself fall back, bracing himself on his hands and spreading his legs for Bet.

For a moment, Bet looked suspicious. "You bend so easily."

Tristram stared at him. "I want you. You know that. I would have the night you came to my room."

Bet unstoppered the bottle and smeared one hand with the oil, shoving his hose aside and running the oiled hand over his cock. Tristram hadn't had the occasion to examine many cocks up close bar his own. When Bet had snuck into his room, he had been grateful to see it was like his. Another way being a dragon didn't make him any different from a human.

Bet grabbed one of his legs and wrapped it around his waist as he moved into the space between Tristram's thighs. He'd never imagined having sex for the first time under such circumstances, with a man he still suspected hated him, but there was no man he had ever wanted more.

Bet's hand found his hole first, spread oil over his skin, and then guided his cock there. With little fanfare and no hesitation, he breached him.

There was the pain Tris had been expecting from this encounter. It wasn't excruciating, though, and it gave him no urge to beg for an end to it. He had already proven his willingness to spill his secrets to Bet, so it weren't as though there was anything left to offer.

He reached for the man's hair again and pulled him in for another kiss as Bennet thrust fully inside him. It hurt terribly at first, more than it was good. He feared his cock would wilt and Bet would stop, and for some reason, even through the pain, he knew he didn't want that.

So he forced his way into Bet's mouth again, thrusting his tongue as

Bet thrust his cock, and whimpering against his will at the feeling of utter vulnerability.

Bet didn't fight away from the kiss, merely kissed back as he slipped his hands around Tristram's hips and down to grab his ass and brace himself as he pushed inside. Slowly, the pain of his forceful thrusts turned into something else altogether.

Tristram's head fell back on a moan, and Bet pushed harder, giving no quarter, taking everything. It was nothing Tristram had imagined, but everything he wanted—needed—in that moment.

"Bet," he moaned as the man pulled back one hand to reach between them and fist Tris's cock. It was just the wrong side of painful, and Tristram pushed that much harder into it.

He felt like an untried boy, but all it took was a handful of hard strokes before he was arching up and releasing all over Bet's hand and his own belly.

Bet continued to hammer into him for a moment more before curling himself around Tris, burying his face in his neck and biting down on the tendon there as he groaned in his own release.

They stayed there like that, panting, until Bet leaned back, wide eyed. He looked surprised, as though he'd merely walked in on the scene instead of having been an active participant. His eyes turned from one side of the room to the other, mouth open and still breathing hard.

When he pulled out of Tris, he took a step away.

As much as Tristram wanted to reach for him, he didn't think it a good idea. There was something lost and confused in his eyes, and Tris recognized it from his own emotions over the last few days.

Tristram, in fact, had yet to do anything quite so strongly against Reynold's orders as Bet no doubt had. It wasn't likely Reynold had ordered Bet to fuck him. Reynold probably did not even know there was anything but loathing between them.

"Bet, are you all right?" Tristram asked once his breath had recovered enough.

With a pinched brow, Bet stared at him. He blinked slow, like he'd forgotten himself. A shuddering breath later, and Bet stepped back into him. His hand cupped Tristram's knee, his thumb circling the bend of it. "You of all people should not ask me that."

"And yet, I am." Tris smiled, but it missed its mark. Bet was too busy staring at his knee to see it.

When Tris sat up, he hissed. He was a little sore, as much from the strain in his own muscles and the pummeling he'd taken from Reynold's guard as anything Bet had done. Nevertheless, any hardness in Bet's expression shattered.

"I hurt you," he whispered. He lurched forward, perhaps to try and provide some comfort, but his dark gaze dropped to the stain of blood on Tristram's tunic. "It—it is what I came here to do."

For once, Bet sounded entirely lost. Tris reached out to cup his cheek, and Bet flinched. "I'm fine," he swore.

But when Bet lifted his hand to cover Tristram's, he pressed it to his face for one second and pulled it away the next.

"I'm sorry. I can't—" He shook his head, but that was all he offered Tris before he stepped away.

While he understood that Bet was stunned, he did not expect the man to straighten his clothes, then go pound on the door and call for the guard. Instantly, Tristram hopped into motion, pulling his hose back on and then his boots as he listened to the guard's approach. His tunic was a loss, but he pulled his doublet over his bare chest in the hope of some vague semblance of dignity.

The guard pulled open the door, glaring daggers inside, Tris wasn't sure whether it was at him or Bet. "You said two hours."

Bet waved him off and didn't even take his daggers with him as he fled.

Tristram frowned and leaned down to pick up the one from the floor and set it with the others.

"Are—are you well, my lord?" the guard asked, watching Tristram rearrange the implements intended for his own torture.

His mind reached for an explanation that would neither uncover him as a dragon nor Bet for what they had just done. Finally, he motioned to the chain he'd pulled out of the wall. "Apparently the chains didn't see much use or upkeep under His Majesty, King Edmund. He attempted to lock me up, and it crumbled out of the wall."

The guard tutted and shook his head, but shrugged it off. "Sorry as I am for it, my lord—"

Tristram held up his hands. "I understand."

He did. While he could not imagine a time he would have agreed to commit injustice in Reynold's name, he recognized that many others did not have that luxury. They, and their families, lived and died by Reynold's whims.

Tristram had never before thought on how dangerous a bad king could be. He'd never imagined that Reynold would become one.

The guard locked him back in his cell and quietly slipped him a handful of dried meat, whispering an apology on behalf of everyone. For once, Tristram didn't have the energy or inclination to wave it away. The situation was ridiculous, and he deserved a damned apology. He would never get one from Reynold, even if the man miraculously changed his mind, but he would take what he was offered, and that included food.

He lay on his cot and chewed his meat, listening to Rhiannon sleep fitfully.

Some time later, when Gillian appeared in front of his cell, he thought for a moment that he was hallucinating.

"He has lost his mind," she whispered, staring at Tris in horror.

As much as he wanted to deny it, that was impossible without more ignorance than he had managed to retain. He had begun to realize the very same thing. His cousin had, in fact, lost his mind.

Had it happened suddenly upon ascension to the throne, he wondered, or slowly, and they had all missed the signs?

She leaned in a little and whispered when she spoke. "I don't understand, Tristram. This is all about you being a dragon? Only that?"

He listened for the sounds of guards nearby, but there was only Gillian. It weren't as though it mattered. He was a dragon. "I don't know why, Gillian. I'm not sure there is a reason."

"He says you are a traitor. It's madness. He must be sick!"

He hastily lifted a hand to stop her speaking. She was not wrong, but if Reynold had gone mad, what would stop him from throwing Gillian in the same dungeon and leaving her to Walden's tender mercies? Maybe they were alone, but there was no reason to take chances.

"You mustn't say anything that could land you here next to me, Gillian." He glanced toward the end of the hall, as though he could see through his cell's stone walls. "Someone needs to look after Roland. And my mother." He hesitated, then sighed. "And Llangard."

"That is *your* responsibility," she hissed back, glaring at the cell door as though she were a dragon who could shift and burn it down. "What I need to do is fix this."

He sighed and shook his head, pushing himself up to go stand at the door, despite how his muscles were starting to protest. "We must all be prepared to do what is necessary for the good of Llangard."

She glared at him and didn't back down. "Allowing my brother to throw you in the dungeon isn't for the good of anything, let alone the entire kingdom." She took a step back and drew herself up, resolute. "Something must be done about this." Turning, she marched toward the door.

"Gillian," he called after her, and she at least paused long enough to look back. "Please be careful. I couldn't stand it if you were hurt because of me."

She gave him a weak smile in return. "I know. The closest thing you have to a sister." Her eyes turned sad. "I hope you're not the only brother I have left."

He scowled at that, but she continued out before he could remind her to be careful, and perhaps explain that implications of the king being either mad or dead were not a part of being careful.

She had been right when she told him that she was an adult and capable of making her own decisions. He just hoped she made good ones.

❧ 42 ❧

GILLIAN

Some measure of Gillian had been relieved when her father had died. She was not relieved that he was dead—of course not! But a weight lifted from her shoulders when his death removed her from the immediate line of succession.

It had felt like an escape, of sorts. She wouldn't have to worry about the throne anymore, so she could do as she liked.

Now, she stood outside her uncle's chambers with the distinct idea that she could not afford to turn her head and ignore all that had happened. She raised her fist and knocked.

A footman opened the door for her. "Princess Gillian," he said with a bow.

"I am here to see my uncle."

She peered past him into her uncle's rooms. They were quiet since he'd sent his family back to his holdings in Aronfort. She wondered if he would follow them soon. There was little reason to stay at court if Reynold did not need him as a counsellor, and if Reynold were to die, Gillian could imagine she would need some time in the country to recover from the loss.

"Let her in," she heard from a private study to the right. As she marched across the entrance, the footman scurried to get to the next door before her and announce her to her uncle.

Seated by a fire, reading, her uncle rose when she came in. With his hand over his stomach, he bowed low when he saw her. "Princess Gillian."

She entered, pursed her lips, and looked around. Her foul mood seemed at odds with the coziness of her uncle's study.

"We should talk about the king," she said.

"Of course." With a wave of his hand, Laurence sent the footman away. "Would you like to sit?"

Laurence motioned to a chair, and when Gillian took it, he returned to his own. "What is it, Your Highness?"

"You said that you would help Reynold."

He nodded. "I intend to."

"When? What is your plan?" Gillian asked.

Her uncle shifted in his seat, leaned forward on his elbows, and propped his chin in his hands. "Are you in a rush to see this done? We cannot simply depose him, Your Highness. He has the right to rule, however he sees fit."

"I'm not saying we—"

"You think your brother will abdicate willingly?" He raised a steely brow at her.

Gillian pursed her lips. She thought of Rhiannon, battered and asleep in the dungeon, and Tristram, locked away as well. She considered all her brother had done—his willingness to send Kyston after his enemies, his ready brutality. "I think that there is something the matter with him, and we ought to help if we can. If that means giving him a break—"

"Can you take a break from being a princess?"

Gillian worried her lips with her teeth. "Well, no . . ."

"And if someone told you to take a holiday at the southern coast and leave your title behind?"

"I—"

"You wouldn't. You'd see it as an insult. A threat. Making any moves against Reynold, even to his benefit, warrants consideration." Laurence sat back in his chair. "We cannot be rash in this."

"Yes, but—"

"I promised you I would handle this, did I not?" Laurence asked. Gillian had the distinct feeling he thought she were still a child.

She sighed, shifted in her seat, and tapped her fingers on her skirt.

They did not have time. Tristram, alone in that dank cell under the castle, did not have time. "So what do you intend to do?"

Laurence frowned and set his ankle over his opposite knee. "I did not think you'd want to be involved. He's your brother, after all. He'll see this as a betrayal."

Gillian licked her lips and locked her fingers together. "Be that as it may, something must be done."

"You think he is a danger to Llangard?" Laurence asked.

Biting her lip, Gillian nodded. "I do."

"Would you be willing to say as much in front of the council? Your assertion would go a long way toward inspiring action." Suddenly keen, he leaned toward her.

Gillian took a breath. She'd grown up beside Reynold, loved him as well as she was able. When she had cast her first spell, she'd seen the first spark of rage in him. But he had never acted on it—not against her. Not in any way that affected her at all, until now. Whatever barrier he had in his mind that prevented him from acting on his worst impulses was gone. Maybe it was just because there was no one left to tell him no. Maybe he'd been cursed. Whatever the case, allowing it to continue at Tristram's peril was no option at all.

"I would," she whispered. "If that is what must be done, I'll do it."

43

BET

Tristram Radcliffe, Lord of Merrick, wanted him. No, he hadn't just wanted him—when Bet had pushed him back on the table and torn his hose down, Tristram had spread his legs and welcomed him.

Nothing had ever terrified Bet more. A lord should not have—and with *him*. It was impossible. And nevertheless, Tristram had gripped his curls and pulled him in, thrown his head back, moaned Bet's name from his strong throat.

He was gorgeous, disheveled, his shirt spread open by the blade Bet had cut him with. Men weren't formed like Tristram Radcliffe—not normal men. Bet might've discounted his fine figure as the result of Tristram's long hours training, but this was something else. His chest was chiseled. The strength of his arms overwhelming. His thighs—gods above, his fucking thighs.

There was not a single part of Tristram that Bet didn't want to dig his fingers into. Not a part he didn't want to own entirely.

But it wasn't for someone like Bet to feel possessive over the king's own cousin. Right then, Tristram belonged entirely to His Majesty.

"What did you get out of him?" Reynold demanded when Bet returned to him the next evening.

Bet's throat clenched shut. He blinked. "Excuse me?"

"What information did you get from the snake, Bennet?" the king asked impatiently.

"Ah, of course—" Bet licked his lips to stall long enough to recover. The king swirled his wine glass from his seat in his private quarters and lifted his brows. Candlelight cast his face in deep shadows. He had already dismissed his servants. "He did not have much to tell, sire. Lady Elinor has no part in this—"

"Doubtful. She knows the nature of her spawn."

A line puckered Bet's brows. "Does she? Only . . . Lord Radcliffe has had ample opportunity to transform himself into a beast. He has not. Can you be certain he is what the woman said?"

"You think Rhiannon lied?" Reynold demanded. "Why?"

Bet clenched his jaw. He had seen what Tristram could do. His strength, like Bet's speed, was inhuman.

It wasn't like he had never lied to Reynold before, but in every other instance, Bet had felt it was in the king's best interest to hear something other than the truth. Now, perhaps, the situation was the same. If Reynold continued to think Tristram was an enemy, it would not end well for Lord Radcliffe, and Reynold would lose a true ally.

That wasn't why Bet felt drawn to lie, however. What spilled from his lips was all for Tristram.

"Because you are close to Lord Radcliffe. She has spent enough time at court to see that. If she wanted to weaken you, she would have you strike out at your friends first. And if Lord Radcliffe were what she said, why would he subject himself to so long spent in the dungeons when he could raze the Spires to the ground?"

"He's not been collared?" Reynold asked, eyes flashing.

Bet shrugged. "No, my lord. I believe the king's guard had some qualms with collaring a lord of Llangard like a common slave."

"Like Tristram's kind would do to us?" Reynold laughed, startling and loud in the dark, warm space. "If they take issue with treating him as a prisoner, I have bigger problems than one traitorous cousin."

Bet drew in a long, slow breath through his nose, but he held it in before it could escape as a sigh. "In any case, the collar seems unnecessary, as does—"

A page rushed into Reynold's drawing room. He grimaced at interrupting them, but Bet fell silent before he could hear anything of import.

"Yes?" the king snapped.

"Prince Laurence, Your Majesty. He wishes a word."

Reynold straightened in his chair. He narrowed his eyes and set his glass aside. He seemed to consider lounging for a moment, but there was a table near the windows that he liked to stand behind. He got up, smoothing his hands over his clothes. Bet couldn't fault the impulse not to show weakness before his uncle.

It was no secret that Laurence coveted the throne. He was genial when King Edmund had not been. The court still spoke of Laurence's impressive showings in tournaments. If they did not desire the same high seat, Bet thought Laurence and Reynold would have gotten along well.

A moment later, Prince Laurence joined them. He shot Bet a dark look, but it only lasted a moment before he swung his arm across his firm belly and bowed deeply to the monarch. "Your Majesty."

"It is late for a social call, Uncle." Reynold turned his chin up. In a moment, he'd gone from slouching in his chair, sulking at the notion that he might be proven wrong while swilling wine, to a king who appeared to have matters well in hand. So the smirk that played at the corner of Laurence's lips was troubling.

"I did not think there was any time to waste," Laurence said lowly. He stepped farther into the room, past Bet, to conspire with the king.

"Wine?" Reynold asked as he approached.

Laurence pursed his lips, momentarily distracted. "No, thank you."

"I thought you'd want some. It is from the bottle you gave me. A fine vintage. I've been enjoying it most evenings."

"There are important matters afoot, Majesty. It is not a night for wine."

His Highness waved his hand for Laurence to continue, not offering Laurence a seat or taking one again himself.

"There is a plot against you, sire. To remove you from the throne and install Princess Gillian in your stead."

Bet fought the urge to scoff. "Honestly, if *anyone* desires to take the throne from His Highness—" He waved his hand at Prince Laurence, who straightened and glared at him.

"Believe me or don't, but if you do nothing, you'll find yourself exiled from your own kingdom by the new moons."

Bet lost the battle to roll his eyes then. But Reynold watched his uncle, rapt.

"Why would you think that Gillian would move against me?" Reynold asked Laurence.

"She intends to speak to the council day after next, sire. She thinks that you are ill. Unfit to rule."

Bet frowned. If the princess had concerns as well, perhaps this went deeper than a friends' quarrel. He had thought only to repair things between His Majesty and Lord Radcliffe, but Tristram did not seem to be the root of His Majesty's fears.

"After all," Laurence continued, his words like oil, "she is the last Cavendish with even a speck of Athelstan's power."

Bet's stomach dropped as he watched a shadow cross Reynold's features. For so long, the king had desired magic. He had trained, retreating to the western monastery to try to find power in himself that was not there. He had no skill in it. Gillian's magic, though faint, was a point of contention between them. It had been since she'd first shown any talent.

The king's nose flared. "There are those who'd rally behind her," he agreed.

"Sire—" Bet only managed the one word before an animal sense warned him against speaking. He wasn't in the habit of correcting the prince, much less the king. It took him a moment to recover himself, but when he did, he glared at Laurence. "I believe," he said, "there is no one less desirous of the throne than Princess Gillian."

"But where does Her Highness's loyalty lie?" Laurence asked Reynold. "With you, or with Lord Tristram?"

That was the final strike. Reynold's gaze snapped toward Bet. "Follow her. If she goes anywhere near the council chambers, I want you to take her to the eastern tower and lock her there until she can be dealt with," the king continued.

When Bet didn't respond, Reynold snapped, "Do you understand?"

"Yes, sire," Bet mumbled. "I'll see it done."

✲ 44 ✲

SIDONIE

Your king, Sidonie had started reminding herself with every step she took. Particularly on the occasion she was asked to protect Reynold, as infrequently as it was anymore.

At first, she worried that he knew about her indiscretion with Rhiannon. Or was it the indiscretions she had wanted to commit?

She glanced down at the braid around her wrist.

Your king.

"There doesn't seem much point to carrying on," Reynold was telling Walden, who looked downright gleeful. Something about the expression made her want to remove his head from his shoulders.

No, that wasn't fair. It wasn't his expression; she always wanted to kill him. He was a tiny little man whose great joy in life seemed to be hurting others, and she wanted to put an end to it all.

It was not that she thought herself so pristine or high and mighty. If the previous days had taught her anything, it was that she was every bit as bad as Walden. Worse, maybe, because she knew very well that what they did was wrong, and yet she did nothing about it.

What she would do if she were the decent creature she liked to believe herself . . .

He is your king.

"And what would His Majesty like to do about the dragon problem?" Walden asked, hands clasped tight in front of himself.

Reynold threw himself into the chair behind his desk and gave an exaggerated sigh. "I'd like to drop a mountain on the lot of them, damned treacherous snakes. But I suppose it is time to do what we must." He turned and faced the window, taking a deep breath. A strange serene look crossed his face before he turned back to Walden. "We'll do it in the courtyard. Not publicly, but enough of the palace servants will see that everyone in the kingdom will know in a week."

By the seven hells, he was talking about killing Rhiannon. Executing her right there in the courtyard as though they lived in those dark and ancient days of political intrigue and unrest. It was barbaric.

"You want the dragons to hear about it?" Walden asked.

Surprisingly, he seemed nervous. It might be the first sensible emotion Sidonie had seen on Walden since this disaster had begun. Angering all dragonkind was one of the most foolish things she could imagine. Humanity had defeated them once, but magic had been common and plentiful then. Now even the line of Athelstan had a mere trickle of power. Even the prince's display had been little more than a child's fancy.

Athelstan had been able to move mountains, and Roland could reshape wood. A little.

Reynold waved away the concern. "They fear us, and rightfully so. They won't come here. They wouldn't dare."

Sidonie remembered the young dragon who had escaped, and she doubted. Rhiannon's friend had seemed a child, but even a child could point out that the humans were defenseless against dragons. Once they murdered Rhiannon, the dragons would have every reason to invade and wipe them out. Perhaps Reynold had already killed them all, and the disaster simply hadn't played out to its end.

And you'll die fighting to protect him, because he is your king.

"And Radcliffe, Your Majesty?" Walden asked. His tone was strange, and it took Sidonie a moment to realize that he was pouting. "Master Kyston doesn't seem to have had much luck with him. Shall I have a go?"

Sidonie snorted aloud, and Reynold looked over at her, eyebrow quirked. She did not much want his attention on her, but it was ridiculous.

She returned the look. "Surely Your Majesty doesn't believe Bet Kyston to have been less than thorough in his work?"

The look that crossed Reynold's face was sheer malevolent amusement. "Indeed, it does seem unlikely, doesn't it?"

It did. But the strange thing was that Rhiannon had seen Lord Radcliffe with her own eyes just that morning, and other than looking exhausted and dirty, he hadn't seemed particularly poorly. He'd been contemplating his cell door, and if Sidonie believed he were a dragon, she'd have thought perhaps he was considering breaking out.

She still wasn't sure she believed Rhiannon. The woman wasn't a liar, but people said strange things when they were in pain. Torture wasn't always the window into the mind people seemed to believe. She'd had injured men under her command cry for their mothers, but she'd also had them try to catch green horses they swore were running through the barracks.

And she had given Tristram every chance to escape, from leaving him to his window, to telling the men they didn't have a spare collar for him. They did, but she had conveniently misplaced it.

Reynold would call it treason, but everything else be damned, Tristram Radcliffe was no threat to Llangard or its king, even when both had abandoned him to his fate. Rhiannon might be both, but part of Sidonie was starting to wonder if—

"Still, Bet has other things to do now. Perhaps Walden should have his chance." Reynold looked at the greasy little man speculatively. "Bet seems to believe Tristram innocent."

"It does seem likely, Majesty," she offered.

Reynold's lips pursed, displeased to hear that perhaps his suspicion was misplaced. "Even if that is so, how can I ever trust him again?"

Sidonie held her hands tight behind her back so that she wouldn't take the hilt of her sword.

Your king. Your king. Your king.

The man was worried about his own trust for Radcliffe, when he was the one who had thrown his cousin in the dungeon and had him tortured by an assassin. Perhaps Tristram looked well, but who knew what Kyston had done to him? She hadn't seen him looking as though he were considering escape until after it, whatever it had been.

Were she Tristram Radcliffe, upon release, she would leave the palace and never return. She might choose to join the Torndals above ever looking at Reynold again.

In fact, she was not sure why she wasn't doing precisely that.

"Tomorrow, I think," Reynold said to Walden, having lost interest in the subject of his cousin. "We'll execute the snake in the morning. And I shall sleep better for it when it's done."

Walden bowed deep and backed his way out of the room. "As Your Majesty wills. I shall make the arrangements."

Odious little man.

"You don't like him," Reynold observed after Walden left. He was looking at her speculatively now. She wondered how long before she ended up under the torturer's hands because Reynold decided her a dragon. Or perhaps he'd stop using excuses altogether and simply order it.

She inclined her head. "He smells bad, Your Majesty."

Her king laughed and poured himself a goblet of wine, as though he weren't about to execute a woman for existing, and then likely his own cousin for having the bad luck to be the name on the tip of a torture victim's tongue.

Your king is a madman.

She clenched her hands so tight together that the tips of her fingers went numb.

45

GILLIAN

Gillian hid her sweating palms in the folds of her skirt. She'd dressed in green and gold, finer than she normally did, not so somber. She thought—hoped—it might win her favor with some of the older council members. Lady Elinor wouldn't be so easily swayed, but there were men on the council who'd respond better if she presented herself like a fine lady. They preferred to see her first as a trinket, then as a ruler, and if she had to appeal to their sentimentality to save Tristram, so be it.

Perhaps she should have dressed like a soldier. Now that she was there, she was second-guessing every decision she'd ever made—most especially the decision to walk down that corridor.

Then she wasn't walking toward the round council chamber at all. Something quick and black crashed into her, pressing her into a tapestry. A hand covered her mouth, and she found herself blinking up into the flat onyx eyes of Bet Kyston.

She struggled in his arms, squirming off the wall. He tugged her away, dragging her toward a set of stairs.

Gillian dragged her feet, hoping her weight would slow him down while his hand muffled her shouts, but Bet tugged her up a discreet set of stairs. Only when they'd crossed two flights did he remove his hand from her mouth.

"What are you doing?" she demanded, haggard and out of breath from her struggle.

He held her fast to his side. "What your brother commanded, Highness."

"Help!" she shouted.

Bet grunted, covering her mouth again. He cut her off with the hard press of his fingers.

He carried her all the way up to the top of the eastern tower, a tall spire meant for a magician to keep watch over the kingdom from above. The window was wide enough, circling the entire room to provide clear vantage to anyone trying to defend the palace. But it was empty now— empty usually, with what few magicians were left in Llangard. Even if she counted amongst their number, Gillian did not have the might to call winds to her aid.

Unceremoniously, Bet shoved her into the room ahead of him. Then, he slammed the door behind her and locked her inside.

She rushed the door, slamming her palms on the wood. "Bet Kyston! Let me out this instant!"

She didn't hear him leave, but he gave no response as she continued to bang on the door.

THE SUN SET and rose again before anyone came to find her. Then, it was only a maid delivering food. Gillian tried to convince her to help her escape, but the maid dipped her head, flinched, and rushed out before Gillian could follow, snapping the door shut just before her fingers.

Reynold did not come to see her. All day, she sat there. And slowly, it began to dawn on her that he wouldn't come. It was on his orders that Kyston had locked her away. Her brother thought her a traitor, and the only way he might come to think that was if her uncle had thrown her to the wolves.

Dread chilled her fingers, turning them into icicles that she pinched between her knees as she sat on the cushioned bench. It curved against the wall opposite the door. She glared at the wood, willing him to come and unlock it. But she knew he would leave her there, just like he had left Tristram in the dungeons.

After a minute of glaring, Gillian gave up. "Damn it," she whispered to her lap.

She thought about attacking the maid next time she returned. But where would she go if she escaped? Atheldinas was her home. The Spires was the only place she'd ever lived. She'd gone on tour when she was a child and her father was young enough to show his family off to his subjects, but she didn't leave often. And damn it all, she did not want to hurt a maid who was innocent in all of this.

The sun was beginning to rise higher in the sky when she heard someone climb the stairs—odd, that she could hear this faint shuffle of feet, but not once had she heard Bet outside her door. Perhaps her brother really did love him for some dark magic he possessed.

There was a scuffle, a click of a lock, and the door swung open on Lady Elinor and Prince Roland.

"Gillian!" Roland rushed in and threw his arms around her hips. He buried his face in her skirts. "I'm so glad we found you."

She brushed her hand through his short russet curls. "I am too," she whispered, sharing a worried look with Lady Elinor, who was straightening from her crouch, something like a hairpin in her hands. "What's going on?"

"Something is happening in the courtyard," Elinor said tightly. The glance she spared Roland said that whatever it was, it was distressing enough that she didn't want to speak of it in front of the child. "A distraction. We thought we might find—" She hesitated, grimacing.

"Tristram?" Gillian asked.

Roland lifted his head and nodded, gazing up at her with wide eyes.

"He's in the dungeon," Gillian said.

"We'll find him," Lady Elinor promised. "And we'll free him."

Resolute, Gillian nodded. If they all fled the castle that very day, she'd do it. The people she cared most about in the world were right there, and Merrick was far enough away that it would take effort on Reynold's part to move against them. Perhaps he would simply let them go.

Once they had snuck down from the tower, though, Elinor gripped her wrist. "You should leave, Your Highness," she whispered, nodding toward one of the servants' doors out of the castle.

"I thought—"

Elinor shook her head. Roland frowned up at her. "It's not safe for you," Elinor whispered.

"And is it safe for you?" Gillian challenged.

Elinor frowned at her—it was a mother's frown—the sort she'd give a child determined to get into trouble. "The king is unwell. There's an . . ." She mouthed the word "execution." Roland scowled so darkly that it wouldn't surprise Gillian to learn that Roland knew what was afoot.

Lady Elinor took off her cloak, wrapped it around Gillian's shoulders, and pressed her purse into Gillian's hand. "You must leave. Go north to Merrick. We will follow you soon."

Gillian shook her head. "I will wait for you at the city's northern gate. I'll try to find horses for us at the inn there."

After a moment's consideration, Elinor nodded, and Gillian turned to sneak out of the castle. She had never been on the streets of Atheldinas without an escort and now, with her dress so fine, she wished she had dressed as a soldier after all.

With her head down, she rushed through streets she barely knew. She had never had to learn the way of things, but in this early hour, the slivers of Penrose and Nye above were just visible to guide her way.

As she moved through the streets, she barely avoided the splash of piss from a window high above—a pot emptied after the tenants had filled it all night.

She was in a dangerous part of down, with the homes built to shadow the cobblestone paths cut haphazardly between them. But up ahead, the narrow path opened onto a square. On the other side, she was sure, was the inn she was looking for.

Before she reached the square, a shadow moved to her right, and a man stepped out and grabbed her. Tall, hulking, with his head shrouded by a hood. His eyes gleamed unnaturally in the dark. They looked too much, far too much, like Tristram's.

"You don't look like you belong here, my lady," he growled.

❧ 46 ❧

ROLAND

From the way Aunt Elinor looked at him after she sent Aunt Gillian away, Roland knew what was coming.

He shook his head resolutely. "No. I'm going too."

"The dungeons are no place for—"

"Me," he agreed. "Or you, or Tris. Or anybody. But if you have to go find Tris, I have to go find Tris. I'm supposed to be king someday. Kings don't just make everyone else do the hard things. Grandfather said so."

Since Tris was in the dungeon, and everyone he loved was sad, it seemed obvious that he should try to copy his grandfather. When he'd been king, there had never been a question of hurting Tris and Aunt Elinor and Aunt Gillian.

Roland was just glad he'd overheard the kitchen maid crying over being forced to keep Aunt Gillian locked in the tower, or he would still be looking.

Instead of arguing, Aunt Elinor nodded. "There are things you don't know about what's happening," she told him.

He scrunched up his face and looked up at her. "Of course there are." No one ever told him anything, after all. He learned everything he knew by listening in, or because adults didn't think he was smart enough to understand things.

It had something to do with Rhiannon, he was sure. And dragons. And somehow, Tris and Aunt Gillian.

"Did you bring Tris's dagger?" he asked. "He'll want it."

She looked at him funny but nodded.

They were avoiding the guards, he realized halfway there. Whenever Aunt Elinor saw a member of the royal guard, she turned the other way. It meant they were backtracking as much as they were moving forward, and Roland didn't like it. He wished Bet were there.

He would make sure no one bothered them.

When he saw Bet, though, looking sad and scared and following Father down a hall, he didn't call for help. If Tris were in the dungeon, it had to be Father's fault. Who else could it be?

Roland remembered when a lord had been executed for treason. They said he'd been trying to kill Grandfather, and Roland hadn't seen that, but he had seen the lord hit a serving maid for being too slow. He hadn't been a good man, and Roland wasn't surprised that someone who would hurt an innocent maid would also try to hurt Grandfather.

Tris would never hurt a servant. He was always saying how everyone should be nicer. He would never have killed anyone who wasn't bad. Not even Father, whom Roland was beginning to suspect might be bad.

No. If there were only two of his father's men Roland could trust, they were Bet and Tris. They were always there, and they never treated him like he was useless, even though they didn't think he had magic. He felt bad for not telling them, but Aunt Gillian had magic, and Father hated her for it. He might say he wanted Roland to have magic, but that wasn't true.

So Roland hid in the shadows of the hall, waiting for the guards to pass so that he and Aunt Elinor could cross to the wooden door that led down into the dungeon. Roland was good at hiding.

✿ 47 ✿

BET

Bet had never considered what he would do if Reynold proved a bad king. When Reynold brutally dismissed his guard, it was because they had failed to prove themselves worthy. When Reynold had dismissed Bet's father, ordering around the kitchen staff when he had no business there at all, it had been to Bet's benefit. When Reynold had thrown a tournament so soon after his father's death, it was the move of a new king looking to consolidate power.

Or maybe each of those instances were warning flags, waving in Bet's face, begging him to think twice about his loyalty.

The truth was: without Lord Tristram languishing below the castle, locked in a cell, Bet wouldn't have cared. It was not as though he had any special tie to Llangard and its people. The reason he'd fallen in so tightly with King Reynold was that he had no one else. His father had hated him, his mother had abandoned him, and he simply was not human enough to find his place amongst the others.

Or if he had been, he'd lost that humanity long ago.

Bet thought of Tris alone down there, so like him—dragon instead of elf. Neither one of them belonged entirely to Llangard. Somehow, until now, Tristram had managed to get along well enough.

On the king's orders, Bet was prowling the outer wall of the palace, looking for any last sign of trouble before Rhiannon's execution. His Majesty remained convinced that something was coming, but Bet was beginning to think there was no threat save ones Reynold brought down on himself.

With a sigh, Bet tipped his head back to look at the sky. High above, the Spires' peaks cut into the air in uneven shards. Legend said it hadn't been built, but that Athelstan had stood on this hill and lifted his fortress in jutting points. The exterior walls were sharp, leaving few spaces large enough for a dragon to land—and each of those had a scorpion bolt waiting to attack. Those, no matter who was king, never fell into disrepair.

If the dragons had meant them harm, why not fly in from above? Rhiannon could have caused far more harm with fire than by toying with the king's heart.

He could not think of her flying; she'd never fly again. Had Tristram ever? He said no, but it served his interest for Bet to think he was an inept monster, rather than a dangerous one.

With a sigh, he dropped his gaze again. There, sulking in the shadows of a spire, Bet saw a dark figure in a shroud, looking for a way in at the bottom of the castle.

Silently, Bet followed the figure as he slipped into a small door—usually used as a private entrance to the eastern tower.

Before the figure could mount the narrow stone stairs, Bet rushed him. The man had height on Bet, and breadth, but Bet took him by surprise and slammed him into the curved stone wall. "What do you want?" Bet hissed in his ear.

With a snarl, the man spun around. Scales rippled over his skin. His eyes flashed red, and when he swiped his hand at Bet, his fingers were clawed.

Bet managed to shift back in time to avoid them, but the dragon lunged, teeth bared. When Bet went for the dagger in his belt and slashed the creature's arm, the fine edge skirted harmlessly across his black scales. The dragon grinned at him.

They danced in the small space, Bet looking for a soft place to hit, the dragon trying to catch him. But Bet had felt Tristram's strength. Getting caught was death. A dragon could snap his neck or crush his ribs with hardly a thought.

Before it could go further, Bet dropped into a crouch, swung his leg out, and sent the enormous man tumbling onto his back with a grunt.

Bet was on him, shoving his knees into the bends of the man's elbows. He pushed the point of his blade into the hollow of the dragon's throat. The scales there were broader, lighter hued, softer. Another day, Bet wouldn't have hesitated to plunge his blade into the man and watch as the life faded from his gleaming red eyes. Now, he considered that the man might be there for Tristram, and he couldn't do it.

"I'll ask again," he said coolly. "Why are you here?"

The dragon took a breath so deep that it lifted Bet, but he didn't try and push him off again.

"Rhiannon," the dragon said. "I want Rhiannon gan Derys."

"The woman who wooed the king?" Bet scowled. "She's set to be executed today." He glanced out the small window, thin and high on the wall, meant for archers or mages. "Soon, I should think."

He did not imagine the shudder that ran through the man under him. "I have Princess Gillian. If your king wishes to see her again, I would suggest you put a stop to that."

"You took her?" Bet pressed the tip of his blade in harder. "How?"

She'd been locked in the tower—an easy place for a dragon to snatch her, perhaps, but someone would have seen him in flight.

The dragon laughed. "I did not have to. Your princess ran directly into me. But I've put her somewhere safe. No harm will come to her if your king returns Rhiannon."

Fighting all his instincts, Bet pulled his dagger away from the man's throat. The scales rippled away as Bet stood. He could've killed the dragon and gone to find Gillian himself, but this—

If Reynold killed Rhiannon, how long until he had Tristram executed as well?

"I will carry your message to the king," Bet said. "I would suggest you wait for me here. The castle is not a safe place for your sort at present."

Reynold was in his chambers after breaking his fast, dressing for the execution. He looked finer than he had any day since the tournament, though his skin was pale, sunken and purple below his eyes.

"Your Majesty," Bet said, bowing low. "I have a message."

"What?" Reynold snapped.

"A dragon has taken Princess Gillian. He demands the release of Lady Rhiannon for her safe return."

For a moment, the king only stared at him. His lips in a thin, firm line.

"We don't negotiate with snakes—certainly not for the release of traitors."

A rock dropped in Bet's stomach. "Sire, are you certain? He could kill her."

Reynold scoffed. "Athelstan was not bothered by dragons. Gillian has his power, does she not? She should be able to defend herself."

Bet's eyebrows furrowed. "Her power next to Athelstan's is hardly more impressive than yours would be, sire."

"Then let her see this as an opportunity to grow. It is nearly time for the execution, Bet. Come."

Bet stepped back, inclined his head. "I have one more errand, sire. Then I will be by your side."

He left the king behind, scowling. His feet fell heavily on the way down the curved staircase of the eastern tower. The man he'd fought continued to wait at the bottom, pacing like a caged cat.

"Dragon," Bet said lowly.

The man's head snapped up. There was hope in his eyes, now a dark, reddish brown.

Bet shook his head. "The king will not negotiate with you. Lady Rhiannon will die today."

The dragon snarled, "Then I will rip out the princess's throat with my teeth."

Listless, Bet shrugged. "You will do as you must."

He left the snarling dragon behind and turned to join his king in watching Lady Rhiannon die.

❦ 48 ❦

RHIANNON

The energy in the dungeons had changed overnight. The guards hastened past her cell, ducking their heads and avoiding her gaze. The maid who brought her breakfast had trembling, worried lips. They'd hardly fed her while she was there; the meal should have been a warning.

Meanwhile, Rhiannon slouched on her cot. Walden had not returned that morning, so she was left in peace to her aching limbs. With her good hand, she twisted the copper lock of Sidonie's hair between her pale fingers.

Had she always been so pale? Perhaps it was the sallow, thin light in the dungeons that made her skin so dull. She had always been gold—more luminescent than Tristram Radcliffe. When she'd seen him in the light of day, he was nearly silver. Now, he looked gray.

And neither one of them matched the sunset beauty of Sir Sidonie. Rhiannon sighed, rubbing her thumb over silken strands. And as if she had called the knight herself, Sidonie appeared on the other side of the bars.

Rhiannon lifted her head and smiled softly. There was no such expression on Sidonie's face, but Rhiannon had few enough pleasures left to her that even Sidonie's frown ranked.

"My lady," she said, pushing off the wall to sit at the edge of her cot as Sidonie unlocked her cell.

The knight's eyes darted around, then she looked over her shoulder to make sure they were alone in the corridor but for prisoners.

"The king would see you executed today," Sidonie blurted out.

That wiped the smile from Rhiannon's face. "Oh."

Sidonie glared at her, her jaw clenched. "That's all? Oh?"

Rhiannon shrugged, the motion small to avoid her aches. "How did you think this would end, my lady? Reynold and that monster have hardly been gentle so far."

Sidonie made a frustrated sigh. In three long steps, she was in front of Rhiannon, looking down at her, eyes shining with . . . something.

Rhiannon laughed softly. "Keep glowering like that, and I'll think you are the tortured one of the pair of us."

Sidonie reached under the curtain of Rhiannon's hair, hanging lank around her shoulders. She brushed her fingers over the collar, whispered words of power, and it fell off.

Rhiannon started. "Perhaps you will be."

"A king doesn't murder indiscriminately," Sidonie said stiffly. She was trying to convince herself as much as anyone, but Rhiannon's lips twitched. In a battle with a king for Sidonie's loyalty, she had won out. That was not nothing.

Another laugh escaped Rhiannon. "A king does exactly what he wishes."

But so, apparently, did a knight—at least this one.

Rhiannon got to her feet. She stepped forward; Sidonie stepped back, but she licked her lips. They fell apart, soft and pink and enticing.

One step at a time, Rhiannon backed her into the stone wall. Sidonie allowed it, despite the sword at her side. Rhiannon's collar fell from the knight's slack fingers.

Rhiannon leaned in and brushed her lips across Sidonie's softly. She'd had water, but she doubted she was particularly fresh, so she left it at that. "Thank you," she whispered.

"I am not sure I want gratitude for betraying my kingdom," Sidonie muttered back.

"Then consider it a goodbye kiss."

Sidonie's strong hand curled around the back of her neck. She pulled Rhiannon in gently, tilting her head. Her eyes fluttered closed, copper eyelashes brushing her freckled cheeks. "I'm not sure I want to say goodbye either," she said before slanting her soft lips over Rhiannon's.

⚜ 49 ⚜

TRISTRAM

Walden hadn't come for Rhiannon in more than a day, and Tristram wasn't fooling himself into thinking they were giving her a break. They had decided she had no more useful information, or at least she would not give it.

Bet had not come back for him, either, but that was less of a surprise. The man was probably as confused as Tris about what had happened. He'd been there to do the king's dirty work, after all, and there was little doubt that had not been what Reynold intended.

Tris had done his best to stop thinking about it, but he didn't have much else to do. Beyond that, frankly, if he were stuck contemplating the ceiling, reimagining the feeling of Bet's body moving against his was preferable to wondering what would come next.

Tristram still had the strength to break out, something he might not have for much longer, but that tiny voice in the back of his mind kept preaching about duty, and honoring king and country.

Was it possible to love Llangard and betray Reynold at the same time?

That morning, when the maid had brought Rhiannon breakfast for the first time since Tris had been dragged down to join her, he knew. He wasn't offered breakfast. Hells, the maid didn't even glance at his cell, like she didn't know anyone was in it. Amazing, how this place could swallow a person and render them entirely forgotten.

He couldn't see Rhiannon's reaction to the woman bringing her food, but there was confusion in her voice when she thanked her. He noted, hopefully, that the girl didn't seem the slightest bit frightened of Rhiannon.

While she hadn't ever cut an imposing figure, and Tristram would imagine she was even less frightening after so much time half starved and left to Walden's tender mercies, that didn't necessarily mean anything. A starving wolf was a dangerous wolf, not one to be pitied or offered table scraps. If the woman was not frightened of Rhiannon, she knew that the dragoness was no danger.

Perhaps it meant that Reynold's hatred wasn't universal.

Sidonie came for Rhiannon, and for the first time, Tristram truly hated his cousin.

Perhaps Reynold did not know that Sidonie and Rhiannon had any affection for each other, but logic didn't make a difference to Tristram's sentiment. Reynold had sent one of the finest knights in his kingdom to lead a woman she cared for to her death.

Sending Sidonie at all was an insult to her station.

Sending her to do this specific thing was like sliding a knife into the gut of one's most loyal retainer. Like sending Bet to torture Tristram, if Bet had truly cared for him.

After she unlocked the cell, she turned and met Tristram's eyes a second before slipping inside. Her expression wasn't what he might have expected, but it gave him a moment's hope. She wasn't beaten or miserable. She was sad, but there was anger simmering in her eyes as well.

All else be damned, Tristram hoped Sidonie followed her heart. And if doing so landed her in a cell next to his, he would break them all out. There truly was a line between what was honorable and what was right, and Tris no longer had any doubt which side he fell on.

They lingered in the cell for a long time before they came out, Rhiannon first and Sidonie following behind. Chains clinked from the shackles around Rhiannon's wrists. She met his eye, and he thought there was something like pity there. Or possibly . . . sympathy?

He nodded to her, then turned to Sidonie, but she wouldn't look at him. He hoped that she wasn't there to retrieve Rhiannon for execution at all, but making an escape with her.

Let Walden come for him—he would say nothing of what he had seen. Sidonie's future was safe with him.

"Sir Sidonie," he called after her, and she paused to turn her head in his direction. She still would not look at him, but that was fine. "I wish you luck. Both of you."

At that, her gaze did snap to his, shock on her face. She swallowed hard and nodded to him. "I am sorry," she whispered to him, then she turned and followed after Rhiannon.

If Sidonie helped Rhiannon escape, he realized, things would go poorly for him, and very soon. He could only imagine the rage Reynold would go into if his "snake" prisoner escaped with the help of one of his loyal knights.

His cousin had been seeing treason in every shadow, and this would prove him right.

If Tristram had been waiting for a cue, that was it.

He dropped to his knees next to the cell door and examined the hinges for what felt like the hundredth time. It would be easier if he had something sharp, or anything at all he could use to pry.

Fortunately for him, while he was hardly a dragon in any useful way, he did have a few tools a human prisoner would not.

He flexed his fingers, stared at them, and willed them to turn into the wicked claws he'd spent his childhood wishing away and trying to hide. It was much harder making them grow, simply because he'd stopped trying. It had been so long since Tristram had wanted to be a dragon, that even his claws resisted.

After a frustrating moment of nothing, he reminded them—well, himself—that he had no other weapon. His hoard had been stripped from him, and unless he escaped, he would never see his blades again.

In an instant, his fingernails shot out into familiar silvery claws, almost as though he were wearing some strange jewelry on his fingertips. For a moment, he was mesmerized by them. They hadn't been so big or shiny when he was a child.

Had he actually stopped to admire himself?

He sighed and rolled his eyes. Apparently, he was every bit the vain lordling some members of court believed him to be. Admiring his own claws, indeed.

He set them at the edge of the door side of the bottom hinge and tried to wedge them underneath. Instead of working them in, the claws sliced the wood like it was no more substantial than fresh bread. He'd pushed too hard, in fact, because a second later, the hinge tore away from both door and wall, and dangled limply in his hand.

For one ridiculous second, he wondered why Rhiannon hadn't done the same, but then he realized: they'd torn her fingernails out.

He shuddered and pushed off the floor to give the second hinge the same treatment, but just as it tore off, he heard soft footsteps down the hall. There was one hinge left, and he jammed his hand against the door to hold it in place, lest it fall aside and display what he was doing.

Instead of a guard or his cousin or even Bet, the next thing he heard was his mother's quiet voice.

"Tristram? Are you here, dearling?"

Tris was frozen for a moment. He did not want his mother to see him like this. He was filthy and hadn't eaten in days. He could not hide from her, though. He should take the last hinge, get her, and run. Perhaps Merrick was lost to him, but did it matter, truly? It was a tiny estate, and it wasn't even his birthright, bastard that he was.

"How are we going to get him out if he's locked up?" a small voice asked, and his heart almost stopped. Prince Roland was in the dungeon with his mother.

He could almost hear the secretive smile in his mother's voice when she answered, "Oh, our Tris is a resourceful boy. He'll manage."

"Mother," he hissed, leaning to try to look down the hall. In an instant they were in front of his cell. He tried his best to glare at his mother, but it was too good to see her. Still, he had to say something. "You should not have brought Roland to this place."

"It was my idea," Roland told him in his best approximation of haughty royalty. He was terrible at it, and Tris had to work hard to hold back a smile, despite the wretched circumstances.

His mother leaned in. "You have to break it, dear. There's no choice anymore. We need to get you away from the palace. He's going to kill that poor girl. He's obsessed."

"He locked Aunt Gillian up," Roland added helpfully.

Tristram sighed and let his head thump against the door. The remaining hinge gave an ominous squeak, and the door rattled.

He looked up to find his mother smirking at him. "Already decided you needed to find your way out, did you?"

"I didn't think there was much choice left," he admitted. He turned his attention to the last hinge and pried it loose before catching the door and gently setting it against the wall.

Roland's pale little face came around the doorjamb, staring in wonder at the door, then the hinge in Tristram's hand. His eyes went round when he saw the claws. Tris probably could have put them away in time to hide them, but he was done with that. Lying to Reynold had caused this problem to begin with.

Instead of demanding answers, calling Tristram a snake, or threatening him with beheading, Roland reached up and grabbed his hand, pulling it close to his face so that he could inspect it.

"You," he announced after a moment, "are a dragon." He looked up at Tristram curiously. "You're still Tris, though, right?"

Tristram nodded and went down on one knee in front of Roland. "I am, Your Highness. I am precisely as I have always been. A half dragon, loyal in every way to Llangard."

Roland gave him a smile. "I know that." Then he got a faraway look. "I wonder if the dragon queen will like it, that we have a dragon here at court."

His mother scoffed. "What Halwyn likes or doesn't like is of no interest to us. Wretched hag."

Tristram and Roland both turned to stare at his mother in shock.

"What?" she asked.

They turned to look back at each other, and Roland let out a childish giggle. "Aunt Elinor doesn't have to talk to her."

"I think that might be for the best," Tristram agreed. "Now, I have to sneak out of the palace, and the two of you need to get back to the royal wing and pretend you've had nothing to do with this."

There was a strange sound then, and for a second, the very walls of the palace shook. The three of them stared at each other, then ran for the stairs.

50

SIDONIE

What had Sidonie done? What was she currently doing? Was it in fact she, and not the king, who had gone mad?

She had given Rhiannon the means to escape her own murder, but that wasn't how the king would take it.

Of course, she'd given Radcliffe every chance to turn into a dragon and fly off, but he hadn't. She had seen the dragon Hafgan fly away as they pursued him, hopelessly behind, so she knew dragons were still capable of the feat.

Was Rhiannon? She was pale and wan, and Sidonie imagined that the bulk of a dragon required immense amounts of sustenance. Rhiannon had been lucky to get any food over the last week, let alone enough to perform impressive feats.

It was a wonder she was capable of walking.

She was though. She marched on in front of Sidonie, like a woman marching to . . . not to her death, actually. Like a woman on a mission. Her shoulders held high and squared, back straight, and chin in the air.

The guards they passed averted their eyes so quickly that not a single one seemed to notice the lack of a collar on Rhiannon. The cuffs around her wrist weren't hidden by her curtain of golden hair, and they should be enough to hold anyone. Any human.

When they reached the door to the courtyard, Rhiannon turned to look her in the eye. "I see no way to return from this."

"Nor I, my lady," Sidonie agreed. Her gaze slipped to the rosebushes. All of their blossoms had shriveled, their petals in wilted red curls, scattered across the dewy grass.

"Then I do apologize for offending your sensibilities. It is bound to be a bloody affair." Rhiannon turned and preceded Sidonie into the courtyard.

Sidonie frowned. Did she intend to harm the palace guard in her escape? Sidonie would never forgive herself if her knights died this day because of her choices. She rushed out after Rhiannon, but the woman was already well ahead of her.

A few guardsmen were assembled behind the king, who had come to watch his brutal spectacle. Kyston stood directly to his left, scowling. Most of the servants, even those who would generally be present in the courtyard in the afternoon, were conspicuously missing.

Walden stood at the block, wearing his usual black, his stance exuding smug superiority. Truth told, Sidonie wouldn't mind if Rhiannon killed him in her escape.

She looked back to Rhiannon, standing in front of the platform where she was meant to die, in time to see the midmorning sun glint off her first emerging scales.

The shift was positively magnificent.

Despite her growing worry, Sidonie couldn't help but admire it. Rhiannon shone like a bonfire, and as her shackles and tattered dress fell away, scales sprouted on her skin and grew, bigger and bigger, to match her size as a dragon. It happened so fast that hardly anyone had a chance to react.

Walden screamed and turned to run, but Rhiannon's enormous tail lashed out and sent him flying into a wall with a wet crack. When he slid down to the ground, he left a trail of blood on the stones. It was better than he deserved.

Two of the guards stepped in front of Reynold, and despite her worry for them, Sidonie was powerfully proud. Those were her knights.

She ran as fast as her armor allowed, yelling at Rhiannon. "No!"

Rhiannon glanced at her, and she was stunned at how much of the expressiveness of her human face remained. There were scales missing, bloody patches from the damage Walden had done to her, and it made Sidonie want to run the man through, likely as it was that he was already dead. To injure such a magnificent creature was a crime.

"Kill it!" Reynold screeched, dragging Rhiannon's attention back to him.

She turned to him, cocking her head all the way to one side, that gesture that had always seemed strange and painful as a human, and for a moment, she considered him as though he were a bug.

She didn't breathe fire or swipe at the knights—her claws were likely still missing, Sidonie realized, her stomach churning. Regardless, her movements weren't vicious. She didn't hurl the knights aside as she had Walden. She simply put a scaled hand on each and pushed them apart.

Then, with one swift, smooth motion, she lowered her head and snatched Reynold up in her jaws. The sound of his screaming only lasted a second when, first, she snapped him in half. Then she swallowed him in two bites.

The guards stared in shock and horror, and so did Sidonie.

Without waiting for anyone to gather their wits, Rhiannon spun and looked at Sidonie. "You will make a nice snack for later," she announced. Her voice was still human, but deeper, more resonant, and she lunged forward. She grabbed Sidonie with both hands as she snapped her gold wings open. The clap they made was almost deafening, and the roar that emerged from her throat even more so.

Rhiannon bunched the muscles in her legs and leapt straight into the air, her wings catching the breeze almost immediately, as she carried them both away from everything Sidonie had ever known.

🦋 51 🦋

BET

The second Rhiannon shifted, the courtyard erupted into panic. The knights who'd gathered jostled Bet back and forth in their desperation to escape, but Bet only stood there, staring as the dragon, mere feet away, bit the king in half.

His mother had told him stories of dragons bigger than houses; she'd sung of fires that engulfed whole towns. Nothing in his imagination had prepared him for this.

She was a soft, creamy gold. Her scales were resplendent, but for the large swathes of exposed red flesh where Walden had pried off her scales and hacked into her flesh.

She might've been beautiful if Bet weren't watching her powerful tail flick through the air. She snapped the king in her jaws, silencing him in an instant. When she jerked him off the ground, Bet watched the muscles in her throat work to swallow him—clothes and all. His crown hit the floor of the dais with a soft thunk. Like Bet, it was elven made, light and graceful.

His breath shook. But she didn't come for him. She took Sir Sidonie, spread her wings, and with a mighty flap that sent some people diving into the grass, she flew.

Everything had changed in an instant, but as Bet stared at the spray of blood where his king had stood a moment before, he didn't feel it. He did not realize that his loyalties had lost their tether but thought first of how Reynold would want him to act.

To hunt the dragon down and slay her? To go to the prince and see him safe?

It took Bet a full minute of standing there, frozen and blinking in the midst of chaos, to realize that Reynold was past wanting anything. Bet could, for once, do exactly as he liked.

Before he weighed what that was, he'd slipped off the dais, moved past Walden's broken body, and taken the path toward the dungeons.

No one knew why Tristram was there. Most of the people who did—who believed he was a dragon—were dead or flying away from the keep. The guards were clearly uncomfortable with the notion of detaining a lord. Tristram could escape. He wouldn't even have to run.

Bet moved on the balls of his feet, hardly making a sound, jogging through the dim corridor. The other cells were empty—they'd been so seldom used in Edmund's day, and Reynold had not had time to fill them with any save his one-time friends.

He'd thought to find Tristram there alone. Instead, he found an empty cell, the door removed and set aside every bit as carefully as Lord Tristram would have.

Bet breathed in through his nose and quelled his panic. If something were wrong, if Tristram had been taken against his will, there would be signs of a struggle.

And slowly, a smile curled Bet's lips. The world could burn—Tristram Radcliffe had broken out.

52

TRISTRAM

They had barely made their way out of the dungeon before they heard the screaming from the courtyard.

Tristram had little enough doubt what had happened, Rhiannon shifting into a dragon and making her escape. He hoped she took Sidonie with her. It was unlikely Reynold knew enough about Sidonie's family to take revenge upon them, and he didn't want Sidonie to stay and face Reynold's wrath on her own.

Rhiannon causing a scene in the courtyard gave him a good distraction to make his escape, but he needed to see his mother and Roland safe first.

He didn't even try to process the urge to go back to his hoard. It wasn't a rational pull. He herded his charges into a side hall just in time to avoid a group of palace guards rushing toward the courtyard.

Perhaps his mother and Roland didn't need to avoid the guards, but if they were in his presence, it was best they not be seen. If Rhiannon had made an enormous spectacle, played upon Reynold's already out of control fears, anyone who had ever so much as spoken to Tristram would likely fall under suspicion, let alone if they'd been seen with him during the upheaval.

"Mother," he whispered to her, taking her by the shoulder.

Before he could speak, she cut him off. "We are taking the princess and going to Merrick. We will figure out what to do from there."

Tris shook his head. "You need to take Roland back to the royal wing. Stay there and pretend you never left."

She scowled at him, but Roland was the one who answered. "We're not leaving you on your own. Someone might hurt you."

He ran a hand through his hair and looked helplessly down at the prince. "Highness, if you are seen with me, someone might hurt you. Your father—he isn't well."

Roland nodded, too solemn by half for a boy his age. "He is not. He put his cousin and friend in the dungeon and locked his own sister in the tower. Someone needs to stop him."

The look in his eyes as he said it, serious and worried and most of all, entirely trusting, told Tristram precisely whom Roland thought was going to stop his father.

It was too late for Tris to stop Reynold the right way, by going to the council and expressing his concerns for the king's sanity. Reynold would need only to announce that Tristram, like the monster who had escaped from her own execution, was a dragon infiltrator.

The only other way for Tristram to stop Reynold was to sacrifice his own life. To kill his cousin himself to stop what he was doing to Llangard.

He would be executed for that, and rightfully so.

But could he run away, sneak out of the palace like a thief and leave the kingdom to its fate, to be ruled by a man who would lock up his own sister for confronting him?

He looked up at his mother. "Do you have my dagger?"

Her mouth fell open in shock. "Tristram—"

"I cannot run away from this, Mother. All of Llangard is in danger."

Her face contorted in anger. "Llangard can go hang! What has this place ever given you but heartache and fear of your own nature? We should all leave."

Roland reached up and took her hand, then Tristram's. "Where would we go, Aunt Elinor? Merrick is part of Llangard. Tornheim? Across the ocean? This is our home."

Tristram nodded at Roland, then looked up at his mother. "Llangard is our home, Mother. Its people are our people. If we don't protect them, who will?"

Her jaw was still set, angry tears in her eyes. He hated to deny her anything, but he couldn't promise her that he would be safe, even if he ran, and that was the only thing she wanted.

"Perhaps the king will listen to me," he suggested, and she glared at him.

She pulled the dagger out of her belt pouch and held it by its hilt, pulling it free of its sheath. "Then this old woman will handle it. I've lived enough for any two women. If you ever meet your father, tell the old bastard I loved him." She broke off and glared at the wall, sniffling and blinking away tears, then muttered, "Even if he is a scaly ass."

Tristram and Roland stared at her for a moment in shock.

Footsteps echoed through the halls, the distinctive clatter of the palace guard. Guiding the king to safety, no doubt.

Tristram shook his head and carefully took the dagger from his mother without injuring himself. "I need that, Mother."

She frowned, but clearly, he hadn't thwarted her plan for longer than it took her to find a new weapon. He'd had no idea his mother could be so bloodthirsty. He was both pleased she loved him so dearly and horrified at the notion of her killing anyone, especially her own nephew. Not to mention making Roland complicit in the whole mess.

He turned and pressed them back down a hall, toward the entrance to the royal wing.

The knights were there, but searching, not standing guard, and all thought of confronting Reynold was lost. This was not right. These men had not escorted Reynold to safety.

"He's not here," someone called from the direction of Roland's rooms, voice panicked.

The two men at the end of the hallway looked at each other, worry written across their faces. Roland made a confused noise that caught their attention, and they turned in unison to him. When they took in the entire group, Roland and Lady Elinor their usual selves and not unexpected, but Tristram filthy and half dressed, they were momentarily relieved, but then looked at him with confusion.

Tristram's mother stepped between him and the guards, ready to throw herself on their swords to protect him, when a silken voice from the shadows caught everyone's attention.

"I see you've returned from the king's mission, Lord Radcliffe, and not a moment too soon." Bennet Kyston peeled away from darkness Tristram hadn't even noticed, met his eye for a long, intense, unreadable moment, and turned to the guards. "You've come to protect the prince?"

At their terse nods, Bet turned back to Tristram, but he knelt smoothly in front of Roland, taking the boy's hands in his own. Roland, swayed by instinct, swallowed hard and announced, "My father is dead."

Bet met the boy's eye and nodded. He glanced up at Tristram, then back to Roland. "I am sorry, Your Majesty." He lowered his head in deference, and the guards followed suit, dropping to their knees before the young king.

Tristram watched Roland for a second, the boy's eyes darting back and forth in thought. He was blinking back tears for the father who had treated him like a disappointment, but he was the cleverest child Tristram had ever known. And there he was, preparing for a task a grown man shouldn't have to live with, let alone a boy of nine.

Tristram's mother turned to kneel next to Bet, but as Tris turned to do the same, Roland caught his hand. "Lord Tristram Radcliffe of Merrick, most trusted cousin and advisor of Kings Edmund and Reynold, we name you regent of Llangard."

Every head within hearing range snapped up to stare, and Tristram was no exception. "Your uncle, my king," he tried to interrupt, but Roland shook his head.

"Laurence Cavendish is an excellent advisor and my dear uncle, but in the case of my"—Roland swallowed hard—"untimely demise, Llangard will need a young king, well versed in protecting our land from the hostile Torndals. You are the regent we need."

In front of Roland, Bet's eyes sparkled with barely contained amusement, but he didn't look up at Tristram. Probably laughing to himself about how Tris had gone from next to be executed to lord regent of Llangard in an hour's time.

Tris wanted to be sick right there in the hall, but instead, he swallowed and mastered his churning stomach, dropping to one knee in front of his tiny cousin, his rescuer, his king.

"I live to serve my king and country."

53

GILLIAN

A round the base of the Spires, where the tallest towers shot straight toward the sky, Athelstan had drawn the stone from deep in the earth. With it, he'd pulled up the bones of civilizations past. Though Gillian had never been allowed to scale the outer walls, she'd heard that there were shards of pottery, tools, scraps from meals.

But there at the bottom were the biggest remains, and out of one stone wall on the western side of the palace, over a craggy area most of the guard didn't bother patrolling, the rib cage of an ancient dragon curved out of the wall and back into it.

The fossilized creature predated Athelstan's rise—must have by centuries or longer. And the gruff man had grabbed her and tied her hands behind her back, around the curve of bone.

"Do you know who I am?" she'd hissed at him as he had dragged her away from the city square and back toward the Spires. "I am Gillian Cavendish, and if you want to keep your hands, you'll remove them from my person immediately!"

He had not listened the whole way back, instead leaving her there, tied to the bone, with a wrapped cloth around her mouth to muffle the sounds of her shouts.

No guards came to this side of the castle, where bones grew from the earth and the Spires dropped in a steep crag toward the river that brushed its western side. There was no sense patrolling where they need not guard.

No sense patrolling here at all, when the "traitors" were in the dungeon already.

She jerked her hands against the bone. The rope the brute had used bruised her wrists, but she continued to struggle without success.

Only when her hands were numb and aching did the man return, crawling over the stone ridges as if he were a mountain goat.

The furious cant of his brow kept her quiet as he moved toward her. Glaring, he paced past, growled, and rounded on her again.

He stalked back and forth for more than a minute before he leaned over her face, enormous and livid. His teeth were bared like he'd snap her in half.

"Your brother does not want you," he growled.

Gillian laughed helplessly, just a breath, and shook her head. She made a sound into the cloth, wet with her spit—she wanted to speak. Surprisingly, he ripped the gag down so it hung around her neck.

"I could have told you that and saved you the trouble," she snapped.

The man's hand slid into her curtain of black hair and pulled her head back. "You think it is funny?" he asked. "I was going to trade you for my shield sister. But your king is going to kill her. So where does that leave you?"

Gillian's morbid smile disappeared. Her breath caught. "Do you mean the Lady Rhiannon? You are a—"

The man's growl rose all the way from his stomach. Gillian flinched back, arching over the curve of the dead dragon's rib to lean away from him.

"Your kind enjoys killing mine, doesn't it?" he demanded. "I should return the favor."

"I can help you save her," Gillian blurted.

He narrowed his eyes. His breath on her face was hot—hotter than it ought to have been.

"She's in the dungeons. There are—there are ways into the castle. I spent my childhood trying to sneak away from my guards. I can help you get to her. Only—" He was still glaring at her. Nerves jumped in her belly, but she pressed on. "Only she's not the only dragon in the dungeons. If I help you, you must also help Tristram."

His eyes narrowed into slits so thin it was a wonder he could still see her, but the faint sheen of his inhuman irises kept her trapped.

"Tristram Radcliffe," she offered. "He's from Merrick. Son of Lady Elinor. He's one of you. I will help you if you will help him."

"You are not in any position to make demands, Gillian Cavendish." He sneered her name.

She pushed up on her toes, leaning forward as far as she was able, until he had to straighten or risk touching noses with her.

"If you will not accept aid, then you simply want to be angry. Fine. Kill me. But that will solve nothing, and your lady will die."

Before he could respond, there was a whoosh of air, the beat of wings, and a grating roar like nails on steel. They both turned to look up at the sky and saw the shining gold dragon fly overhead.

A smile slid across her captor's face.

"We're leaving," he said. Behind her, he made a move, and the ropes that bound her fell to pieces.

"What about Tristram?"

The man arched a brow. "That lordling belongs among his own people. His place is here."

"They'll kill him!"

Already, he was dragging her down the rock face. "I don't care. Radcliffe is not my concern."

"But he needs your help."

When she slipped in her silk shoes, the man grabbed her, hoisted her up, and slung her over his shoulder. She bounced against his broad back as he carried her down toward the river, where a small wooden boat waited to carry them away from her home.

❀ 54 ❀

SIDONIE

Once, when she was ten summers old, Sidonie had been helping her father thatch their roof and fallen off the side of the house. It had lasted less than a second, the fall, but she would never forget it. The rush of air against her face, the dropping sensation in the pit of her stomach, and the sick realization that there was nothing she could do to control her immediate future.

She had broken her arm, and the village healer said she was lucky she hadn't broken her skull.

Sidonie had never climbed up on the roof again. Instead, she'd always let her father and younger siblings handle that chore.

For the first few moments, flying was exactly like that moment of terror.

The wind in her face, staring helplessly down at the ground, even that horrible swoop in her stomach. When the ground got farther away instead of closer, her body started to unclench. Thanks especially to the way Rhiannon held her so close, but with such a tiny amount of pressure.

There was no doubt Rhiannon could have either dropped her or crushed her, and easily, at that. Instead, she cradled Sidonie against her. Like she was precious.

Sidonie had never been precious to anyone before.

When they were speaking ill of dragons, humans always compared them to snakes and lizards and other cold things, but unlike those creatures, Rhiannon was warm, and despite the scales, somehow soft.

Sidonie lay her head against one of Rhiannon's huge hands, stayed as still as possible, and watched the miles of farmland go by beneath them. The patchwork of fields and towns below them passed in a blur, and she lost track of time.

The sun was starting to dip on the horizon when Rhiannon finally descended, and Sidonie didn't know if it was the normal way to land, or if Rhiannon was being especially ginger with her, but she glided down slowly to the top of a hill, setting Sidonie in the grass and then landing beside her.

In a few seconds, Rhiannon was human again, small and hurt and even more pale and unhealthy than before. It was hard to reconcile the sickly woman with the enormous dragon, especially when she practically collapsed onto Sidonie.

"Can't anymore," she rasped out. "Too much energy." Her stomach grumbled loudly in demand. Of course. She'd been left hungry for days in the dungeon. The only reason she'd had any energy at all . . . Well, that didn't bear contemplation.

Sidonie cupped her cheek in one hand and smiled. "Then it's my turn." She pointed in the direction they'd been headed. "This way?"

Rhiannon nodded. "There's a monastery in the mountains. Even if Halwyn is angry with me, they'll take us in."

That was strange. Sidonie knew a monastery in the mountains. She'd never been there, but every child in Llangard with magical aspirations knew it. It was the place where mages worth their name spent at least a few years training. The monks themselves were not mages, but they knew more about magic than any other living creatures, and people said they could look inside a person's soul and know if they had magical talent.

They were heading in the direction of that monastery, she thought, with some surprise. "The Hudoliaeth?"

Leaning heavily against her, Rhiannon nodded again. Sidonie reached down, slid her arm under Rhiannon's legs, and hoisted her up. She was more substantial than someone so wispy should be, but Sidonie could manage. They would stop when she found something Rhiannon could eat.

Hopefully they would pass a village where she could trade her heavy armor for more useful things. Clothes for Rhiannon, for instance.

Sidonie had started with less, though. They would make do, and they would find their way to the monastery.

"I didn't realize the monks there were friendly to dragons," she said conversationally as Rhiannon rested against her. She probably couldn't keep up a conversation and any kind of pace for long, but she would do her best.

Rhiannon gave her a tiny, secret smile. "Oh, they are. Whatever humans and dragons have ever thought of each other, the monks have remained as neutral as possible. It used to anger both sides."

"During the war?"

Rhiannon's eyes went far away and glassy, and she gave another short nod. Then she looked up at Sidonie once again. "Are we at war again? Because of me?" Her voice was smaller than Sidonie had ever heard it, and it was little wonder. She'd come to the land of men to try to talk to them. Instead, she had nearly been killed, and in turn, killed the king of Llangard.

Sidonie dropped her head down to lean against Rhiannon's. "I don't know, love. But there's nothing we can do about it this moment. For now, we need to get you somewhere safe, so you can heal."

With a soft chirring noise, Rhiannon snuggled into Sidonie's chest and proceeded to fall asleep.

55

TRISTRAM

I n the days that followed, Prince Roland had a quiet ceremony to take the throne. No tournament, only a small feast, and a somber one at that.

Laurence pretended to understand Roland's choice of Tristram as regent, even as he glared daggers at Tris and pointed out to the king that he was not a Cavendish.

The wiliest nine-year-old of all time, King Roland had simply smiled and said, "Llangard is more important than our family, Uncle Laurence. It must always come first."

That had been the end of it. Tristram's mother, long a member of the council, told him that it had required very little debate. Few members of the council liked Laurence or his political maneuvering, and they were far more concerned about preserving the nation than Athelstan's line. So Tristram was in the very position he had always—very happily—thought he would avoid. There had been half a dozen people between him and any hint of the throne, and now there was one.

Tris would die before he would allow anything to happen to Roland.

They sent out a group to hunt for Gillian after Bet told them she had been taken, but there was neither hide nor hair of her in the castle, in Atheldinas—anywhere.

For the first week, Tristram's time was consumed with the day-to-day running of a kingdom. It turned out that Reynold had spent more time stockpiling weapons for a yet-to-happen war than food for the coming winter, and Tristram was terrified that people were going to starve. It would be a black mark on the first months of Roland's rule, whether it was his fault or not. The people wouldn't blame the dead king, but the living one.

They needed a short, mild winter. Little else would mitigate the coming disaster.

That, for better or worse, left little time to deal with the subject of Bet.

Not that Tris didn't want to deal with him. Didn't dream of him and wake with that cursed, beautiful name on his lips. The possibility of people starving was more important than Tristram's tiny problems.

Six days after he had taken on the job, he was on his way out of a meeting with the council—discussions of sending unapprenticed youths to work with fishermen at the coasts to increase food stores—when he saw Bet returning from the practice yard. He was half clothed and sweaty, but Tris forced that out of his mind. He needed to deal with this now.

Bet Kyston was a distraction Tris could not afford, and he invited a reputation King Roland could not have.

"Kyston," he called, and sped down the hall to catch up, Ewan and another guard trailing behind him. Every time he was reminded of it, he tried not to groan. He had personal guards. Gaspar, in charge of the king's guard following Sidonie's supposed death, had assigned him the youngest, least experienced of the guard. It was supposed to be an insult, but it was mostly a waste of their effort.

"Can I help you?" Bet asked as Tristram approached. His black eyes were, as ever, a mystery. There was an expression on his face, but it was as impenetrable as everything else about the man.

Tristram turned and waved for the guards to hang back a few paces, continuing to walk alongside Bet as he headed toward the servants' wing of the palace. "How did you know that Gillian was taken?"

"I spoke to the dragon that took her," Bet replied easily, as though it were a thing he did daily. Tris supposed he did often speak to a dragon, but he didn't want the reminder that Bet was one of the only people in the kingdom who knew Tris's secret.

"You knew she was in the tower before that," Tristram hedged. He suspected he knew what had happened. He hoped he was wrong, but—

"Of course," Bet admitted. "I put her there."

Tris had to sigh. Bet was a professional assassin, a master at lying and murdering people. He couldn't have lied about this one thing?

"King's orders," Bet added defensively.

"Why?" His voice came out a whisper, but he had to ask.

"Prince Laurence convinced the king she meant to betray him. Laurence wasn't wrong—I suspect it was on your account she did it."

He had known. He had asked Gillian not to put herself in danger on his behalf, and he had known even then that she would not listen to him. Tristram took a deep breath and girded himself for what was to come. "I think you should leave the Spires."

Bet blinked. "Excuse me?"

"You betrayed the princess of Llangard—"

"Because its king commanded me to—"

"You killed Jarl Jorun—"

"Do you miss him?"

"The gods only know what other atrocities you've committed—"

"In the name of king and country."

Damn the man for making every point Tristram had made to himself trying to find a way out of this discussion. "King Roland is not his father. He'll have no need of a . . . a shadow."

Bet's brows shot high under his shaggy hair. "You think not?"

With a shift of is shoulders, Tristram summoned his full height and tipped up his chin. "As lord regent of Llangard, I am telling you to leave."

Bet smirked at him. He didn't glower or bare his teeth or growl. If anything, he seemed amused. "Lord Radcliffe, you will have to do better than that," Bet whispered. His dark gaze flicked down to Tristram's lips. "If you want to banish me, prove you are the steel-hearted man a king needs at his side. Levy charges against me."

Tristram's gut churned, and his head swam. They both knew Bet's crimes were many. Listed publicly before the realm, they wouldn't see him banished—they'd see him executed. Tristram was in no way capable of sentencing Bet to death. He hadn't even wanted him to leave.

But he needed him to.

He tried to speak, to find any words to convince Bet to go, but nothing came. Even for the good of Llangard, his first priority in so many ways, Tris couldn't be the end of Bet Kyston.

"Until you do, I'm staying right where I belong," Bet leaned over to whisper in his ear. "The shadow behind the throne."

"At your peril then," Tristram growled.

They turned a corner into the servant's wing, and before Tris could think about spinning in the opposite direction and marching away, he nearly tripped over something—no, someone. Bet reached out a firm hand to steady him as they both looked at the man on the floor before them.

"William!" a woman cried from the top of the staircase in front of them. She rushed down and knelt next to the man on the ground. "I told you to see the healer, you old fool."

She rolled him onto his back, and his pale eyes stared sightlessly up at the ceiling, deep dark furrows beneath them as though he hadn't slept for many days before his death. His skin was waxy and yellowish, unnaturally so. The woman clapped a hand over her mouth and buried her face in the dead man's tunic, sobbing.

Tris recognized him then. The king's food taster.

ABOUT SAM BURNS

Sam is an author of LGBTQIA+ fiction, mostly light-hearted romances. Preferably ones that include werewolves, dragons, magic, or all of the above. Most of her books include a little violence, a fair amount of swearing, and maybe a sex scene or two.

She is a full-time writer who lives in the Midwest with her husband and cat.

For more information:
www.burnswrites.com
Sam@burnswrites.com

ALSO BY SAM BURNS

THE WOLVES OF KISMET

Wolf Lost

THE ROWAN HARBOR CYCLE

Blackbird in the Reeds

Wolf and the Holly

Fox and Birch

Hawk in the Rowan

Stag and the Ash

Adder and Willow

Eagle in the Hawthorn

Salmon and the Hazel

Wren and Oak *(Coming Soon)*

WILDE LOVE

Straight from the Heart

Sins of the Father

Strike Up the Band

Saint and the Sinner

A Very Wilde Christmas

ABOUT W.M. FAWKES

W.M. Fawkes is an author of LGBTQ+ urban fantasy and paranormal romance. She lives with her partner in a house owned by three halloween-hued felines that dabble regularly in shadow walking.

For more information:
www.fawkeswrites.com
waverly@fawkeswrites.com

ALSO BY W.M. FAWKES

LORDS OF THE UNDERWORLD SHORT STORIES

Heart of the Sea by W.M. Fawkes

Made in the USA
Coppell, TX
03 September 2020